QUIET UPON SHENBYRG'S DAWNING

Second in the

Night Skies Over Valhallow series

by Dan Osarchuk

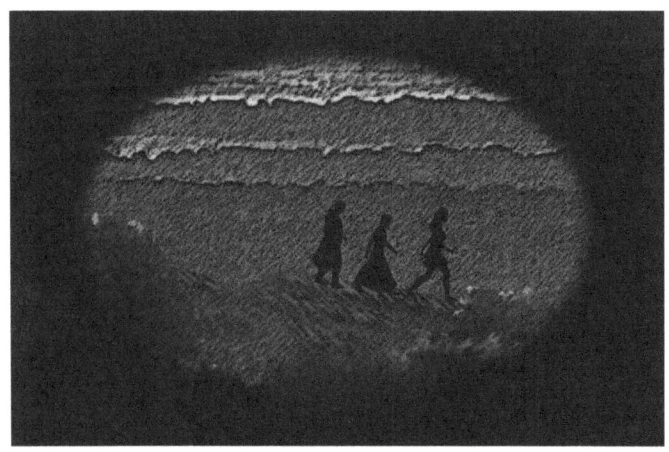

Written by Dan Osarchuk

Cover picture by Traci Meek
Cover design and conversion by Rachel Bostwick

Special thanks to those who support my work.

Note that this is a work of fantasy fiction and no characters, places, or situations in this book are intended to represent actual, real-life people, places, or situations, though the themes that they represent certainly might be.

Loki's child
from life summoned
to her thing
the third liege-lord,
when Halfdan
of Holtar farm
left the life
allotted to him

- Heimskringla

TABLE OF CONTENTS

Dan Osarchuk

PART 1

Chapter 1

Strass Hill

How did he keep getting himself into such places?

Oborren sighed as he crawled in yet more mud as the rain came down even more torrentially. Small rivulets began to invade the sanctity of even his supposedly waterproof outer gear as well as his supposedly inviolate undergarments underneath.

Why enduring such trials of Mother Nature was necessary when hunting the unnatural, Oborren might never know. He certainly would have preferred to be *killing something* rather than lying in this Gods Forsaken muck. He only guessed that it took a special type of person to be a hunter.

Ah yes, Oborren certainly felt special. Here he was, answering yet another Wanted poster, this time to slay 'Something that keeps killing my peasants'. The local Jarl, Egelbert, had offered a very fair bounty, most likely due to the fact that his own huscarls could not capture the monster so far. Why the creature seemed to have only attacked this particular hamlet had intrigued Oborren at least as much as wondering where the creature was *when it wasn't attacking this particular hamlet.*

Quiet Upon Shenbyrg's Dawning

So Oborren had begun to investigate. Some hunters might rush into a situation, crossbows firing, but such hunters rarely lived for long. Despite the stories to the contrary, fighting monsters was never some 'shooting-festival'. Unless one was dealing with large groups of goblins or orcs, *real monsters* usually required certain methods to be truly *cleansed*. Any 'shooting' would then necessarily be limited in amount, of a very specific variety, and also quite precise.

Another occupational hazard unique to hunters during an investigation was the questioning of peasants. Oborren often had the distinct displeasure of having to ask the local folk about any monsters that might be in the area. Of course, the peasants had no shortage of creature-stories, but identifying the *real ones* took no small measure of finesse and a resolute willingness to hold back from throttling those being questioned. Was the shadowy presence that dwelt in Canute's outhouse an *actual* wraith or simply the product of poor digestion? Was a screeching woman's voice that carried off Erika's brother screaming into the night an *actual* flying-thing or just one's fratricidal wishful thinking? Maybe it was true that the woods a few miles away *actually were* some sort of gargantuan fiend's backbone, but any real proof might be hard to make.

One clue that the peasants weren't imagining things was the presence of actual gore. And the nice thing about most monsters was that they were sloppy. When a true *flying-thing* struck, there was plenty of blood, carcasses, and remnant pools of urine to dispel any chance of such tales being the result of an overactive peasant's imagination.

Yes, *flying-things:* that was the official hunter name for them. The commoners would certainly nod knowingly whenever Oborren would use that term, though of course, the peasants knew little else about what it meant. Whether it was a wyvern or a demon or a manticore or some other beastie, it could make a significant difference as to what the flying-thing's capabilities and motivations were, not to mention how to kill it.

Dan Osarchuk

The fact that the creature had also been consistently referred to as female had certainly given Oborren some idea as to its actual type. Not only that, but because all the victims were male made that line of suspicion even more compelling. Oborren therefore felt that he had a pretty good idea of what he was dealing with. It then only became a matter of providing the proper *bait.*

What sort of lure was needed depended on what type of *female-flying-thing* he was dealing with. Being thorough, the hunter opted for very broadly appealing bait. It didn't take much coaxing to get a number of local norsemen into one of the barns that were within the creature's feeding area. Chances were that any number of them could easily be drunk, womanizing, and or remorseful, if not before entering the barn, then certainly afterwards. Oborren set them up with a few kegs of *Strassmen's Beast* and the misleading promise that 'some woman would be joining them soon' to make sure. Such an arrangement would draw in all sorts of *female-flying-things.*

So here he was in his present circumstances. He just hadn't counted on their being so much rain. Oborren knew he had to stay out of sight, but then again, he didn't want to drown or be washed away in what appeared to be an areal flood.

Risking some noise, the hunter dragged himself out of the muck, his black garb and hair making him nearly invisible except for his pale, clean-shaven face in the night rain. The light popping sound that his removal made didn't bother him as much as the realization that his trusty crossbow was now caked in mud- unusable until at least a good quarter hour of cleaning. Oborren simply didn't have the time for that now. And his trusty dagger had also been missing since that business at the Schoolhouse last year. He had only replaced it with a small knife- not much use against a *flying-thing!*

The hunter glanced back over at the barn. The norsemen inside didn't seem to be bothered by the rain. Based on his expert assessment, nearly all of them were drunk, roughly half of them were now ready for the 'woman' that he had promised, and one or two seemed a little withdrawn. He wondered who the flying-thing would attack. He felt some pity for the Norse, but that was soon overcome by his excitement over being able to correctly identify the monster.

Suddenly, Oborren felt something grab his shoulder. Half expecting it to be a drunken norseman who had escaped being barn-bait, he turned and caught a glance of a wicked-looking woman's face! He instinctively twisted his body and let out a girlish scream. Whether surprised by his quick reflexes or startled by his unmanly reaction, the creature lost its grip and vanished from the hunter's sight.

Rain and incredulity were all that remained. The dark sky continued to emit upon the hunter's wide hat as he stalked over to the side of the barn to give himself some cover from a return of the flying-thing and to hopefully prevent a heart attack. The constant shower made his gear hang heavy and uncomfortably from his body. He cursed the innkeep at the Strass Hotel for selling it to him. Oborren had to remind himself that even though an item might be, in the innkeep's words: 'Specifically Colored Black and Specially Made for such a Capable Hunter as Yourself', it most likely had its flaws.

Then as suddenly as before, the thing was upon him again! A large bird's talon came out of the dark and nearly scratched off his face. Thinking quickly, Oborren whipped his flail around the thing's other talon and was carried into the air with it. The she-beast screamed and flapped towards the barn roof with great speed. Oborren, being able to do little else, hung on for dear life and tried to take note of the creature's characteristics. It smelled awful and was certainly avian. And Oborren could have sworn that he had seen the thing's face before, but on a woman, not a monster. If he could only tell if it had wings on its back and human arms or instead had *wings for arms*, it would- WHACK!

Before he could match the face to a name or identify what type of flying-thing it was, the hunter experienced a brilliant flash of light when his own face connected with the side of the barn. All went dark.

* * *

Oborren awoke to an even heavier downpour. The Gods had not deluged the land enough apparently. It was still night and his clothing was sopping wet. He tested his aching body, but nothing seemed broken. He regained his footing and, looking around, assumed that the creature had smashed him into the side of the barn; that is, if he hadn't dreamt the whole attack and had simply fallen asleep in the muck. His body was becoming so numb from the chill and dampness that he had trouble telling.

The raindrops struck him harder now. They felt sharp and painful upon his weakened hunter's body. Dark Night herself seemed to be tearing at him, ripping away at him, preventing him from catching his quarry which seemed so near.

Was he dreaming again? A terrible shriek erupted, forcing the hunter to cover his ears in pain. The norsemen inside the barn too must have heard the racket, for they also began to yell. Their voices were not nearly as loud as whatever was making that horrible screeching though. Was it the *flying-thing*?

Oborren took off and sprinted around the barn, struggling to see if he could locate the creature in the dark night, wondering if all the peasant stories he had been listening to had been causing him to experience things that weren't really there. One never really knew with monsters and the unnatural...

But then he heard it: SMASH. It sounded like something had crashed *inside the barn.*

For a moment Oborren stood transfixed, unsure which way to go.

Quiet Upon Shenbyrg's Dawning

He soon decided and sprinted back around to the barn's entrance, perspiration mixing with the falling rain. The hunter, finding it hard to run, began to discard his outer sloshing black raingear, revealing no less soaked, but somewhat more maneuverable dark garments and a colorful necktie beneath. He rounded the corner and took in the sight. It was lit well by the many barn lanterns. Roughly a dozen drunken norsemen, weapons drawn, were squared off against *something* inside.

What had its back to him looked like an enormous falcon, standing the height of an adult human with a woman's head on top. Oborren's hunter training had him stop there. He needed something to slay this creature, something that was unfortunately still outside the barn and caked in mud.

And though many of the Norse inside would now fit the description of drunken men, a number seemed so inebriated that they were also intent on womanizing: they *were promised some woman* by the hunter, after all. Oborren doubted that the flying-thing would react well to their wooing her.

So, Oborren did the only thing that seemed right: he stepped out of the barn, closed the doors, and locked them from the outside.

He hoped the girlish screams inside were from the female-flying-thing and not from any terrified norsemen. It wouldn't do for them to die that way.

* * *

Around a quarter of an hour later, Oborren returned. With his crossbow now cleaned and the *special* bolt ready, he positioned himself a few paces from the barn doors. No sounds emanated from inside and lantern light still flickered through the cracks. He was fairly certain who had won the battle; he doubted victorious norsemen could be this quiet.

Dan Osarchuk

With a pull from one of his heavily gloved hands, Oborren unlatched and forced open the doors, quickly pointing his crossbow back inside. To his surprise, the men were still alive, and only slightly bloodied. They looked over at him sheepishly, powerful emotions apparently surpassing even the intensity of their earlier dipsomania and lechery.

Oborren stared at them questioningly. One of them finally made a reply, "it hjauled away Sven."

"What... took Sven?"

"Whjoo knows?" he replied.

The hunter paused a moment to ruminate. He believed the man who was talking's name was Bjartar- though he wasn't sure. Oborren often found it best to try to not really learn the names of those he used as bait for a man-killer: he might grow too attached to them.

"What did it look like?" enquired Oborren, attempting to refocus on the investigation and assuage his own guilt.

Bjartar and the other men all gave varying accounts of the creature, but three descriptors remained universal: bird, woman, and scary. Oborren was not surprised. It wasn't just peasant superstition that could confuse the facts of a monster sighting- the fear generated by actually seeing a monster could rattle one's senses, making rational thought difficult for most, if not downright impossible for drunken norsemen. And there was also the disbelief that most had in the unnatural to account for, whether it be some impossible creature or sorcerer's spell.

Oborren cast his head downward. It had been a hard night and a failed hunt. His clothes were soaked and he didn't even get a chance to use his special bolt. Bjartar bent down to meet his eyes and pointed up. Following his guiding finger, Oborren guessed that the foul thing had fled back up through a hole in the roof.

Quiet Upon Shenbyrg's Dawning

The hunter couldn't decide what was more disappointing: that he hadn't gotten a chance to slay the monster or that he hadn't even collected enough information to *fully identify it*! For simplicity's sake, he decided that the flying thing must be a harpy, one of *falcon ilk*.

As the norsemen returned to their beer and solemn vows to avenge their snatched comrade, Oborren shook his head and, with his sight clearing, noticed something lying upon the ground directly beneath the roof hole.

Moving closer, he saw that it was a short, cylindrical leather object- a case of some kind. The thing stunk like the harpy, suggesting that it had been carried by the monster and was possibly dropped during the melee with the norsemen.

The hunter sat with his new possession. The mood of the room had begun to lift as each man tried to outdo each other in their claims of what they would do to the flying-thing when they caught her. It was quite colorful, even for norsemen. And Oborren's mood lifted too when, to his great satisfaction, he opened the leather case to find a parchment inside.

He smiled. Tonight's hunt might not have been a total loss after all. The other norsemen, sensing a change in the hunter too, paused in their tales of promised revenge, Bjartar asked what he had found.

The dark-clad hunter smiled back at him and only said, "It must have been a *harpy*."

And he suspected he knew from where it had come.

Chapter 2

The County Castle

Elfriede glanced over at the new Count's visitors: a delegation from the Schoolhouse. She was surprised that the Committee to Investigate the Recent Unpleasantness took less than a year to finish with its findings. Now these tutors sat, seemingly more pleasant than the year prior thanks in part to a change in Administration. Some may have even been present during the Infamous Brigand Raid that was rumored to have destroyed a Notable Guest Speaker, some sort of Enlightened Automaton at the Schoolhouse.

A brilliant panorama shown through the large window across from her desk. The sun had dipped low beneath the curled purple-blue mountains beyond. What beautiful, golden glowing lands had been revealed in West By-Golly? Closer seen was the larger town of Walstock. The many buildings, older and new, stood like some sort of child's play town from this angle, far and below. In the toy streets, the cold autumn winds called to the toy villagers that it was time to return indoors, lest they catch a chill and imbalance their vital humors. This Count's meeting was certainly late in the day; Elfriede knew she should be with those toy villagers, returning to her apartment in the town.

Seeing that the door was now open, Elfriede notified the visitors, who promptly got up and joined to entreat with the Count. Ironically enough, he had only been their Monitor Director a few months prior. But thanks to R'ti becoming the newly official Faith and Law of the Town, he now had a title of peerage to go along with his Cult one.

She sighed and pulled out a small mirror from within her desk drawer as they left. A pleasant Dinglesfuhrian face smiled back at her: deep blue eyes, high cheekbones, pronounced forehead, fair skin with a few freckles, and shimmering blond hair styled back into a bun. Elfriede felt it good to keep a smile on, even though things were not going as well as would merit one.

The new Count seemed a fair enough man, though she didn't trust this Cult of R'ti that had taken control of the town. When she had herself attended the Schoolhouse as a youngster, it was up to the tutors to teach and the pupils to learn. Now it seemed that arrangement had been turned upside down.

To make matters worse, R'ti and other Multicult dogma had begun to inculcate themselves into the daily life of the adults in the town, beyond the walls of the Schoolhouse. Folks weren't really allowed to say what they really thought anymore. Any questioning of R'ti's hold over the pupils and tutors, the heavy taxing for new *County Initiatives*, or even of the Funboxes and Required *Friendly Talk* would lead to a visit from the Watch or the Hounds of Vigilance, the latter being the physical enforcers of R'ti and other Cult doctrine. She had heard that other towns were going through even worse.

Elfriede's real home to the south and east, Dinglesfuhr, seemed to be losing all manner of reason. Some of her own people even wished to give up not just their own sovereignty and defense, but also that of everyone else in the town, as well. It would appear that they would not only declare peace with their ancient foes in

10

Sylvania and Gobington, but might even give them the keys to the city! And she had heard grim tidings to the north as well- it wasn't just Mauriatown and Helltowne at each other's throats that had her worried.

But what could a country lass such as Elfriede do? She returned her attention to the documents that she had been working on earlier. One would think that Orders for running the Schoolhouse might be different than running the entire County, but it wasn't really true. Policy needed to be Followed; Employees needed to show Annua Incrementum... *or else*. And not just the tutors: stewards needed to sweep out the Schoolhouse at an increasing rate with Improving Precision, waggoneers had to transport pupils with Increasing Efficiency and Friendliness. The same was now being applied to all within the Count's employ. She could almost laugh when stewards were commanded by R'ti to develop Vision Statements about how well they could clean a privy or scour a pot.

From watchman to milkmaid to shopkeep to letter-bearer, all had to show Exceptional Performance and Annua Incrementum. The idea of *Full Accountability* might seem reasonable at first glance: everyone could conceivably see the wisdom in the idea of 'Improvement'. Unfortunately though, she saw first-hand what effects that *Improvement* had on those that the High-Monitors of R'ti wished to *Improve*. It was never-ending and ever-changing. It never was enough, and it could destroy lives, especially when one fell out of favor with R'ti.

* * *

"I think the Committee's findings are Sufficient, Sigismund."

"But my Lord Count, many feel that just moving the former Head Monitor to another Schoolhouse was not sufficient for the amount of suffering she caused."

Quiet Upon Shenbyrg's Dawning

Count Remus, Monitor Director of Shenbyrg R'ti, stared at the tutor representative.

"Do you share this sentiment, Sigismund?"

Sigismund's face turned bright red.

"Of... of course not, sire!"

Remus frowned. "You know, Sigismund, everyone needs to *Bear the Same Banner... you Can't Fight the County Castle*, you know-"

Sigismund interrupted nervously, "OF COURSE!" It looked like he was having trouble breathing. The other tutors glanced around nervously.

Remus smiled to put them at ease. "Please remember that anything can be said at this meeting. And, rest assured, Mdme Carve has been given a new... position." It seemed that he had something else to say about the matter, but looked at the Schoolhouse tutors instead. "What were the complaints regarding the former Head Monitor?"

No one spoke except for Ms. Candun. "She screamed at me and many others on many occasions. She targeted tutors to get them to resign. She ruined tutors' lives. Do you know how hard it is for older tutors to find new employ nowadays?"

The Count looked nonplussed, "Oh come now, Ms. Candun-those must have just been Misunderstandings! Don't you remember all the Don Your Dungarees to Work Days she allowed?"

Ms. Candun said nothing. Ms. Dervnel jumped in, "Yes, and we're oh so happy with the Schoolhouse now! Having seven Assistant Monitors makes things so much easier... and we're even allowed to wear our Dungarees More Days Than Ever Before!"

About half of the tutor representatives nodded at this; the other half sat quietly. Mr. Sigismund looked ill.

Dan Osarchuk

"So it looks like everything is going well at the Schoolhouse now. Isn't that right, Mr. Sigismund?"

Sigismund smiled weakly. One of the non-smiling tutors, Ms. Jerminone nudged him.

"We...," he began, "we... still don't feel like we're being treated as the Honored Instructional Artisans that R'ti claims we are."

"And why is that?" asked the Count.

Sigismund went on to describe a litany of scurrilous observations, blatant missteps, and overall lack of support from the Schoolhouse Monitors. He looked so nervous under the Monitor Director's gaze that it seemed he might collapse right there. Perhaps he was a Tutor-Under-Review: such tutors had good reason to fear the Wrath of R'ti.

At that and to everyone's surprise, Remus broke out in laughter.

"Well yes, Mr. Sigismund, it's a Learning Process For Us All!"

The Count then stood up, signaling that the meeting was over. The tutors made their way out the door. Some had to support Sigismund on the way out, since he was now finding it difficult to walk.

As they left, Remus turned and stared at the wall, reading a golden plaque upon it:

> Labor for Tutors (ever-increasing)
> Loyalty to the Monitors and to R'ti, above all else
> Lasting Innovation- Everlasting Change

It was good, but being over a year old, also outdated. He would need Elfriede to make a new one with different slogans: Everlasting Change required it.

Quiet Upon Shenbyrg's Dawning

Reaching into his desk drawer, Remus pulled out a strange shard. He looked around to see if anyone was watching, but he appeared to be alone. Returning his attention to the object, he shifted it to and fro, and it gave off amazingly hued chromatic lights that seemed to dance of their own accord. The Count and Monitor Director smiled as he heard it speak to him quietly. It spoke of Eternal Growth and Everpresent Change... how wonderful...

* * *

"No, thank you, that will be all for today."

With that, Elfriede knew that she was granted leave to depart. It had been a long day and she wondered at what the tutors and the Monitor Director... ahem, Count... had discussed. She would usually spend this time to take a quick ride in the woods towards Fjord Vallee. But the days were getting shorter and it was dangerous for a lone woman to travel at night, even in supposedly a safe land of Men such as this.

So instead, she traveled west into town to do some shopping before returning to her Walstock apartment. Along the way, the villagers greeted her and she bowed in turn. She smiled: perhaps the townsfolk had not been truly corrupted by R'ti or the other Cults yet. Common village politeness and etiquette seemed to still be in effect.

Elfriede gazed at the various storefronts: dark wooden beams accented the white painted walls of quaint window displays. Though most of the shops were closed, she enjoyed seeing all the cute handbags and scented candles in one window and the designer garden trowels and pruning shears in another. Elfriede's onkel would tell her stories about the Ancients when she was little, stories handed down for generations- she wondered if the Ancients had commerce like they had now.

She noticed that one shop was still open and hurried inside. The scent of fine herbs, poultices, and something undefinable filled her senses. The old woman behind the counter smiled at her in grandmotherly fashion.

"What will you like to find today, Dearie?" she asked.

"Oh, just looking," replied Elfriede. She smiled and began to browse through all the goods.

Knowing that it was now or past closing time, Elfriede glanced around quickly and saw a beautiful pendant with a silver stag upon it.

"How much?" she enquired.

The old woman smiled and held up 5 fingers. Elfriede reached into her handbag, but realized she had only 4 silver coins left- the rest of her wealth had gone to recent charges at the Hospitalia.

As if reading her mind, the old woman smiled once more and said, "Four will be fine."

The younger woman thanked her graciously and wished her a good evening.

Entering the street again, it was now completely dark. A watchman walked by, nodded at her, and began lighting the street lanterns. Though she felt nervous about it, Elfriede began walking in the direction of her apartment, even though those streets did not have lanterns.

Rounding the corner, some youths approached, perhaps six in all. Expecting them to tip their hats, Elfriede was shocked when they made rude gestures and remarks at her- some seemed just 10 years of age!

Quiet Upon Shenbyrg's Dawning

"This is *our street*, wench!"

Regaining her composure, she gritted her teeth, strode up, and smacked one of the errant boys right on the backside. Now startled themselves, the youths broke and ran, even the older ones.

Elfriede smiled to herself; it looked like some old-fashioned discipline was just what those youths needed. She continued on her way. The temple of Minerva stood ahead- she was sure the priestesses would be amused at how she had done some justice this evening.

To her horror, she realized that the temple had been defiled. The entrance and windows were boarded-up. Graffiti was painted over the warrior-maiden statues that had so often given Elfriede solace. Tears began to well up in her eyes- who would do this to the temple?

Elfriede studied the area more carefully. The graffiti was mainly sayings of R'ti that appeared to be well-painted and prepared, indicating that this act may not have been the work of opportunistic ruffians. Indeed, what ruffians would espouse such jargon as 'Constant Change is the Foundation for A Stable Realm' and 'Ergo, Why Don't We Have Some Eternal Happiness'?

But there were other cults at work here too. Elfriede was no priestess, but she spotted a symbol of a smiling face holding a syringe, indicating worship of the foul Shield Ghul, who would steal one's health if one didn't pay inordinate sums and great periods of time. If fear of that Demon Lord wasn't enough, his knightly order of Hospitaliers certainly was.

And that wasn't all. Other cult symbols were visible throughout the temple face. It looked like someone was trying to indicate some sort of fell pantheon.

16

Her thoughts were soon interrupted though by a familiar voice. It sounded like that youth who had insulted her earlier.

"Yes sir, Mr. Hound of Vigilance, sir, she hit me right here and said that she enjoyed Violating My Pupil Rights!"

It sounded like the voices were approaching.

Terrified, Elfriede fled. As she made her way through the darkened streets, she could have sworn that she also heard a hissing sound, as if something was stalking her.

She rounded a bend and hid behind some brush. Though her heart was racing, she struggled to hold her breath. The voices sounded distant now, but the sense of being followed, the sense that something was after her, was increasing. Something slippery and poisonous and vile moved between the brush and the trees and porches on the street.

The air was cold and she shivered as she hid, but the chill was not enough to slow the snaky sickness that stalked her. Her skin began to crawl as she sensed it grow closer, slithering unstoppably near, empowered by the false accusations of the rude youths.

The uneasiness within her own flesh began to intensify almost in answer to the approach of the unspeakable horror. She could barely contain herself any longer when her body froze: what looked to be a long, serpent tongue was curling around the porch directly ahead. Too terrified to react, Elfriede saw that it was attached to a woman's face, but then it changed, and appeared to be the face of a huge serpent.

At that, she fled again, and did not look back. Something watched her with alien eyes as she ran; something that knew it would catch her eventually.

Chapter 3

Caelum Mount

"Oh, I see! Oppressing the Mundane Proletariat now are WE?"

The hoplite's shield struck the Karlist in the face again. Tepson was mostly glad that the guard hadn't used his spear or short sword to silence the cleric. Maybe they were used to dealing with rabble-rousers, which Kolveig certainly was.

Of all the places that he had revisited since his return to the Valley... ahem, Vale, Caelum Mount certainly seemed the most different so far. What was once a sleepy, almost backwater hamlet had been converted into some sort of Wizards' Resort. A number of tall, white brick towers arose from the town center, setting off an air of impeccable authority over the remaining, more normal-looking buildings that surrounded them. Even those had tile roofs and Olympian columns out front, strangely enough. Tepson stroked his short beard as he thought.

A *Magocracy,* Kolveig had called it. Tepson would have asked him more about what he meant, but the cleric could only repeatedly spit out that single word, so the gnome didn't want to press his luck... or smack the Karlist in frustration. In fact, it had taken all of his midg... *ahem, gnome* sensibilities to keep the cleric from getting killed in this place, as he would run up to and challenge anyone in the town that was wearing a robe, whether they claimed to be a wizard or not.

And of all his companions that had saved him from the Chromatic Light nearly a year ago, it was ironic that Tepson had stayed with Kolveig. Oborren had become increasingly obsessed in rooting out any remaining taint of the New Strangeness, the *Insolitus Novus* as they called it. That Halfdan fellow was apparently rotting in the Gaol. And Brymanah, well, *being Brymanah*, she returned to her amazon home to 'get away from all these ridiculous males'.

So Tepson had ended up wandering with perhaps the most insane member of the party. Returning to Maury-, ahem, Mauriatown, was still not an option, since both gnomes and left-wingers did not fare very well in that land at all. Tepson sometimes wondered what had happened to his family, but it had been centuries since he last saw them- how could he possibly find out now?

It was therefore fitting to venture with the most insane member of the party, because the current state of the Vale seemed so insane itself. Each locality apparently suffered from its own particular brand of psychosis. Whether it be amazons in Stephania or fascists in Mauriatown or dwarven Bolsheviks in Helltowne or savages in Pentagram Tannery or vikings in Strass Hill *or whatever*, most of the people seemed to have gone quite mad! Why not travel around with the crazy marxist cleric? He fit right in!

Caelum Mount suffered from its own type of insanity, though it might not have been as unpleasant for Tepson to bear as other places. Here he was simply one of the Mundanes: people without any apparent magical powers. Even after seeing many strange things for about a year now, Tepson doubted if 'magic' was truly real or just more mass hysteria. Down below, in the underground, so-called *spellcasters* could even demonstrate great displays of lights and sounds, but was it really magic? Maybe it was just swamp gas.

Whatever the case, this certainly was a New World. Even though the geography, climate, vegetation, animals, and general ethnicity of the people remained the same, things certainly were different. There was no electric power, for one, as well as no internal combustion engines that worked. That changed everything. And whether by luck or design, the people in the Vale today survived without what seemed to be such necessities to Tepson in the past. In fact, they seemed quite occupied with their own particular brand of psychosis.

Speaking of psychosis, it appeared that the hoplite's beating had finally quieted the cleric. Kolveig now lay in the alleyway, dazed. Tepson couldn't tell whether he was more surprised that the local police in this Vale town dressed as Olympian warriors did millennia ago or that Kolveig had finally stopped talking. Everything from the Corinthian helmet to the breastplate, greaves, and weaponry still shown polished, silvery metallic, though the hoplite himself seemed somewhat winded from beating the Karlist. He stared briefly at the gnome before he went back to the street.

Tepson then did the responsible thing and checked on Kolveig. Though he was a biologist, there was little more he could do than study him. It looked like he might be out for a while. So the gnome propped the cleric up a bit, gave him a comfortable sack to rest on, and went to explore some more of the town. He assumed he would get more ground covered if the cleric wasn't trying to start a revolution at every street corner.

* * *

The Karlist shook himself awake from an intense dream. Where was that Fascist Pig Oppressor who had beaten his Karlist Self?

21

Quiet Upon Shenbyrg's Dawning

Kolveig stood and tried to regain his bearings. And where in Tarnation was that blasted gnome? Still oozing some blood from the corner of his mouth onto his large black beard, the cleric stumbled into the street. He adjusted his battered olive jacket and hammer and sickle lapels.

The architecture of the town reflected the cultural motif of the hoplite who had beaten him. White painted wooden pillars lined the streets as townsfolk walked about. The cleric saw them as Foppish Dandies in Yet Another Inane Capitalist Attempt At Finding Happiness Through Acquisition Of Material Wealth. Some called it 'shopping', but Kolveig knew better! Still, he couldn't blame these folk too much. Let them have their measly Ornament Squash, Painted Wagons, and Lemon Tea. He could see the True Dictators in this town!

His eyes rose to glare at the white towers looming in the distance. He went to Raise His Hand In Defiance, the way that all true Just Warriors of Justice did, until he spotted more of those confounded hoplites. Four of them stared at him, perhaps one of them was the one who had beat him- he couldn't tell; they all looked alike with their stupid helmets on.

Another time, he conceded. He stalked down the street further, making sure to stare at those hoplite Fascists while he was walking! No matter if he kept bumping into villagers as he did so.

But despite how hard he focused on his Righteous Outrage, Kolveig couldn't stop the memory of his dreams from returning. He had been having the same dream for months now and it bothered him greatly.

"Oh yes, back in Mauriatown, thank you very much! Just the place where I would want to dream about every night! It's even worse than those Counter-Revolutionaries in Helltowne! Dreaming... dreaming about..."

Kolveig stopped, realizing that he was clearly talking to himself out loud and that he had squarely bumped into someone. Not that he would ever apologize, no a Karlist would never admit-

"Just what do you think you're doing?" said the man.

Kolveig sized up the individual. He had to: it completely dictated what he would say in reply. It was obvious from his starrified robes and pointy hat that the man was a Wizard.

"Attempting to Overthrow the Ruling Class," said the cleric as a matter-of-fact. He smiled evilly at the man.

The Wizard frowned back: his meaty jowls, ringed hands and perfumed aroma also certainly styled him *Bourgeois*.

Kolveig smiled more wickedly- it looked like even the Wizard's traveling companions were taken aback.

"So- what are you going to do now, WIZARD OPPRESSOR?" said Kolveig finally. The cleric's yelling drew the attention of passers-by around them.

The Wizard continued to frown at the Karlist, but his gaze showed anger, not fear. Some more hoplite watchmen approached, spears ready.

"Oh, I see! Hiding behind your HOPLITE GOONS are you, WIZARD!"

At this, the Wizard raised his hands suddenly. Kolveig nearly fell over as he reached for his trusty Marxian hammer and sickle. Unfortunately, they had been confiscated the first time he had been beaten by the watch.

But to Kolveig's relief, the Wizard was not raising his hand to cast a spell. It appeared he simply did so to have the watchmen stand down.

Quiet Upon Shenbyrg's Dawning

At this, the cleric began his Just Chastisement.

"I Hereby Declare a REVOLUTION to Commence Immediately! HEAR ME, TOWNSFOLK?!"

A few hundred feet away, while eating a delicious meal at an elegant food-house, Tepson could tell that Kolveig had finally regained consciousness.

"What More Opiates of the Masses Are We Willing to SUFFER?!" continued the cleric.

Kolveig glared at a villager passing by; the man attempted to edge away from the obvious maniac agitator.

"You, sir! Don't you feel OPPRESSED?"

The man glanced at the agitator and then the Wizard and the hoplites. All stared at him expectantly.

"Umm...."

"EXACTLY," continued the cleric, "this man can't even be allowed to speak his mind, what with such STUPID WIZARDLY SCUM AND THEIR FASCIST HOPLITE LAPDOGS around to OPPRESS him!"

All stood quiet for a moment. The villagers knew that insulting wizards was the most heinous of crimes- *they did rule the town.*

The hoplites looked at the Wizard. The latter smiled and raised his hands again. This time he *would be casting a spell...* on Kolveig!

* * *

Tepson nudged the chair further away. The squirrel kept jumping up on it to stare and chatter at him; apparently, it wanted a better vantage point. *Sciurus carolinensis* might be cute, but the situation was certainly beginning to freak the gnome out.

24

That the Wizard's pretty assistant kept coming in to feed it nuts didn't help matters either.

Finally back upon the chair, the squirrel began to stare at the gnome even more intensely. Its dark beady eyes looked at him accusingly when he did not reply to its irate chattering. It then took one of the nuts that the assistant gave it, cocked its little head to the side and flung it right at Tepson's head. The gnome could have sworn that the squirrel chattered something to the effect of "*Bourgeois.*"

Enough of this! Tepson went to get up out of the oversized chair in which he was sitting and nearly fell face first out of it, he was so irritated. Who did this *supposed Wizard* think he was? To keep us here, just because the stupid Karlist said one of his stupid remarks again? Magic? Pah!

The Wizard's assistant entered the room smiling. There was something to her eyes and face, strikingly like how Lynda or even Gillian looked in their heyday that Tepson remembered from his previous life of television: even-set clear eyes with a perfectly short nose, a warm smile, and flawless skin. Perhaps the Wizard's magic wasn't real, but the assistant's certainly seemed to be so. What else could make such a seasoned gnome like Tepson feel just like a silly schoolboy again?

"Master Antraxus will be with you in a few moments."

The squirrel chattered something accusingly at the assistant. She smiled back at him in return. The squirrel stopped chattering- she *was* truly magical indeed.

The room began to grow a strange color as the Wizard entered. Even the assistant's effect began to wear off- the squirrel began shaking and hissing in anger. The Wizard pointed a finger at it and it quieted somewhat, but its resentment could still be seen even on its simple squirrel features. Tepson was just glad that it hadn't the ability to talk.

Quiet Upon Shenbyrg's Dawning

"So... what to do with you two..." Master Antraxus tapped his nose in thought.

His assistant smiled and whispered something in the Wizard's ear. Antraxus grinned and nodded, then began to laugh. Perhaps she had not learned her magical skills of relaxation from him, because then the Wizard's laugh began to become maniacal. The assistant simply smiled disarmingly. Tepson knew that this wouldn't be good.

* * *

Lloyd Dingle hit the gas on his cruiser. Here he was again- another call to the ATV trail. Couldn't these people just stay in town where it was safe? His irritation mixed with a little joy at making the trip. Peeling up the switchbacks, siren blaring at such a high speed on his cruiser, it felt like he was ascending into the clouds.

His car flew around a bend, the crisp leaves on the trees fluttered in the cool autumn wind of the cruiser flying by. Dispatch sounded: "Suspects spotted at a residence off of FR 74."

Whatever was really going on at the location was most likely an understatement- he needed to be ready.

Like everybody, Lloyd had heard the news- the fall of D.C., 66 was clogged, *people fleeing west on foot*. Where was the fairness in that? People out here in the Valley, we were keeping things together. We lived a simpler life, without all that D.C. nonsense. Now, when things got rough and their crazy town fell apart, they had to *come out here and spread the misery*?

He slowed as FR 74 approached and made the turn. The cruiser bumped as pavement turned to dirt. It would have been good to have his partner, Dakota, with him, but with all the commotion going on- every deputy was needed for separate calls. Lloyd ventured a glance at his shotgun mounted in the center console as he slowed at the residence.

Dan Osarchuk

'Suspects' was right. Roughly thirty older teenage youths had surrounded a trailer and they seemed really ticked-off. They looked like D.C. folks too- how the hell did they get out this far? So much for the Valley having a 'Fort', thought Lloyd.

He pulled over and got out from his vehicle. Lloyd's brown car and uniform blended better with the cedars and oaks that surrounded the area than the garish colors and clownlike clothing of the city-slickers.

"Hey pig!" exclaimed one of the youths.

Lloyd sized up the situation. Most of the suspects seemed occupied with the trailer. It occurred to him that even though the fall of D.C. had caused this mass migration, it might also free up his *flexibilities as an officer of the peace.*

Testing that theory, he whipped out his pistol and pointed it right at the youth. He knew that he couldn't shoot him right away, but maybe the youth would give him a chance.

But unfortunately for Lloyd, the other youths noticed what was happening and turned in unison. To his increasing dismay, Lloyd saw that most of them were armed too and they were dragging a dead local couple out of the trailer.

"It's our trailer now!" they shouted.

The closest youth smiled wickedly as the others started laughing and yelling, converging on Lloyd. They didn't even raise their weapons, they knew they had the deputy outnumbered.

Lloyd knew it was over for him. He'd never get to see his wife or kids again, that it might take days or even weeks for his death to be avenged. But he also knew that there would probably be no crazy news stories about 'police brutality', since the reporters would be too busy with the fall of D.C.

He wondered how many of these bastards could he take with him?

Lloyd's shots rang out as the youths rushed him. They punched and beat and kicked the deputy mercilessly. He felt his body shatter as they laughed and took his own gun. They held it to his head and asked Lloyd what was he going to do now. They took his silver star badge and shoved into his face.

Holding back the rage and tears, he could only utter one promise before they executed him.

"I'm going to come back one day, and people like you are going to meet justice."

Chapter 4

Dinglesfuhr

The majestic peaks of the Nuttens framed the area as if they were a great, frozen ocean. At times coated in white or a green vestment, now they wore oranges, browns, and reds. All held a fiery effervescence, mixed with an earthy, crisp withdrawal in the quickening of fall.

Frau Mekla returned to the confines of the Darkastle. Oh, what pride she had in her land. Carved by a great wizard a century ago, her people stood in distinct grace, apart from the varied lands that abutted hers. Whether it be the strange politics of Walstock to the north, the savage Fjord Vallee to the east, mad-struck Ever Lur to the south, or the tyrannical magocrats of Caelum Mount to the west, Dinglesfuhr stood apart. Today, it kept its politics to itself and was not lost to primitivism, nor was mad, and though founded by a wizard, did not hold such types above any others.

In short, Dinglesfuhr was a wonderful place for even the commoner to dwell. Mekla, as Dinglesfrau, believed in food for the poor and helping all young Dinglesfuhrians have a chance at a meaningful profession. Dinglesfuhrian *"fuhrniture"* was an especially popular export to the adjacent lands, one of the many that brought prosperity to her small realm. It was not always so, of course, but it was now. She was glad to count Dinglesfuhr as one of the few Enlightened settlements in the Vale.

She walked through the gothic halls of the kastle. Carved gargoyles leered back at her, as well as sundry sculpted pikes impaling stone statue heads. She remembered how her father, a vizier to the Dinglesherr before her, had told her that this prosperity, this freedom for their subjects, had come at a great cost. Mekla never really understood her father's words. Instead, she felt that her tutors had a more reasoned argument: Dinglesfuhr was more prosperous now, *because it had abandoned* its Amaranthine Reign of Terror decades ago.

She entered a large and ornately appointed room. A stained glass dome shown overhead, reflecting the autumn sky just perceptibly beyond. Fine, dark leather and light wood *fuhrniture* was spread throughout, though most notably around a great central table with six great chairs. The scent of leather mixed with the ancient aroma of polish and a slight hint of dust.

Seated in all the seats but one were Mekla's advisors: Kurt, Van Dwick, Eind, Helka, Esmerre, and Frollicke. All wore the high-collared, dark violet formalwear so customary amongst the Dinglesfuhrian upper class. Commensurate too were their pale complexions, perfectly straight hair, and wide foreheads, the latter being noted especially by whispering outsiders. Otherwise, they bore either very light-colored hair, such as with Kurt and Frollicke, or very dark hair, even pure black, such as with Eind and Helka. There seemed little trend for middle ground here.

"What business have we today, Interior Minister Kurt?"

"Mein Dinglesfrau, your itemized listings of the various Fjord Vallee tribes is nearing readiness."

"Nearing?" Mekla smiled at Kurt teasingly.

Kurt smiled back. "Yes, the savages do not take kindly to receiving Census."

At this, Eind exploded. "Savages? How dare you label them that!"

The rest of the advisors began to argue. Mekla could see that the believers in Underreign were certainly opinionated. They held the sentiment that Dinglesfuhr was *too* prosperous and should necessarily *repay* some of the neighboring lands that they had defeated, especially Fjord Vallee and haunted Sylvania beyond. Those believers now certainly included Eind and Frollicke; the others did not seem so convinced.

"Enough." Mekla stopped the conversation in classical curt Dinglesfuhrian fashion. "And what of the *fuhrniture* and food production, Minister of Trade?" she continued.

Helka gave her report. "Frau, though the various Administrators complain that the workers demand too much in salary, we have nearly reached 100% capacity in the silos, *including the salt mine.*"

All the advisors began to applaud in appreciation.

Van Dwick attempted to interrupt, "Mein Frau, the expenditures for additional troops-"

At this, Mekla cut him off, "Later, Herr Van Dwick. The future of Dinglesfuhr lies in its capacity to make peace, not in its capacity to make war."

The advisor's face turned red in frustration, but he said nothing and nodded.

Quiet Upon Shenbyrg's Dawning

All the advisors then arose, except for Eind. He waited expectantly as the others would leave Mekla and him alone in the great room. Van Dwick took his time departing.

"Mein Dinglesfrau," began Eind, "I must salute your chastisement of Van Dwick. His is an outdated sentiment."

Mekla smiled at him, her pretty blue eyes showing a warmth that his harsh steel grays did not. She waited for his next statement.

"A gift, mein Frau." He produced an exotic-looking shard.

"Is it glass? Is it metal?" she enquired.

"Unknown, mein Frau. I found it in my travels and thought you would find it pleasing..."

She smiled and took it from her advisor- it generated such amazing spectral colors; *it did seem very pleasing.*

* * *

Elfriede, tired and distraught, made her way to the Dinglestor. The dark violet-clad Dinglesguards approached and asked for her papers as she approached the gates. The older one looked at her with an almost fatherly concern. Being a classic Dinglesfuhrian, he said nothing out of decorum, but his concerned smile made her reddened eyes and saddened face soften somewhat.

The scrivener always found it odd that even though she was born in Dinglesfuhr and returned here quite often, she always had to show her papers to regain entry. On the other hand, *certain* others, especially halflings and mountain folk, didn't. The younger guard nodded and let her pass.

Soon Elfriede was walking upon the fabled Dingleplatz. She smiled as the townsfolk milled about the place, engaging in energetic commerce and polite conversation. A few halflings were interspersed, wearing the black clown clothing and jester's hats of their Sylvanian heritage. The short people were also unfortunately falling into their stereotypical *pocket-patting* and *food-staring* ways. Most of the Dinglesfuhrians ignored them.

The tall mountain folk could be seen walking about in small groups too, their bluish hair setting them apart. They were strong but few. Elfriede didn't know much more about them, except that there were also rumors of Cults that even worshipped them as the true heirs to Dinglesfuhr.

At least there were no obvious signs of fell Cults yet. Certain Dinglesfuhrians might sometimes turn from the High Ones when things seemed bad, but they might only do so secretly. When harvests failed and when dreams died, even the most devout might question their faith in the Gods. Some might even begin to look to strange or even dark entities for succor instead. Though fairy bargains might be more common in other parts of the Vale, here in Dinglesfuhr, the *dead* were far more likely to be called upon for assistance.

But those who actually fell in with Demon Lords were quite rare indeed. She had only heard of a handful of such accounts in Dinglesfuhrian history. Elfriede still shuddered at what she had seen at the Temple of Minerva in Walstock last night. How could such madness and evil be allowed to corrupt the home of such a forthright and benevolent Goddess?

Following Demon Lords required a certain kind of madness. Obviously, ideas of *Permanent Improvement* or Having Health Treatment at the Complete Expense of One's Livelihood were insane. Few would follow such beliefs on their own merits. The problems arose though when Demonists took control of an area and began to *force others* to follow the madness too. Then such evil would take on a life of its own, growing like a cancer to dominate with its terror, to crush far more dreams than the initial turning from the True Gods ever initiated.

Quiet Upon Shenbyrg's Dawning

Elfriede made up her mind to be more wary, at least for Dinglesfuhr's sake. She might *work* in Walstock, but Dinglesfuhr was her home. She began to cheer up when she spotted her old friends Kalla and Gudre. Before long, they would be laughing like schoolgirls once again.

* * *

Night began to creep into the windows of Mekla's platzhaus. Her mug of hot ale stood in her lap as she stared mesmerized at the shadows on the walls. Ever since she was a little girl, Mekla had been afraid of the Dinglesfuhr shadows. In some lands, parents would tell their young that ghosts and spooks weren't real. Of course in Dinglesfuhr, everyone knew that was a lie.

Before the year 306 ALO (After Lights Out), Dinglesfuhr was quite the haunted place: dangerously so. It seemed that the dark reach of Haunted Sylvania had jumped across the Fjord to hold Dinglesfuhr in its black hand. Few would venture outside at night and return to tell of it. It certainly had an effect on the local economy, which remained a backwater. The Darkastle was nothing but a semi-abandoned watchtower in those days, a leftover of the failed Narquay Imperium. There was no Dingleplatz, nor any *fuhrniture* for sale- few in other lands had even heard of Dinglesfuhr.

After the Amaranthine Wizard came in 306 though, he broke the power of the Night, being highly skilled in such necromantic arts himself. He was even rumored to be one of the legendary Party of the Vale. What were once horrid wraiths and wights now only became whispers and bumps in the night- still present, but just not nearly as real and luckily, not nearly as deadly.

But the Wizard didn't stop there. A great treasure was rumored to be held upon Mill Mountain, which as part of the Nutten range, runs north and south of Dinglesfuhr and forms the eastern wall for most settlements in the Vale. It was said that the mountain folk who dwelt there held *schatz*, treasure of exceptional value.

Marshalling his forces, he marched upon the mountain folk. Men came from Dinglesfuhr and from some of the surrounding towns too, answering the bloody cry for fame and fortune. The Amaranthine Wizard *claimed* that the mountain folk were tainted and evil, that they held the blood of giants within them, and that they worshipped the Fell God Thrym. Such was the power of the Wizard and the response to his call that the mountain folk were defeated in only a day and over a thousand were slain by the conquering men. All for the *schatz*, the treasure!

Mekla started weeping at the story. Granted, it had occurred over a century ago and yet her tutors had imbued in her the great shame that Dinglesfuhr still merited to this day. Strangely too, this was the first time that she had actually cried over it.

As her tears abated, she recalled how others had said how fearsome the mountain folk were, that their giant blood not only gave them great strength, but also great savagery as well. Some even claimed that they had actual Frost Giants helping them-monsters known for their taste for human flesh.

"But did it matter? What right did Dinglesfuhr have in slaughtering them?"

No one knew for sure what the treasure was that the Wizard claimed the mountain folk held, but most wept for the many brave sons of Dinglesfuhr that perished upon the mountain top. There was certainly no shortage of legends of the treasure's true nature or of all the ghost stories of phantom soldiers seeking to return home or of spectral giants that might toss off any Dinglesfuhrian foolish enough to venture back upon Mill Mountain if they weren't careful.

Mekla, having grown up in this land for over five decades had certainly heard all the stories. But strangely now, the sadness grew stronger. She stumbled in her grief to her platzhaus window and looked at her people enjoying fine food and conversation at dusk. Families strolled passed the shops, walking close together in the chill autumn air. The scene would have normally filled the Dinglesfrau with great happiness, but all she could feel now was black despair.

She looked down at the paved walkway below and considered jumping. All her land was a lie! The Amaranthine Wizard didn't just destroy the mountain folk- he had even conquered the Fjord and invaded Haunted Sylvania- all for the 'Glory of Dinglesfuhr'! And look at us now! Walking around and shopping!

Anger started to fill Mekla as she glared at her home. Screaming now, she began knocking over vases, ripping apart books, and throwing cups and candles at the walls until they shattered. Before long, two of her Secret Police bodyguards rushed inside.

"Mein Dinglesfrau?"

She waved them away and regained her composure. *How could we ever make amends*?

Mekla sat in her chair again and sighed at the mess. Then she remembered the shard that Eind had given her. She took it out of her pocket. The lights still shone vividly when she turned it to and fro.

She smiled: she knew now how Dinglesfuhr could be cleansed.

* * *

Hymnir approached the hidden temple entrance, pulling his long bluish hair back over his broad shoulders. Though hidden by a vividly-colored blanket, the entrance was intentionally taller than others on the Dingleplatz: it was made for Honored Guests such as He. The aroma of incense and laughing women excited his senses. He strolled inside.

"A Great One!" exclaimed one raven-haired beauty when he entered. Her voluptuous body fluttered with spectral designs; her eyebrows dyed blue like the people that she worshipped.

Dan Osarchuk

"My, he is *grosse!*" exclaimed another with blue-dyed hair in a rainbow dress. She was becoming visibly excited that he made no demand for her to avert her eyes. She looked up at him and swooned.

Even the males in the room bowed low. They had rainbow masks placed over their faces that read 'Return the Land to Them'; their pants read 'No More Descendants for Me.' Hymnir smiled and kicked one of the men in the face. He enjoyed belittling the Oppressors and taking their women. All clapped and others bowed closer to receive a kick, as well.

Hymnir did not indulge them though and instead went to one end of the room to begin his sermon. The others looked at him in adoration.

Behind him, upon the entrance it read *'Underreign: for the Cleansing of Dinglesfuhr'*.

Chapter 5

The Gaol

"Exercise Yard: 1 hour."

Halfdan had to admit that life wasn't becoming any easier. He had surrendered a great deal to God and to himself during his Odinnic practice, but it seemed like the world wished to take its revenge upon him in return.

Life in the Gaol could be called agonizing. Apparently, his usual social awkwardness did not drive off large and upsetting male inmates inside like it did with attractive females on the outside. That many of the former had taken Halfdan to become his plaything only forced him to disidentify with his mind-body even more. He could therefore witness the agony, but it didn't cause him as much suffering as he might otherwise experience. And yet the agony was still there nonetheless: very unpleasant sensations with a very unpleasant narrative occurring in his mind.

Halfdan missed his children most, but the Gaol was of course certainly no place for them to visit. And he realized that seeing his children might force him to identify with his emotions and personable self again, making it more difficult to ease back into witness consciousness when they left. So it was probably best that they didn't come by, though he often wondered how they fared without him. It helped immeasurably to know that his former wife's family could take care of them while he was imprisoned. It was also probably best that his children did not see Halfdan like this.

Between the beatings and worse by the other inmates, Halfdan attempted to find some solace in writing. He had found an old parchment and quill and had taken to recording his life's adventures and misadventures, however meagre, so that he might pass his story on to his children somehow. Being Odinnic, scribing runes upon the parchment came easily to him. Writing also helped Halfdan because he otherwise seemed to have very little control over what occurred in his life- a life that often seemed difficult and even sometimes hostile.

His current drear and isolated circumstances reminded him somewhat of when he was younger and had first entered this world that was *around the bend*. Feeling unwelcome in the outside lands and with outside people, Halfdan would often isolate himself in his room and play with toy knights and dragons for hours, narrating epic quests and daring sagas. Like today with his writing, it allowed him far more measure in what happened, as well as a much greater degree of sense and relation than when interacting with the world outside his room.

Scribing runes upon the parchment also helped somewhat to occupy his mind with the question of why life in the Gaol was the way it was. He understood full well that most of society had eventually become medieval after Lights Out, but he wondered why gaols in the manner of the Ancients remained. Halfdan had studied at Southbyrg that the condemned were simply tortured, thrown into dungeons to die, or executed during the First Dark Ages. That did seem like an effective enough deterrent to Halfdan: why worry about the expense of a more modern style of incarceration?

But after his own interrogation of the Least Offer nearly a year ago, it had dawned on him that deterrence was only a minor reason for the continuance of gaols in this current age, the Second Dark Ages. Those really dangerous criminals would most likely *excel* in a gaol, while less dangerous ones would truly suffer at the hands of the dangerous ones. If criminal punishment returned to quick torture, execution, or even the restitution of the Tribal Days, then it would have served as a more equitable and fair punishment, no matter how large, aggressive, or deranged the offender might be.

No, there persisted a desire to *keep the ones who have offended those in power* under control and isolated from the larger public for decades at a time. Whether this intention came from a genuine desire to 'rehabilitate' the offender was debatable. As Halfdan had come to discover, most so-called 'good intentions' actually caused more problems than they solved. And, as he had learned more about the creature that once was high in the Watch Command, he realized that the Gaol was an even more twisted form of punishment than being locked in the stocks for a few days or simply getting one's own punishment and suffering over with via beheading.

Psychic vampires aside, the true reason for the continuance of gaols could be to further the power of Cults and their Dogma. Even before R'ti had come to overtly dominate Walstock, the Churches of Tyr and of Athena felt it best to delay execution and other hasty punishments, so as to have a better pool of candidates for their own interrogations and redemptions respectively. That witch hunters could find more heretics to burn, thanks to 'tips' from the inmates, or that knights falcon could lead more villains to redemption, was just too tempting an opportunity to pass. That the Least Offer had capitalized on this arrangement placed him more in the role of a parasite or a predator than as an orchestrator of the current state of gaols.

Quiet Upon Shenbyrg's Dawning

With the Monitor Director now being named the new Count of Shenbyrg, Cult domination of the Gaol, as well as any other institutions in the region, would be complete. The more benign and subtle cults of Tyr and Minerva were already being replaced by the more malign and blatant Cult of R'ti.

And since he was quite despised by those now assuming greater power, Halfdan had been moved from a more solitary cell to dwell with Brotus, a particularly large and unpleasant individual. He was rumored to even have orcish blood. Some thought he was close to an ogre, due to his size and obstreperous bearing. Halfdan would have much preferred to be put in an oubliette: at least the walls did not abuse and belittle him like Brotus did.

And Halfdan couldn't help but hope that his demise would come soon. Each day was a struggle even to arise from his broken cot and to not just allow Brotus or some other inmate to beat him to death. It was an exhausting game of wanting to remain alive vs. not, which made it even more exhausting. He longed to see the open welkin once again, to have some peaceful quiet, to lose himself in the solace, and to spend time with his children and see how they were faring.

He remembered how he had originally entered into the Odinnic practice to meet the blonde woman of his dreams. How ironic that he seemed further from that than ever before, even after all these years of practice. Yes, he had found a great deal of serenity in *holding the* eye (*the I*), but his life, if viewed objectively, was far worse for the measure now. When he had started, he still was at least reasonably enjoyably employed at the Schoolhouse and had a number of compatriots to associate with. What did he have now? Nothing but loneliness and suffering.

He wondered why Odin hadn't just let him die for good last year when that ghost had frozen his heart. Perhaps he was meant to come back and help defeat the automaton Enak and the madwoman Carve, but now that was done. Rumors were that the

Schoolhouse was all better now, with the cruel Head Monitor being moved to another capacity and one of her subordinates promoted- probably one who despised Halfdan. Sometimes he even dreamt that he still worked at the Schoolhouse, happily instructing pupils, enjoying the respect of the Monitors and friendship of the other tutors.

How strange it was that dreams could seem more real than the waking world.

* * *

Halfdan was shoved out the door into the Gaol Yard. Feelings of hope mixed with dread as he stared at the beautiful sky, only to lose the relative protection from the guards. The other inmates started to jeer and shout as they saw Halfdan standing there alone in his slender, aging, intellectual sensitivity. He fell to his knees, hoping to let go of all the fear and humiliation as the others began to get line up to beat and belittle him. Perhaps they would finally kill him this time. At least he didn't have to worry about making them feel uncomfortable.

"Oh look! It's *girly-man!*" they said. Many began stretching so that they wouldn't unduly strain their limbs as they pommeled him.

Halfdan felt deserted by everyone, including God, and wondered when the end would come and what would occur afterwards. As the inmate thugs worked out their frustrations and aggressions on the defenseless cleric's body, Halfdan remembered how he thought he had seen his true love when he had died in the Schoolhouse basement. Perhaps he would see her again?

As his vision turned red and finally dark though, he feared that even she might be repelled by his presence.

To fly so high
And to fall so far

Quiet Upon Shenbyrg's Dawning

Makes one wonder
What to trust
And who you are

* * *

The throbbing in his cheekbone awakened the battered Odinnic back to consciousness. He couldn't help but smile as a beautiful face shined down upon him. There she was, fair and kind: Carsanna. The Gaol Nurse was quite a beauty- Halfdan had even thought that he had died and returned to Valhalla when he first saw her. But no, he quickly recognized her and Carsanna appeared to be mortal, even if she was a breathtaking priestess of Freya.

She cared for him with an amazing degree of sympathy; he felt that he could be himself with her, that he could surrender. She smiled back at him as she rose to leave, her curvaceous, white-clad body giving the impression of both caretaker and vixen.

Halfdan remembered his dreams of the blonde woman. And though Carsanna's hair was instead chestnut, she did remind him of her. Perhaps it was her manner and her mien? There was something so satisfying in being cared for by a beautiful woman, to be able to let one's guard down with one completely.

Feeling her presence strangely felt so right, so normal for Halfdan, and yet so heavenly. What made it strange was that he had never really known that connection in this life for long. He sometimes wondered if, in fact, he was only viewing this life as if upon a screen and that his true love stood behind him in some realer world, smiling at his overactive interest in his own imagination.

Of course, as in nearly all of Halfdan's relations with the fairer sex, things were over before they began. He often said the wrong things to women his age and would even undergo *mild inquisitions* from time to time when he misspoke. Halfdan was unsure whether he was avoided by women because he was suffering

44

under some curse or if it was simply that he did not harmonize with this world because he had gone *around the bend* at an early age. Or it could be that he was simply unattractive.

Carsanna glanced back at him. Halfdan smiled at her, but said nothing. It wouldn't be wise to put himself through more heartbreak if he had flirted with her and he couldn't bring himself to subject the woman to his presence more than was necessary.

As she ventured off, Carsanna smiled at some of the other inmates. Whether it was simply her beauty that calmed them or some more supernatural blessing of Freya, Halfdan could not tell. She obviously got a better response from them than the more puritan Sister Aelstad of Minerva. Though jealousy began to arise as the other inmates flirted with Carsanna, Halfdan dropped it, knowing that it was best. He realized that it seemed a little easier to drop his feelings lately, especially when he remembered to notice the *one who was experiencing the feelings*.

A short fellow with a mustache approached the cleric as they watched Carsanna leave. Terrance was one of the few inmates that didn't beat or do other awful things to Halfdan- and not just because he was short. In fact, the two chatted fairly easily when their paths crossed, making them full acquaintances in the Gaol. They seemed to have a lot in common.

"She is a quite the looker, isn't she?" Terrance winked as Carsanna finally left the room.

Halfdan nodded. "Shall we play some more *civi-chess* later?"

"Wouldn't miss it for the world. Glad they didn't break all your knuckles- so yes, we can still play."

Halfdan raised his hand in salute as Terrance ventured off. He often wondered why he could connect with some people in this world, while others seemed so alien. Perhaps it was because

Terrance seemed different too. He apparently was a changed man since he had entered the Gaol.

In fact, Terrance had only arrived a short while before Halfdan did. And even though he had lost a great deal of weight and was very despondent during the first few months, his spirits had seemed to take a turn for the better lately. He certainly enjoyed playing civi-chess and even discussed more technologically advanced model soldiers than the knights and archers in the game. It made Halfdan wonder at where Terrance really came from- the witch hunters of Tyr certainly seemed to visit him often; perhaps he was some kind of warlock?

During the games, Terrance would also discuss stranger things. The topic of *world-walking* came up once, so Halfdan shared his *Around the Bend* tale. Terrance would listen intently, but added very little, though it seemed to Halfdan that he wanted to say more.

Halfdan took a moment to examine his wounds from the attack in the Gaol Yard earlier today and was happy that they were fairly well-healed now. Carsanna certainly was talented, though he wished that such care might have triggered some of the more amorous Freyan healing side-effects in her at least. Still, all magic had its drawbacks, whether visible or not. The Odinnic wondered if he or the Freyan priestess would be the one to pay it.

As the guards came to bring Halfdan back to his cell, try as he might, he couldn't stop his mind from wandering back to Carsanna. Unfortunately, his impending destination was with Brotus, which was not quite the same thing. All he could do then was surrender and watch the I. Drawbacks or not, it would end his suffering. What other choice did he have?

He knew that he would be beaten and worse by that brute, again and again. It might be that there was a strange, hidden something inside Halfdan that *wanted him* to be abused too- some sort of secret self-hatred. Brotus certainly seemed to agree. If Halfdan was truly controlling his own reality in some fashion, as those who believed in Attraction's Law claimed, then why else would terrible things happen to him? It could explain why reality very often failed to do what he actually wanted it to do.

Halfdan of course wished that he could *share the cell with* Carsanna or someone more pleasant at least, but he knew that could never be. Once he really began to fall for a maiden, she would either be repelled immediately or leave him eventually. It seemed ever a pattern, a law of life for Halfdan.

But whether he was being beaten by a horrible man or lying with a beautiful woman, it was really all just a story: a person doing something with *or to* another. In the clear-minded state, the "I" all alone, it was all bearable, if not altogether fine. It helped Halfdan to know that was *what he truly was*.

And Halfdan knew that he might tempt Reality, tempt Fate with such bold sentiments. All Hel could break loose if one let go of one's fear completely, testing the faith of an Odinnic who knelt ready as a sacrifice to Odin, to himself.

But he was done being afraid; he was already in Hel. The only truth in his life, the only one to *always* hold true, no matter what, was that there was never any suffering in I.

Consciousness itself was always available; it was always there. And the I alone could be aware of Consciousness, and of itself, and thereby be always at peace. Always.

Praise Odin for that- thank God.

Chapter 6

The Hold of Kern

Poy and Jeg couldn't help but be impressed by the manslaves that their Northern Sisters had provided. Perhaps there were more males in Middlechest to draw from... or were the males that they captured actually larger in size? Being from Stephania, Poy, Jeg, and others like them were limited in their selection of males. They were stuck with only those manservants already in their land, plus any new males that were born, as well as others captured from Fairfacts Lordship. Boring, in Poy and Jeg's eyes!

Poy dismounted her chestnut steed as she moved closer to examine the merchandise: large men, muscular, and a look of quiet obedience on their faces. Outstanding! She knew this deal would turn out well. The Shell Oracle had wanted some Hippolytes to investigate the Hold- pah! What did they know about having *fun*? Poy and Jeg were Dames, not Hippolytes, and took it upon themselves to check in on their Northerly Sisters.

One of the manslaves stared back. Poy was a scarlet-haired beauty, shapely in form, and clad in a tight leather bodice and tall riding boots. She gave off an aura of power and arrogant confidence that men might find appealing in a lady. The sharpened horsewhip at her side showed that she rarely took 'no' for an answer, even if they didn't.

Poy smiled at her Dame Sister. Jeg too was quite shapely in face and form, as well as similarly attired, though she was platinum-haired, lighter-eyed, a bit fuller figured, and had more angular features than Poy.

"Looks like quite a catch," she said, marveling at the strong slaves.

"Yes," Poy began to massage one of the manslave's arms seductively and smiled, "they will serve our Sisters well..."

The Hold of Kern amazons looked on. Unlike those of Stephania, the Kern Womyn had not developed the same three castes of Hippolytes, Dames, and Matrons. The *Kernazons*, as they were nicknamed, instead had taken to styling their society as one akin to bees, even painting their arms and armor yellow and black, as well as mimicking the structure of bee society. The drones were of course their manslaves; they were used for breeding and hard labor, but were also treated far worse than the Stephanian manservants. The Womyn, of course, were Warrior-Workers and their Queen remained secured and secluded.

"Perhaps you'd like to sample them," suggested Melyssa, the Kernazon captain. She looked at the two visitors, her finely styled yellow black hair and imposing figure giving off an air of unmistakable authority- strangely intense for only being a Warrior-Worker.

Poy smiled provocatively; Jeg smiled back. They selected a few of the more massive males in the group and the entourage of Stephanian and Hold of Kern amazons walked to a nearby structure, which was shaped like a bee hive fittingly enough.

Dan Osarchuk

What struck Poy was how much this land had changed recently. As a young girl, she remembered the Hold of Kern as simply being an outpost ceded as more neutral ground to the burgeoning successes of Stephania by the Count of Middlechest. It was said that he and other adjacent Counties wanted to secure a peace in this area with the amazons as they faced greater threats from *Septentrional* Amland and Metros to the east.

In those days, her mother had taught her to ride in this area, even having access to some of the famed Boycian war ponies. One could ride across the length and breadth of this land with little more than an isolated outpost and nothing but wilderness for miles around.

As the Hold began to take on its own character, it grew in size and eventually split into a separate, but allied Queendom. Some said that it was due to the necessity of the threats the Hold faced, while others claimed that Stephania did not want to go down *exactly the same* path as their Northerly Sisters. The 'bee fetish' that her Northern Sisters had was only restricted to simple heraldry and nuance at that time. Within the last few years though, the harshness of the Kernazons to their male subjects was certainly noticeable, to such an extent that rumors had begun to circulate that something had *changed* them. They had begun to act like bees themselves.

The Shell Oracle had even begun to warn her fellow Stephanian amazons of the changes in the Kernazons, but Poy and Jeg hadn't heeded it. In fact, a sizable number of Dames were beginning to grow tired with the Oracle's limits on man-control. It was no wonder that they were beginning to gravitate to the Hold, where Womyn might do what they wish with males.

And many males seemed to want it too! Even ones as far south as Madisonburg would travel to the Hold at great expense and great risk of life to be 'slaves' to the exotic Kernazons. They wished for all manner of strange exchange and the latter would give it to them, as well as even more than they would ask for. Many would pay their coin to return, though there were rumors that some of the Kernazons kept these 'volunteer slaves' against their will.

There was something in a man that *needed to be* controlled by a Womyn. Even many of the mighty warlords of Strass Hill had mighty, *domineering* wives. A number of men especially seemed to need a strong Womyn to lead them through this world, even if that Womyn wasn't the particular one who had brought them into it.

All men knew this, or if they didn't, they would soon find out. And the ones who realized it and accepted it were happier slaves in the end. The Dames could bring *such happiness* to men by showing them who was in charge and who could inflict the pain. At least, that's what they thought.

Poy and Jeg tied up their horses outside the beehive structure and the Kernazons stared at them. The manslaves looked to be afraid now. Poy was surprised: didn't these slaves know what Dames *liked to do?*

* * *

Dusk fell upon the Yonitarian Yoniversalist Church. Brightly armored Hippolytes patrolled the grounds, eyes wary for any intruders. The watch had been increased of late, especially at night- it was said that there were strange things afoot.

Inside, the Shell Oracle presided over the mass for the assembled Womyn of Stephania. The tall goddess statues stood vigil over the many worshippers- women singing choruses of joy and feminine grace. The manservants sat in the back, in the darkness, out of sight for now.

As the singing drew to a close, the Oracle sat to hold auspices for the amazons. She moved her hands gently through the fine sands to perform her augury.

"The tidings are still very dark, my Sisters. Something unclean not only dwells at our borders, but is even gaining strength!"

The assembled amazons gasped at this; the Oracle was usually more optimistic.

"Is it another incursion of men?" asked Gwyre, a particularly talkative Matron.

"It could be," replied the Oracle, "all I'm getting is a sense of uncleanness, proximity to Stephania, and growing strength."

"It must be men on the loose!" exclaimed Miggle, a Dame in a striking red dress. "Men are very disobedient!"

At this, the other amazons became increasingly agitated. Some argued to close the borders immediately, others insisted that they must begin questioning the manservants of Stephania instead, while a few urged patience and calm to at least let the Oracle finish. Many of the manservants who remained awake in the back pricked up their ears in concern.

The Hippolytes were silent, of course. Theirs was not the place to discuss or debate- only to defend. And yet one very strong-looking one with long, brown, curly hair arose. All fell silent, knowing her to be a true Heroine.

"I will go," said Brymanah.

The manservants relaxed: questionings could be so unpleasant.

* * *

Poy and Jeg emerged from the hive building at dawn. They certainly felt different. The two stared at their Kernazon Sisters- now as true Sisters, no longer just in a symbolic way. They looked at the brightly-shining sun and picked up the intoxicating scent of distant autumn flowers still blooming. They were almost as intoxicating as the thought of returning to Stephania.

Quiet Upon Shenbyrg's Dawning

Making the necessary adjustments to their armor, they remounted their horses, which then began to panic. Quickly though, the amazons of Kern rushed forward and rested against the mounts. The horses calmed again, though their eyes now looked dazed.

Poy and Jeg stared into the eyes of Melyssa. Something passed between them that defied explanation.

Then, without another word, the Dames rode south, back to their homeland. They had so much more to tell their Sisters, so much indeed.

* * *

The amazon had enough of these mad males. Did they think that their inverted pentagrams and false animal heads scared her? *They didn't!*

Those very same 'mad males' came at the amazon again, screaming their blood-curdling war cries. Upon their shoulders rested the heads of stags, bulls, horses, and even a rabbit or two. They slashed at her with savagely-crafted axes and spears and screamed to their foul Demon Lords to spill her blood.

But it was to no avail. Brymanah had wisely positioned herself on a high point to better slay the horde of pretend animal men that had surrounded her. Perhaps she stood on the actual Devil's Spine that these stupid males claimed this land to be; the bestial men certainly seemed a little hesitant to attack at first.

"TIME FOR YOU TO DIE!" howled an especially large bull-headed one. He must think himself a minotaur!

"You'll get no meat from me, *cow-wisher!*" was her retort.

If it were possible, the savages became even more enraged, launching yet another wave of attacks, only to be repelled with her mighty cutlass slices. It appeared that they had lost all of their hesitancy.

Dan Osarchuk

Bull-head continued to direct the attacks in his illiterate way. Brymanah was not disturbed by these males' fruitless rage and fruitless attacks, though she was disturbed by their terrible odor and lack of clothing.... *ugh!*

This time, a pair of stag-heads rushed her with a net, while a third attempted to hit her with rocks. She nearly laughed as she batted them aside. The primitives had strength and ferocity, yes, but their lack of coordination was pathetic. As they fell from the high point, she grabbed one of the stagheads by the antlers.

To her surprise, the helm which she thought he wore did not come off. Instead, the entire stagman: horns, head, body, and all, remained suspended by the amazon's grasp. Her great muscles flexed as she held him. Perhaps these primitives were using some sort of glue to hold the animal masks on?

Seeing her stumble under the weight, the others began to clamber up the rocks again. In response, Brymanah gave a forceful hack with her cutlass, taking the stagman's head clean off. The body and gushing blood dropped on his fellows, toppling them back down to the lower ground.

The amazon then held the decapitated staghead aloft, gore still dripping from its brainpan, all-to-human eyes lolling back. The other savages recoiled for a moment, as if Brymanah held some fell totem of their death. The murderous look in her eyes only added to their fright. And yet their intense bloodlust caused the animal men to come at her again.

A horse-head was next, very brazenly so as his fellows chanted for his success. He held a huge spear, possibly fashioned from an iron spit, and neighed at her in challenge. She was impressed by his horse impression, but found his attempt at pointing something big and long at her to be yet more typical manly nonsense.

"Keep your spear to yourself; and don some pants, *male!*"

Horse-head merely snorted and neighed, closing in with the spear.

As the amazon moved in to silence this horse-boy once and for all, something struck her from behind. To her shock, it was one of the smaller, rabbit-headed ones; it looked like he had stabbed her in the calf with some sort of petrified carrot of all things. Somehow, even though the scoundrel must have been masked, she saw him smile. An outrage!

It was now Brymanah's turn to smile. She swore viciously as she grabbed rabbit-head by his long ears, but then recoiled at how little else he wore. She then attempted to shift, sensing yet another impending attack from behind, this time from the direction of the massed animal men.

The amazon swung rabbit-head into the group. His not-clad-enough body smashed into them and knocked them off the Devil's Spine.

Exhaustion mixed with exhilaration as Brymanah realized that her attack had landed rabbit-head right onto horse-head's spear, impaling the former and knocking down the latter. The stench of man-smells and sound of man-wailing nearly drowned out her righteous amazonian sense of victory.

Something was wrong though, for Brymanah began to feel a numb coldness in her calf where rabbit-head had stabbed her. She had not lost that much blood, but then she realized that she had been... poisoned! Stupid rabbit-head!

She leapt down to die in the mass of bestial, wailing manness below- she would take as many down with her as she could!

But it was too late. Something massive and heavy impacted with the back of her head, turning everything dark. Her last thought was that she had failed in her quest to find the corruption that threatened Stephania.

Dan Osarchuk

She had been defeated... defeated by a carrot.

* * *

Melyssa stared at her Kernazon Sisters. Soon the whole area would be *buzzing* with activity and, thanks to their new Sisters, Poy and Jeg, Stephania would be too. She stepped into the hive house and admired the slain manslaves. So meaty, so... predigested: they would provide excellent meals for a true Queen such as she.

A glint of light caught the necklace around her neck. A shard of some substance was affixed to it, shining in scintillating colors, so strange; so pleasing.

Chapter 7

Minas-Ninona

The two sat by the riverside, warming morning autumn sun making the grasses come alive with birds and bugs.

"I can't, Tared," the blonde woman's voice broke with sorrow.

"We are to be wed tomorrow, Em, it's only fitting if I *spend some time* with ya." Tared toyed with his engagement ring.

"I love ya, Tar, but ya know we can't be together, I tell ya."

"Why not? Because of some silly curse? Oof-dah!"

Emhild made to touch the dark-haired norseman beside her, but stopped herself.

"I don't care what hjappened at the river! Those Malwood Boys were attacking ya!"

Emhild's eyes turned red and tears began to form.

Quiet Upon Shenbyrg's Dawning

"Oh Em, yar the sweetest maiden in all of Vinland: why do ya weep over such scum?"

"Because... Hjel's bells..." Em's clear blue eyes shone bright as more tears flowed freely.

"So what? I don't believe in curses or Hjel or all the wrath of the Gods! We all know ya as nursemaid, Em, that's all that matters. Yar beauty shouldn't be unappreciated."

Tar moved in for a passionate kiss, but Em held him back, her face turned pale.

"I might as well be the Beauty Queen for All the Norse Plains Kingdoms, I tell ya, but people don't say that I'm just the nursemaid, dontchya know?"

"But ya *are* hjer, the Beauty Queen I mean, you betchya!" Tar smiled and moved in for another kiss attempt.

Emhild cursed herself but gave in. They were to be married tomorrow: perhaps this time would be different?

* * *

Cattle lowed as the wind swept through the rolling hills. Blue skies shimmered above, white clouds swirled, all held in a crisp cold that foretold the coming of winter. The villagers of Bjeiland worked the fields as they had done for centuries now. Perhaps their distant forbears, the Ancients, had hurtled across the land on the *Fitty-yoo* in their *drivecars* to the *Mall* of *Vinlandia* and had flown upon birds of steel, but the people now only knew such things as myth.

Today, they worked the land and raised livestock. They crafted the items that they needed or traded for them. It was simple work, but it had meaning. One could see the fruits of one's labors immediately, if not by the end of a season. A person's life had purpose, something to do, and it made sense- only Hel herself could take it from them.

60

Folks knew each other and trusted one another. They had to: anything less would mean their mutual demise. Neighbors had to get along and they had to work as a community, there simply was not enough time, skill, or resource for individual families to make it for long on their own. People followed the Old Ways and families stuck together, for to do anything else just didn't make sense.

And it wasn't dull. Though the Ancients might have had their viewing screens and their play-songs, the people today had *real adventure* and *real suspense* to deal with. Granted, sometimes it might become *too real*. Even though the people were usually able to make a good living off the land from their farms and shops, dealing with *other dangers* could be another matter entirely. Raiders, both human and otherwise, could descend upon unprotected villages at any time. And nocturnal attacks by dangerous creatures and foul spirits were not unknown. The common folk were wise to keep a weapon at their side and the Gods in their prayers.

Bjeiland was no stranger to such attacks. Just a few dozen miles south and east of the Ruins of Roch-Medsitar, these mostly peaceful folk were easy pickings for raids. It was by the grace of the Gods that none had been too devastating yet.

In the distance, a village boy named Evann spotted a group of riders approaching from the north. He ran to the central *hof*, yelling the alert. Outside, the Guardians at the Doors, Thor and Heimdall, stood embossed in metal bas relief. The boy ran passed them on his way inside, passed the startled priest to the stairs leading up.

Nearly out of breath, Evann felt a cold clutching around his throat. He gagged as he reached for the bell's pull-rope. The priest raced upstairs and was startled by the presence around the boy. To see such here in a holy place in broad daylight did not bode well. He glanced out the cupola as the boy still tried to sound the warning. The priest reached out and stopped him, uttering a prayer to the Gods to spare them from what awaited.

* * *

"We're seeking a maiden," said one of the raiders with a rust-colored beard. His great horse snorted for added effect.

The villagers were not surprised that the riders were well-armed norseman- such things were commonplace. What did surprise them was what they had come for: just one woman. In fact, many of the eligible womenfolk had already begun to line up for the warriors, it was simply easier that way. Some of the menfolk had even begun to bring out kegs of beer. They hoped that there would be less damage done to the village if the villagers gave the raiders what they thought they wanted right away.

"Just one?!" asked the village priest incredulously.

"Ya," replied the grizzled rust-beard.

These riders were not intent upon rapine and slaughter. Just what kind of raiders were they?

"Whjoo?" said Evann finally, since all of the adults seemed too afraid to speak.

The raider smiled grimly, revealing a number of missing teeth. He shifted in his saddle, displaying a black and white skull emblazoned upon the tunic beneath his cloak and a deadly viking sword at his belt.

The priest walked forward, pointing to a lone house down by the river. He had recognized the mark. These raiders followed Hel, Goddess of death, and must be looking for the one so blessed by her.

* * *

Dan Osarchuk

Ragennar dismounted from his warhorse as his men began surrounding the dwelling by the riverside. He reached into his saddlebag and removed a firmly secured iron coffer. Producing a key from his cloak pocket, he unlocked its bonds. Inside was grave earth, which Ragennar judiciously began applying to his face and hands.

No signs of life from the lone house could be seen. Ragennar completed his ritual and readied his battle axe, sharp and well-worn. The magic of the Gods might be one thing, but he could always trust his axe if they failed him.

His men ready, the raider yelled at the house, "We know yar in there! Come out easy- or we'll come in with the taste of our axes!"

Still no sign of life inside.

Ragennar nodded and his men began to approach. It was a well-practiced tactic. Why be a hero and get oneself killed or, even worse, badly injured and days away from the nearest healer? Raiders knew that the application of overwhelming power made their job easier... and safer for them.

They were no cowards- they looked forward to dying in battle someday and being carried to the Valhallan Halls. But they also weren't stupid and were in no rush for that day to happen.

That's why eight warriors were moving in on one woman.

Torsteinn, a sallow-haired raider, glanced inside a window and spoke, "She's in there, you betchya."

Another with a great brown beard, Konigsgild, replied, "Then why don't ya get her out?"

"She's crying."

All of the norsemen sighed- it could be far less fun to raid when a woman was crying.

Quiet Upon Shenbyrg's Dawning

Ragennar moved forward and burst open the door. A strange scent filled the air, he couldn't place it, though he might have just been smelling all the grave dirt still on his face.

Seeing the heavily-armed, dirt-faced norseman bearing the heraldry of Hel enter her home made the smaller woman stop crying and stand in fear. He towered over her and her delicate hands shook.

"Ya don't want to come any closer!" She still seemed afraid, though perhaps more afraid for the men than for herself.

All about the room, what looked like bridal dress stood in tatters, some parts had even been stuffed in the woodstove at the north end. Otherwise, the place had a strange mix of a dismal air with a pleasant light radiance, like a steely Minas-Ninonan morning when the sun peeked through.

The rest of the raiders came in. Em backed up against the wall, grasping for her stove-poker.

"We need to test hjer," said Torsteinn.

"Ya don't want to do this!" Em pleaded.

Konigsgild rushed forward, but was repelled as Em nearly took out his eye with the poker. She may have been short, but she was feisty!

"Ya- stay back," said Ragennar.

The tension in the room relaxed for a moment, until all realized that Ragennar was still advancing, his eyes staring straight into Em's.

"NO!" Em started screaming now- the sound of a woman whose life had collapsed. She knew what raiders would do to a lone woman. Some of the raiders even began to feel bad for her, strangely enough.

Ragennar rushed at her and knocked her poker away. He grappled her as they fought to the ground. She punched him in the face and narrowly missed kneeing him in the groin. To Em's surprise, the norseman only took out his hand and placed it against her lips.

She would have made him stop; his hand was really filthy. But she also sensed that this large man had no intention of hurting her.

The woman was surprised again when the raider let her go and arose. All eyes were on his hand, which had started to smoke. It looked like the norseman was in intense pain.

"Beer!" He gasped as his face contorted in agony.

Torsteinn rushed forward and dosed his leader's hand with malty hops. Ragennar began to relax, though it still burned red from touching the woman's lips.

The norsemen turned and gazed at Em in awe. All except Ragennar knelt.

He spoke, "Ya are truly blessed by Hjel, my *Dróttning*. We will now bring ya back to Winnonar."

Em didn't know what to say: first she thought these men had come to horribly attack her and now they were calling her *their Queen*.

Finally, she replied, "I don't want to be blessed by Hjel!"

The norsemen smiled grimly- no one *wants to be* blessed by Hel, they conceded. They began to collect Em's belongings and brought her extra garments for her trip. Some of the other raiders even broke out hammers and nails and began to repair her door. Others discreetly returned the materials for a witch pyre that they had brought. The raiders hadn't known whether she was genuine or not.

Quiet Upon Shenbyrg's Dawning

* * *

The day grew late. Em looked at Ragennar again. Despite her concerns, it seemed like the matter was settled. The others hauled most of her possessions to the horses and secured her house. She glanced back at the river sadly. Ragennar put a hand on her shoulder and then helped her up to her mount.

Some of the other raiders were doubling up on their horses, giving Em and her possessions their own. Perhaps they really did see her as their *Dróttning*?

The group began to trot away. Em ventured one last look back at her home, at the river, and her village. She uttered a short prayer to Freya that she *would* find love again someday, *a love that would remain with her for eternity, like the one that she dreamt about.*

Back at the riverside, dusk was approaching. The birds had fled south at the darkening winds and the bugs had died. The grasses had already begun to feel the icy touch of winter, which came soon here in Bjeiland, in the northland of Minas-Ninona.

And upon the bank, in the light of the dying sun, a corpse could be seen: a man with an engagement ring still upon his finger.

Chapter 8

Pentagram Tannery

A vivid blue autumn sky shone over the pines ahead. Dried leaves crunched beneath the hunter's black boots. The day had warmed to a pleasant temperature, in an especially pleasant time for the Vale. Gone was the pollen, the gnats, and the humidity. All that was left was the clear, pleasant air and the quiet of the woods.

Oborren shook his head. It was never a good idea to let one's guard down, *especially* in the woods, even if the weather was nice.

Apparently, he had been breaking many of his own rules lately. Not only had he let his guard down, but he had also broken his rule of working alone, one that he had made for himself after the business with Brymanah, Kolveig, and the rest. At the conclusion of the harpy incident, Bjartar had volunteered his services in helping to avenge the abduction of Sven. And of course, all the other remaining Strass Hill norsemen had volunteered too, but Oborren only allowed Bjartar to join him. One henchman was enough. Still, the others had been so insistent that Oborren and Bjartar had to lose them in the woods. The hunter was fairly certain that they would find their way back to Strass Hill eventually.

Another one of his rules that he was in the process of breaking was asking for directions. The parchment that he had found in the harpy's satchel indicated that someone named 'Director in WS' wanted to coordinate with 'Bee Queen in HK'. Hunters were trained in using codes- it was essential for their profession, lest some unnatural being capture one of their communiques and get the upper hand. Oborren suspected he knew that 'WS' meant 'Walstock' and that the 'Bee Queen in HK' meant the Hold of Kern, since they were noted for their Bee heraldry. He just didn't know who the 'Director in WS' was, so they were traveling northwest to meet with someone who might.

Oborren glanced back at Bjartar: he seemed to be a skilled enough woodsman. He wasn't making too much noise as they travelled, and he looked to be alert with his long bow out and his hand axe at his belt. For now, the norseman seemed to remain cooperative enough, as long as he was under the impression that Oborren was doing something to avenge Sven.

So they ventured further into the broken fields and forests that was Pentagram Tannery. The nefarious name was certainly intentional. Here Baphomet and other Fell Gods and Demon Lords were worshipped. Oborren made sure to avoid the sinister Devil's Spine area itself- that was certainly heavily infested with such monsters, even if it wasn't *actually a devil's spine* like some claimed.

The hunter could remember not too long ago when his own brother had returned from this place. Perhaps he had made his final transformation with the other degenerates upon the Devil's Spine? The *'bestial men'* issue could be perplexing in light of the prevailing notions of what was supernatural in the Vale. Unlike ghosts and dragons, more human-looking creatures could certainly be *seen and believed by* the common folk- even in their own towns in broad daylight. The townsfolk of Walstock certainly *saw* the goblins as they battled them upon Restaurant Row last year.

But the issue was still unclear on the bestial men, otherwise known as *beast-heads* or *atavars*. Were they an actual race? Or were they magically created from some unnatural force? Or, as some claimed, were they simply savages who donned the *masks of beasts* and acted accordingly?

Oborren knew the truth of course, at least in the case of a *certain stagman* that he had dispatched last winter, though that may not necessarily have been the case with *all* bestial men. The hunter adjusted his colorful necktie as a wave of sorrow rose up from his throat at the memory. The hunter hoped that his new henchman did not see his rising sadness.

The matter might have seemed academic, except that they were entering deeper into the very land overrun by such folk.

* * *

The pair halted at around noon. Bjartar still didn't say much, but kept his eye on the road ahead to the west, while Oborren glanced back east. Here a red earth embankment rose to the north, revealing the roots and rocks beneath the many cedars and oaks. Higher still, a wall of green, orange, and brown leaves stirred in the midday breeze.

A 'snap' off to the south caught Oborren's attention. It was ever so slight, causing Bjartar to miss it, but his own trained hunter's ears didn't. He strode over to his henchman quietly, his lunch of deer jerky and hardtack still in hand. Bjartar caught Oborren's gaze and both lowered their meals and readied their weapons.

They waited for a moment, but there was no other sound. Bjartar resumed eating his rations quietly; longbow in his lap. Oborren reluctantly went back to his own lunch as well. He didn't take his eyes off the woods though.

Quiet Upon Shenbyrg's Dawning

All else remained quiet, except for the rustling of the fall leaves in the breeze. Some had even begun to land upon the road, making travel potentially noisy- at least for the hunter's sensibilities. The two packed up their gear and continued west.

Something watched them from the nearby woods- something with all too human eyes.

* * *

The road dipped into a small valley as the day grew late. Oborren could tell that Bjartar was beginning to tire. He couldn't blame the man- he was a henchman, not a hunter. They passed a broken signpost to the left. The claw marks on it made any clear indication of what it said indecipherable. To the sides of the road were the ruined remnants of farmhouses and barns. They seemed destroyed long ago with only broken shells remaining.

It was said that during the early years of Lights Out, some in the Vale, especially the isolated ones, had fared quite well. Protected from the initial bands of raiders, they had access to both space and succor. These Ancient homesteaders were even rumored to have foodstuff so well-made that it would last for years or even decades, if only minimal care was taken with its storage. Coupled with a good land to farm, supplies, and weapons to hold it all, they did better than the towns and cities, at least at first.

They fared well, that is, until they were discovered. Having one's own isolated farm helped immeasurably during hard times until others experiencing their own hard times found one's own isolated farm. How long could a single family hold out against a large group of determined raiders? Eventually they had to rest or even just reload their weapons- firearms of incredible precision by today's standards still could not be shot indefinitely...

It didn't help either that the folks in these parts never coalesced into a true nation, perhaps because they didn't re-embrace the Old Ways, such as the Norse of Strass Hill, the Teutons of

Walstock, or the Olympians of Caelum Mount. Those settlements and certain others survived as small civilizations because they were able to band together under a common culture.

Unfortunately for those in what would become Pentagram Tannery, many were overrun, slain, *and eaten* by the malevolent and the starving. If they were lucky, it happened quickly and occurred in that order. And it wasn't just human raiders that would attack these hapless farmsteads in those days. Orc and goblin tribes erupted into the Vale to conquer and kill too, and those who were repelled from the human towns and cities sometimes ended up in places like this.

Granted that orcs couldn't stand the forests long and any goblins that might remain would become less organized and more savage, but it was the *humans* who survived the attacks and remained in these woods that were *changed*. It was said that they fell into some form of *Animalia*, living as insanely wild men and women, in a manner even more savage than those who dwelt in Fjord Vallee. Legend had it that they would don the heads of beasts to gain their power and protection, no longer needing shelter or supply. The few explorers that returned from this area hence only told more tales of 'beasts that walk as men and engage in all manner of heinous pursuit'. Little more was known.

They were officially classified *'Atavars'* in hunter lore, for they were certainly atavistic and reflected the opposite, *preternatural* direction, as opposed to the *superhuman* 'Avatars' that would represent humanized gods, rather than beasts. And though they were apparently born in the dark days soon after Lights Out, they might have been known to humans long before that, if the sages were to be believed. It was no coincidence that the Minoan, Antediluvian, and Arcadian varieties of bestial men were named after such pre-Ancient times and places, even if they were mainly known to now occupy Pentagram Tannery.

Quiet Upon Shenbyrg's Dawning

And nowadays, it was the perfect place to remain isolated, if one were so inclined and had such craft to keep the bestial rovers at bay. After the incident at Restaurant Row and the Schoolhouse, Oborren had befriended one of his former enemies, since he did save his life during the Yellow Goblin invasion. Oborren was aware that 'Old Sieg' had a place out here, guarded by his elite Poultry Protection Squad. Sieg had said that he considered Pentagram Tannery to be the perfect place to hide his Secret Recipe. What thief would dare to venture *into these woods*?

Oborren's thoughts stopped when he noticed Bjartar sitting down. Not a good idea he thought, since his back now faced one of the farmhouse ruins, which was only a few hundred feet away. The Gods only knew what nasty creatures might lurk onside. Though the bestial men might no longer need such isolated structures to survive like their homesteader ancestors did, they could still dwell in such ruins all the same.

"Come on," said the hunter, breaking the hours-long silence, "let's find a better place to rest."

Suddenly, they heard a commotion coming from behind. Half expecting a horde of rampaging stagmen to be barreling down upon them, a single raven cawed loudly and landed on the broken signpost. Oborren had seen this before and he knew it was unwise to defy the will of the Gods, even if he had other business to attend to.

* * *

The thing's stinking breath lingered in the air. Try as she might, Brymanah could not loose her bonds. Though they had the heads of beasts, they still had the hands of strong men, making the thickly corded rope well-tied and quite durable, no matter how hard she struggled.

As she worked to push the thoughts of all the terrible things that the bestial males did to her, Brymanah could hear the sounds of the *others* in adjacent stalls. At first, she thought it was

72

just her head wound, but no- she was now beginning to think that the sounds were real. What she heard was nearly as disturbing as the outrages she had suffered at the hands of these beasts-with-man-bodies.

Though her view was mostly obstructed by the crude wooden pen in which she was kept, Brymanah guessed that other humans had been captured and were being abused just as she. The only difference though was that they seemed to be broken. One even uttered a strange sound like a goat. She could see their tormentors above the stall, since they were ironically walking upright, while the humans remained close to the ground.

In one case, in the stall to her left, she saw a horse-head repeatedly enter what sounded like a man's stall. As the days went on, it would whip him and spit on him until the man became a sobbing mess- *typical male weakness.* Earlier today though, the man had begun to make a sound like a horse himself and the actual horse-head just smiled and left, rather than abusing him. Brymanah expected him to be released soon.

Bizarre? A similar phenomenon occurred when she had first arrived, except in this case it was a Womyn making a cow sound before she was later released. Brymanah knew that the Womyn wasn't Stephanian: no self-respecting amazon would ever let herself sink so low. In fact, Brymanah had heard tales of how female cattle were mistreated in the lands of Men, so as to serve as unwilling mates to bulls. *Such things never happened in Stephania* and certainly would not happen *to a Stephanian Womyn!*

Why these beasts were treating the humans in such a way didn't matter to Brymanah. She had first thought them to be actual men with masks on. Her close encounters with them had shown that to be otherwise though. Whatever the case, most seemed to be *male* and Brymanah knew just how to deal with them!

Quiet Upon Shenbyrg's Dawning

Brymanah paused and shivered when a human in the distanced uttered the goatlike sound of "Baah-phomet."

* * *

Father Farhred stared at the Gaol guard. The aging cleric's white robes covered the heavy armor that the faithful of Tyr wore almost as religiously as their tyrswords. Farhred knew the guard from his many trips to the Gaol to 'meet with those incarcerated'. With a cold, steely stare from the Tyrian witch hunter, the guard held back the request for him to surrender his tyrsword before entering.

"Faith precedes duty to any mortal master," reminded Farhred.

The cleric strode through the Goal block, accompanied by his assistant, Brother Freundel. They passed the cells of the incarcerated, noticing the odor of the unwashed and the defeated. Farhred removed his witch hunter's hat, though Freundel kept his own iron kettle cap on. They stopped for a moment outside the cell of one inmate, some sort of Odinnic upstart, part of that business at the Schoolhouse last year. The man's body showed defeat, but his eyes showed something else. Perhaps there was something to it... and him, thought Farhred.

The Tyrians strode on to another cell. A black "T", like that of a longsword pointing downward, shown clearly on their robes in the torch light here. Producing a key that the guard had surrendered to him, Farhred unlocked the cell of a short mustached fellow, who had recently lost some weight. Farhred was impressed at how much the man had changed. The fellow's face remained unmoved as the cleric entered. No matter how unpleasant the Tyrian found it, he had a duty to perform. It was time for *some more questioning.*

* * *

"I say, where might that confusticatin' fella be!? I got his message that he would be a-coming here this mornin'!"

74

The gnome ladyservant shrugged her shoulders; Old Sieg reached for his whip. The gnome ran out the door shrieking with her little arms waving in the air.

"Don't let the beasts ett yeh!" spat the Colonel sarcastically.

A uniformed and lightly armored gnome glanced in the window. His helm was that of a stylized chicken and he bore a sharpened frying pan as a weapon. The heraldry on his tunic even showed a chicken being thrown in a pot with a characterized version of Old Sieg looking on. "Do you want us to round her up for you, sir?"

"Nah," conceded Sieg, "she'll either be back or she'll be *ett*." He smiled malevolently.

Seeing the cruelty rise in the old man with the whip, the guard quickly saluted and went back to his patrol.

The Colonel returned to his desk and sat down. A breakfast of fried egg and hashbrown stood still steaming there. He poured a tumbler of Maurian Whiskey to begin his meal.

He sighed. The hunter hadn't shown and the Colonel would like to be in a better mood for his trip back through the Tannery.

There were just too many damn atavars for his likin'.

Chapter 9

Fjord Vallee

"What did that blasted wizard say we should do again?"

Tepson cursed. His squirrel companion stared back at him. It looked angry.

He had heard the warnings about the Fjord: magic acted strangely here. The gnome reached into his pack and pulled out an ornately carved wand. Magic acting strangely? Did it matter? Magic isn't real!

And Tepson had heard about the great reptilian beasts that *people claimed* to roam here, as well. More psychosis: it sounded like something right out of Land of the...

The gnome's thoughts were cut short as the squirrel leapt up onto a rock and began chittering madly.

"The heck with this!" Tepson pointed the wand at the squirrel, but then hesitated. "I'm *not* going to say it."

The squirrel stared accusingly; it chittered at him.

Quiet Upon Shenbyrg's Dawning

"This is ridiculous!"

The squirrel leaped right in front of him and made an even more vicious chittering sound. Some froth began to emit from its little mouth. He hoped that it hadn't turned *psycho*.

"Fine: *'Ápage, O Kúrie Hekás. Khaíre.'*"

Nothing. Just an angry squirrel. It even began to wave its little fist at him.

"Alright already! *'Ápage, O Kúrie Hekás! KHAIRE!'*"

Again, no result. Tepson shook his head in discouragement. He stared at a scenic mountaintop in the distance. He wondered why he had believed that self-described wizard in Caelum Mount. But when he returned his gaze, there the Karlist stood again. He couldn't believe his eyes! The gnome reached back into his pack and retrieved Kolveig's uniform. Perhaps this magic was real after all?

"Certainly took you long enough."

The gnome shook his head again: *how was that for gratitude?*

"And if that Stupid Bourgeois Capitalist Wizard thinks that we're going to do his dirty business for him-"

Tepson cut him off- "Listen: that 'Stupid Wizard' could have killed you and now he's even given you a chance to do what you do best in exchange for your freedom, so I suggest you just suck it up. And put on some pants!"

Kolveig stared at Tepson in confusion. Suck what up? *Gnomes could say such stupid things.*

The gnome grabbed his pack in disgust. Whether the Karlist cleric would follow or not, he didn't care! Tepson would get the primitives to rise up by himself if he had to. And if he was lucky, maybe Kolveig would even get eaten by a dinosaur.

Dan Osarchuk

* * *

The rolling vistas, so closely framed by the mountains, truly set the Fjord apart. It was like the Vale itself, and yet smaller and simpler. Not a building could be seen, not even a road larger than a game trail. And, as much as the scientist in him protested, it *did feel* different here.

Tepson knew the tales about the Fjord being *different*. Even though the Vale had somehow reverted to the Bronze or the Iron Age, the Fjord had somehow reverted to the Stone Age- but not the Stone Age that any self-respecting scientist would espouse. For some reason, it also included aspects of the Mesozoic, as well, which defied all logic, but seemed to be par for the course in this crazy world.

He glanced over at his cleric companion. Kolveig seemed much calmer now and was thankfully wearing clothing. They had agreed to continue with Antraxus's quest to locate a savage Fjord Vallee tribe. And, with no signs of civilization or even literate people to trigger the Karlist's fanaticism, the walk so far had been surprisingly pleasant.

Soon the duo spotted a traveler walking upon the trail, roughly half a mile ahead. The fellow was dressed in little more than a loincloth and carried what looked like a set of javelins. The man otherwise had an unkempt and mighty beard, but also fairly well-styled long brown hair. He looked to be in especially good shape too, even considering how much leaner the people in the rest of the Vale were. It must have been from all the walking.

Kolveig's mood lit up too upon seeing the primitive. Tepson imagined that the Karlist could barely contain himself at the sight of a True Proletarian Noble Savage. Unfortunately though, something blocked the sun for a moment and the poor savage, most likely being painfully superstitious, yelled and went to hide behind a rock.

Quiet Upon Shenbyrg's Dawning

The Karlist went immediately into action. Tepson knew that the cleric couldn't help himself: here was a Wayward Primitive to be Rescued from his Own Superstitions. Unfortunately for all of them though, the gnome glanced up at the sky to identify what sort of cloud it was that had blocked out the sun- only it wasn't a cloud. Though it was difficult to see, it appeared to be some great bird. Perhaps it was a vulture?

It must have been pretty close, because it seemed to fill a large part of the sun from his standpoint. As it moved though, Tepson realized the 'bird' was actually quite large and *not really* a bird at all. He couldn't believe his eyes. It dove towards the cleric and the primitive with alarming speed.

"KOLVEIG! LOOK OUT!"

The monster descended faster, its great claws extended. Tepson was amazed that something so large could be so silent as he sprinted to help his comrade. He remembered that his hunter friend from last year, Oborren, had said that people couldn't see monsters in broad daylight. Apparently, he had never visited Fjord Vallee!

What looked to Tepson like a *Pteranodon longiceps* nearly grabbed Kolveig, only to recoil at the last moment. Apparently dumb luck was upon him, because it looked like Kolveig had turned and threw something at the pterosaur just before it could snatch him. The monster then flipped around, flapped its huge wings, and was now heading right in Tepson's direction!

The wily gnome then made the enlightened biologist's decision to leap into some bushes and hold on for dear life.

Luckily for Tepson, the pteranodon flew passed him, heading back towards the mountains to the west. He picked the sharp brambles out his clothing, left the brush, and glanced back in Kolveig and the savage's direction. The scent of fall foliage mixed with the aroma of his own, terrified sweat.

Any fears that Kolveig was injured during the encounter were dispelled when he heard the cleric proselytizing.

"You shouldn't allow yourself to be so Oppressed by Aerial Phenomena, Noble Proletarian Savage! The sun will return! See?"

Tepson made his way down to the two. Kolveig continued his Diatribe Against Superstition, while the savage simply touched different parts of the Karlist's uniform. He apparently had no comprehension of personal space.

"How did you drive off the pterosaur?" asked the gnome.

"The WHAT?" replied Kolveig.

"The pterosaur."

"What in Karl's name is a 'pterosaur'?"

"It's that thing that nearly grabbed you!"

"My foolish gnome," Kolveig laughed condescendingly, "that was obviously a wyvern!"

"I thought wyverns had tails- and that they had reptilian heads..."

Kolveig just shook his head and laughed mockingly as if sharing some personal joke with the savage. The savage moved on to checking the cleric's hair for bugs.

"How did you drive it off!" Tepson's patience was nearing its end.

The cleric didn't reply, he simply held up a walnut, he must have had a small sack full of them. Maybe the wand hadn't completely removed his *squirrelhood* after all?

* * *

Quiet Upon Shenbyrg's Dawning

Tepson and Kolveig were eventually led back to a cave entrance that was also set in the mountains to the west. There they had met a tribe of savages, all mostly unclad and illiterate, and yet appearing ethnically similar to most civilized folk in the Vale. Kolveig claimed that he had convinced the savage to show them his Karlist Paradise, but Tepson doubted that the savage could understand a single word that Kolveig said.

An honored seat near the cave remained empty as the tribe greeted them- perhaps it was for their chieftain? Around the entrance were many deer etchings. Tepson was no anthropologist, but he guessed it was their tribal totem. The rest of the tribe quickly distracted the gnome from his thoughts with all their poking and prodding.

What struck Tepson as odd about these people was that even though they were savages, their hair seemed well-groomed and even styled to be short in the front and the sides, but long in the back. He hadn't seen anything like it since his Ancient Days. Most of the folks in the Vale now either wore their hair shorter or longer, but not *both at the same time.*

Of course, Tepson did enjoy the savage women's attention. They were all in incredibly great shape and great health too, mostly likely due to the constant exercise and lack of refined sugars in their diet. And, just like the savage man that had groomed Kolveig before, their complete disregard for personal space caused them to groom Tepson intensely. He found it a little ticklish, but also exciting. And since he was a midg... er... gnome, the savage women seemed especially smitten with him. They called him 'Tep-Tep' and even argued a little over who would get to groom him next.

If Kolveig minded that the savage women weren't showing as much interest in him, he made no indication. In fact, he just walked around the tribe, patting members on the back and commenting on how wonderful it was that they had done away with Material Wealth. The gnome had never seen the cleric so happy. It made Tepson smile too, since a number of the tribal children were following Kolveig around imitating him. He just hoped that they wouldn't become Karlists.

Eventually the duo stumbled upon a member of the tribe who they could understand and who could understand them. His name was Mohee.

"I reckon you be in these parts for mighty a-purpose."

Tepson sighed: maybe 'understand' was an overstatement.

Taking an immediate liking to the eccentric man, Kolveig replied, "We always have a Mighty Purpose, Friend Proletarian."

Mohee smiled back. He looked noticeably older and in worse health than the rest of tribe. He also wore more clothing. Unlike the tribesfolk that wore only loincloths at most, Mohee also wore a jacket vest and sandals.

"Well, I'm a-thinkin' that this here tribe would be more than a-willing to help ye with that purpose, by and by..." Mohee spit over his shoulder.

Tepson was beginning to suspect that this 'Mohee' wasn't a member of the tribe at all!

"Where did you learn to speak Eng... er... I mean Amercian?" the gnome asked.

"Why, I'm a-from the Vale *proper* just like ye! Came out here to the Fjord to avoid them... Authorities. Matter of fact, I knew the whole Party of the Vale, ever heard of them? Well... I got them started on one of their very first adventures, mind you. Afterwards, I had to a-come out here." Mohee gave a sly wink.

Tepson wasn't sure of what to make of the old man, but he didn't seem that trustworthy. Wasn't the Party of Vale active around over a century ago?

Quiet Upon Shenbyrg's Dawning

"Don't get me started on the Authorities," exclaimed Kolveig. "But yes, tell us how we can get this tribe to help us- I assume you know how to communicate with them?"

"Oh yes sir," offered Mohee, "and even though they sure a-taken a likin' to yer gnome friend, I can tell ye what would really float their boat."

Tepson couldn't wait to hear what this strange old coot had to say.

* * *

The short, bright yellow-skinned creature scampered over the rock face, its little, twisted mind racing. Those giant bird-things were terrifying, almost as bad as those human savages who were barely wearing any clothing! Goblins running around in loincloths was one thing, but humans doing the same was just disgusting!

Snik Snak rested for a moment as he tried to catch his breath. That stupid sun was shining down on him again- PAH! He had heard his stupid human former captors mention that the land he was going to was cloudier- anything to get him out of the blasted sun! Maybe he might find a new cave...

The former goblin chieftain sighed and slashed a tree with his dagger, knowing he couldn't return to his home cave, far to the north and west. He had fail... er... all those miserable warriors of his had failed! It wouldn't do to return, but he could still enact his revenge on the humans- one way or another!

His stupid human former captors, the ones who had caught him and led him around on a leash, had even let him go! How stupid! And he even stole the black-clothed one's dagger! It was only through luck that they weren't all dead!

"Humans!" Snik Snak spat out loud. "Me wrench their necks and drink their sorrows! HUMANS STUPID!"

Snik Snak stopped himself, realizing that he had been shouting. He knew that orcs dwelt in these hills and that the lands beyond were haunted.

He hoped he could stab whatever it was before it could stab him- he might finally make it to Sylvania!

Chapter 10

Gaol-break

The massive Gaolwagon lumbered up High Street, passing the homes and landmarks that many of the prisoners dimly remembered as if from former lives. Four great workhorses pulled the hulking wain, well-armored and loaded with men. Two watchmen drove in front and four more were mounted, riding their own horses at its sides. The great hoof beats echoed upon the paving stones below and the buildings nearby the street.

Halfdan sat uncomfortably next to Brotus, who kept pushing him against the wagon inner wall and getting a cruel laugh from his nearby friends, Burb and Ivnok. Halfdan had noticed lately that his own mood had shifted from one of depressed acquiescence to one of murderous patience, which only compounded as Brotus kept elbowing him in the gut.

The plan had been arranged for months, with so many inmates involved that Halfdan suspected a number of the watchmen were even in on the scheme. It was possible that those guards failed to respect the new authority of R'ti so much that they wished to be done with it themselves. Since it was a Cult designed to brainwash and belittle tutors, it had noticeably less of an effect on watchmen. Some might have even become so disillusioned that they wished to depart for other lands and having a few escaped convicts for the remaining authorities to deal with would certainly divert attention from their own escape.

The guards were otherwise fairly honorable men at least; they didn't let the beatings and abuse of Halfdan go too far. And it was also doubtful that the dregs, which many of the prisoners were, would have any way to bribe them. The cleric had trouble reasoning why else a group of 30 prisoners was allowed to work at the edge of town with only six guards. He caught a glimpse of his friend Terrance at the back of the wagon and nodded quickly before Brotus saw him.

The prisoners emerged from the Gaolwagon and their eyes took a few moments to adjust to the brightness. There around them were the sights and fresh scents of nature with just a few townhouses back to the east from which they came. Otherwise, the crisp wooded realm of fall was here, with few other signs of civilization amidst the rolling hills and trees, except for the road and the bridge.

A familiar white tower also stood a quarter mile away to the west- it seemed like another life when Halfdan had last visited it. The open air, the touch of the outdoors, all brought such a great sense of relief to the Odinnic that he nearly came to tears. Not a good idea he realized, since it might attract more unwanted attention from Brotus and his friends.

But it would seem that Brotus, Burb, and Ivnok had more pressing matters. They were drawing straws as to who would be released first. Even the guards, if they were complicit, knew how dangerous these men could be together, so the agreement might be to release them only one at a time, and even then, they were to only go in different directions.

The other prisoners began removing the shovels from the Gaolwagon to ostensibly begin work. The story was that they needed to dig some ditches around the causeway to the bridge to improve drainage and also fortify the causeway itself. All except Brotus's crew moved up to begin work. Halfdan picked a spot to work next to Terrance, at least as much out of companionship as mutual protection.

Halfdan's gaze lingered on the tower, which of course was Mistro's. Few of the other prisoners would even venture a glance at the place out of fear of getting hexed. Halfdan had not only glanced at the tower but had even gone inside to confer with the Wizard just last year. Mistro was certainly an eccentric fellow, but he did steer Halfdan in the right direction for ending the threat at the Schoolhouse. How ironic that the results of that liberation had ended him up here.

As the prisoners began their work in earnest, Halfdan's mind lingered on the ways of fate and magic in the world. He could do little else sometimes when engaged in simple toil. Odinnic teaching maintained that all worked in the end for the best for the aspirant: that even life's vicissitudes helped in removing one's eye (I), so as to better uncover the Runes, the mysteries of Life. The Norns spun their threads of destiny and it was up to Odin's faithful to sacrifice oneself to oneself to be free.

Of course, wizards like Mistro were not Odinnics. Theirs was more the path of great personal power through force of will alone. True, the approach was not altogether different- that of gaining greater freedom and ability by sacrificing what held one back, but the applications and results of that power would differ even more so.

As a follower of the Odinnic way, Halfdan might be guided on the right course of action or receive other help and succor from On High. Such miracles would often become more common the more connected the aspirant became with one's patron God. The resulting greater peace of mind and harmony would even allow the enlightened to help others in similar ways and to become more inured to dark forces and creatures that were antithetical to their God's purpose.

And while most wholesome clerics would see the Gods or God Almighty as supreme, their power was further variegated by which divine patron they followed, their own personal god. In other words, while a cleric of Odin might gain deep insight or be able to travel in an extraordinary manner, a cleric of Freya might be especially charming and skilled at euphoric healing. And on it went: there was no shortage of patrons in the Vale to follow, nor in the other lands of Amercia for that matter. Just as there were many paths to enlightenment, so were there many types of manifestations of that power. Followers of each divine patron followed a particular theme, above and beyond that of just helping and testing the faithful in times of need.

And it would seem that a time of need had now arisen. Still lost in thought and digging, Halfdan was only vaguely aware of a commotion back at the Gaolwagon. Terrance slapped him on the shoulder and pointed in that direction. Apparently Brotus had grown impatient with the guards and surprised them with his shovel. He and his friends laughed as they began bashing the fallen guards on the ground. The sickening thumps of breaking bone mingled with the cries of the dying men.

"We need to get out of here!" pleaded Terrance.

"Not yet," countered Halfdan.

The other prisoners had begun to sprint away in various directions, though none headed due west for the tower nor east back to the Gaol.

"Are you crazy? The guards are done for!"

"No," replied Halfdan firmly.

The cleric grabbed his shovel and approached Brotus and his men.

"Look who's here! *Girly-man!* Come to take a swing at the guards, too?"

"That's enough, Brotus."

The brute stopped in mid-swing. His large friends stared at him in disbelief. This scrawny, aging reject certainly was showing some bravery.

"Oh yeah, *girly-man?* Will you stop me?"

The hulking Brotus strode forward, standing head and shoulders over the cleric. His comrades, Burb and Ivnok, also of nearly the same size, began to laugh sinisterly and encircle Halfdan.

Brotus smiled. "Now, I'm going to *really have some fun with you, girly-man!*"

The brute reached out with surprising speed and grabbed Halfdan by the throat. The cleric's vision began to grow dim as he was strangled, Brotus was just too strong. The others approached with their shovels ready, laughing about what they would do to the cleric next. Brotus tossed him on the ground.

"And then, you're going to die!!!" finished the brute viciously. His friends laughed.

To all of their surprise, Halfdan returned to his feet and said quietly, "I'm already dead."

Suddenly, a number of ravens cawed loudly and rushed at the large prisoners' heads. Dumbstruck, they began to drop their shovels and move away from the fight- all except Brotus.

Quiet Upon Shenbyrg's Dawning

"It's going to take more than a bunch of birds to stop me, girly-man!"

The brute snapped his arm forward again, but this time Halfdan parried it with his shovel's haft. Not to be outdone, Brotus followed through with his other fist, knocking the wind out of the smaller cleric as he smashed him in the chest. Brotus continued his assault and smacked Halfdan down with a hammer-hand strike to the head.

The brute grabbed his own shovel and thrust the haft into Halfdan's throat, choking him again. The aging man gasped and choked as Brotus laughed and spit in his face. He then spun around to bring the shovel's point down upon the cleric's chest, but something bright blinded him at the last moment.

Feeling invigorated, Halfdan leapt to his feet and thought he saw an armored maiden, winged helm and all, standing next to him out of the corner of his eye. She shimmered brightly, but the cleric couldn't tell if she was real or not. Brotus then lunged with his shovel, but Halfdan was quicker and brained the thug with the side of his own. Brotus tumbled over and was silent.

Halfdan rushed over to the fallen guards- they looked badly beaten and were still. He called upon Odin, upon God to heal them. Feeling led, he closed his eyes and laid hands on their wounds. He felt the presence of the armored woman, a Valhallan aid, and heard the cawing of the ravens. His mind clear, the cleric arose and smashed his shovel upon a nearby stone. The edges broke clean off, creating a spear point.

Now it was time to wash this spit off his face.

* * *

"It's just a little bit farther," insisted Terrance.

"You said that an hour ago," replied Halfdan calmly.

Dan Osarchuk

The orange and brown leaves shown dimly in the setting sun, scattered amongst the fragrant cedars. What was a mild, clear day now brought the concern of a chilling night. Dry air could be as much a menace to the unprepared traveler as bug swarms and rains.

Still, it was quite a relief to be out of the Gaol and here in the wild. Halfdan didn't recognize these particular woods, but it didn't matter- one might find a spot that seemed familiar and sometimes even be transported thereto. The cleric stopped and examined one of the white oaks nearby.

"We need to LEAVE!" implored Terrance.

Halfdan looked at his companion. The latter was frowning, so perhaps he hadn't intentionally made a pun. Halfdan had noticed that not just his companion's mood, but his entire demeanor had changed once they had escaped. Terrance had seemed mild-mannered and patient back in the Gaol. Now he seemed insistent and beseeching ever since they had headed into the woods. He had said he knew of an 'escape'; Halfdan was beginning to doubt what he truly meant by that.

"How much farther could we go, Terrance? The Walstock Watch wouldn't look for us this far away. We must be half-way to Stephania by now."

"I know, but we need to *get out of here!* Don't you understand, Halfdan? We don't belong in this world!"

"What are you talking about?" Halfdan remained perplexed.

"You of all people should understand, Halfdan, this world is not meant for those like us!"

"*Like us*- how?" replied the cleric.

"Halfdan: I read what your rune parchment said back in the Gaol. I'm not from this world either."

Quiet Upon Shenbyrg's Dawning

"How could that be, Terrance?"

"My name... isn't really Terrance."

"What?" Halfdan noticed concern arising with the realization of deception. "What is your real name then?"

"It doesn't matter. Just a little farther, then I know of a place where we can escape this world forever. Ha!"

"No, Terr- or whoever you are. I'm not going to leave this world forever, at least not now. There are too many things that need doing, and I hope to see my children, Larnen and Kelne, again."

At this, the man who Halfdan had known as Terrance became enraged: "How dare YOU! I thought you would UNDERSTAND!" The man shook his fists at Halfdan.

The cleric simply stared at the man, smiled, and shook his head in reply. He walked a few paces into the woods and began circling a tree.

Realizing what the cleric was doing, he shouted, "NO! STOP!"

Halfdan passed around the tree again, eyes closed, but did not come around the other side. His former companion shrieked.

The man known as Terrance sprinted to the tree to see if he was hiding behind it, but he already knew that Halfdan was gone. He fell to his knees, rage mixing with sadness as he realized that he had been deserted by his comrade... and that the witch hunters would be coming for him soon.

If he only had his tome...

Chapter 11

When Haircuts Go Wrong

The three fair-haired maidens rode through the hinter hills, laughing and chatting. Elfriede, Kalla, and Gudre all enjoyed such rides over the pass from Dinglesfuhr into Fjord Vallee. Though they cherished their home, it was a welcome change to be out where the great beasts dwelled and to catch the eye of savage men, being shapely women that rode by them bareback upon their steeds.

It was welcome for Elfriede especially, in light of all the strangeness befalling Walstock of late. Here in the Fjord, the warm noon sun nourished her skin; she could forget her troubles and enjoy a pleasant day with her friends. And though Kalla had a wider face, shorter hair, green eyes, and a more slender frame, and Gudre was more a golden blonde in pigtails that complimented her many curves, the three could have been mistaken for sisters in appearance as much as they acted so.

The blonde patrol made their way to a tribe they knew that wasn't very far: *the Deer Watchers*. They had heard that their new chieftain had gone missing recently and wondered how they could be of assistance.

* * *

"That there big fella should be just over that there ridge a-yonder." The old man spit where he pointed to punctuate his remark.

The Karlist and the gnome arched their necks to look in the direction that the old man was pointing, but the rise in the land made it impossible to see.

"Are you sure that the Errant Proletarian is really over there, Master Mohee?" asked Kolveig.

'Master Mohee'? Pah! Tepson didn't trust this guide or the cleric's strange admiration of him. Kolveig had been much less belligerent lately- was it moreso because he hadn't seen any 'Capitalist Oppression' or was it because he had only recently been a squirrel?

Tepson had to shake his head at his accidental insinuation that magic was real: how ridiculous! Still, they had a mission to accomplish and doing something to aid the 'Wizard' Antraxus seemed as good a reason as any to the gnome. Why not help the Karlist *agitate the savages* against their rival, Dinglesfuhr? Nearly everyone was mad in this Vale anyway!

The pair made their way over the hill as Mohee remained behind to chew upon some rocks. According to him, a 'big fella' had captured the tribe's barbarian chieftain after a falling out over some transaction. Tepson hoped that this 'big fella' wasn't a dinosaur.

As they cleared the ridge, the land opened into the side of a large foothill covered in tall grass that showed bright green in the warm autumn afternoon air. Birds (of normal size, much to Tepson's relief) fluttered overhead and the scent of the woods behind the hill was quite fragrant. The two tramped to what appeared to be a giant shed with a door and window openings that seemed twice normal size- four times normal size in Tepson's case. It stood in front of and abutted into the hill.

Triggered by this sign of civilization, Kolveig's Karlist persona began to return to the fore. He marched up to the door and knocked on it ceremoniously. Tepson readied his pickhammer. He doubted that a dinosaur lived in a shed or would answer a door knock for that matter. But even though birds still chirped in the distance, the situation certainly did not seem safe.

"This door shall be opened in the Name of Great Karl Above!"

No answer. A gentle breeze blew, causing waves to form in the tall grass around the shed. The cleric shrugged his shoulders and glanced at the gnome. Tepson signed and clambered into one of the window openings, taking care not to let his pickhammer bump the side. The Karlist followed soon after.

The shed was quite spacious within, no doubt due to its oversized construction, but also because it covered a tunnel further beyond, set into the foothill itself. The scent of earth and a strange, mannish odor permeated the place, where a large wooden table set was found. Another large chair to the right lay broken upon the floor and bits of large, dark hair and blood led down into the tunnel. The massive hole yawned nearly 15' tall and wide.

Tepson began rummaging around in his pack to see if he had brought a lantern or even just a torch. Kolveig knelt and gave prayer to Karl. It seemed that this quest would be more than a simple knock at the door.

* * *

Elfriede and friends were growing increasingly concerned as they stood mounted in front of Mohee. The old man was already on his fourth chewing-stone and the outlanders that he had sent into the giant shed had not yet returned.

"They are still a-checking on the place o'er the hill."

"Why would you send them in with so little warning, front-long into Vertagern's home, Herr Mohee?" asked Gudre. She patted her steed's neck to calm the beast at mention of the name.

Mohee just chewed his rock and spat, staring lasciviously at the mostly unclad beauties before him.

Elfriede huffed a sigh of frustration and spurred her steed with her bare ankles. The horse galloped off and her friends began to follow.

Kalla paused for a moment to take in the old man. "It is bad form to let the unwary meet their doom unprepared, mein friend."

To this, Mohee made a reply. "If it's doom ye be a-seekin', then it's a doom ye shall get! Why, I remember the time when Cortas himself asked me the very same..."

The last remaining blonde rider sped on her way before the old man could begin another yarn.

* * *

Gnome and cleric stalked the large tunnel with all but a dim candle to give them light.

"Can't that made-up deity of yours create some imaginary magic illumination for us to see by?" asked Tepson sardonically. His voice echoed strangely upon the packed earthen walls.

"You're pretty new to this world, gnome, so I'll let your Counter-Revolutionary Prattle go Unchastised this time," replied Kolveig.

Dan Osarchuk

At this, something stirred in the deep: a roar, quite thunderous in volume, yet like that of a man. Almost imperceptibly, another voice, not quite as thunderous and also muffled, made a reply.

Guessing that the tribal chieftain still lived, the duo sped down the passage. Strange lights danced on the walls ahead- Tepson hoped that the creature they would face needed light to see too.

They came around another turn and found themselves in a large, hollowed out room. Kolveig put his finger to his lip and stared at the gnome, as if the need for stealth wasn't obvious enough.

Before they knew what happened, something large was upon them. A massive man came at Kolveig from behind. He held a club that was the size of a small tree trunk. Seeing the terror in Tepson's eyes, the Karlist ducked, narrowly avoiding a heavy wooden doom. For his part, the gnome tumbled back and ran to find some cover from the giant- a GIANT!

What the gnome had seen in his year here in the future had often given him pause: throwback civilizations, supernatural phenomena, beasts of unnatural size and now... this! What looked like some sort of savage man, nearly 15' in height, who luckily wore more garb than the more normal-sized savages outside. Strangely too, it looked like one side of his head had a mullet-cut, though the other side didn't.

Tepson's biologist mind recoiled at the revelation- how could this be? As he watched the giant chase the cleric around the room, the gnome remained hidden behind a pile of broken boxes, wondering at the impossibilities of this world. Perhaps it was some sort of radiological cause that had triggered such growth in a human body? He guessed that in most end-of-the-world scenarios that D.C. would have been nuked, so it stood to reason that such prolonged radiation might have spawned such monstrosities as a giant.

"Sure! Chase me, Imperialist Scum! You won't squash this Warrior of Justice anytime soon! Why can't you be more egalitarian, like a Procrustean Giant?"

At least the cleric had gotten his Orthodoxy back.

Still, Tepson doubted that neither he nor the cleric had any chance of defeating such a foe. They simply lacked the necessary strength or weaponry to inflict any serious wound upon a man of such serious size.

The gnome looked around the large room desperately. Braziers burned at the walls near the edges, causing the shadowy lights that danced upon the ceiling. At the far side of the room, Tepson could see a large, muscular man of roughly human size tied to a wooden frame near the wall. He looked vaguely familiar and though he was wearing overalls, he did have a mullet haircut in an identical manner to that of the savage tribe that they had met earlier.

That must be the chief!

The giant continued to lay its attack against Kolveig. It smashed at the cleric repeatedly, showing little concern for the boxes and sundry other items that were battered into splinters by its strikes.

"HOLD STEEL, LITTLE MAN!" roared the giant.

"I'd rather not," replied the cleric.

SMASH! Its great club collided with what looked like an armoire, shattering the massive piece of furniture with ease. The club had come within a foot of Kolveig's head. The gnome noticed that the cleric was now momentarily pausing whenever he spoke. Tepson hoped that the giant didn't notice this fact too, or else it would most likely slay his comrade when it goaded him with a question that required a longer answer. He thought about calling out a warning to the cleric, but decided that it would only draw attention to himself.

Instead, Tepson moved closer to the man who was tied up. Where had he seen him before? Maybe somewhere else that was underground? Tepson's attention was distracted by the booming voice of the giant.

"WHY YOU HEERE, LITTLE MAN? YOU HEERE TO SELL ME SOMETHIN'? NOVER HAIRCUT?"

Not good, thought Tepson. He could already see the cleric tensing up for a long-winded reply to the giant's challenge.

Thinking quickly, the gnome dashed the rest of the way and began untying the muscular man. He seemed to be a barbarian warrior. A battle axe and pair of pruning shears rested at his feet. Tepson used the shears to cut the bonds and made ready to give the man his axe. The gnome noticed though that the large man winced when he had cut the bonds- perhaps they had injured him somehow?

Now released, the chief looked at the gnome and said sternly, "That's not how you use shears- they for GIANT!" His manner and visage quickly changed from one of focused explanation to that of unbounded rage as he saw the giant closing in on Kolveig. The cleric had stopped, turned, and made ready to debate the giant.

"Sell you something? Sell YOU SOMETHING? What do you take me for, giant, some sort of DOOR-TO-DOOR MISAPPROPRIATOR OF WEALTH?"

The giant didn't seem impressed by the Karlist's explanation; it strode forward for the killing blow.

Suddenly, the chief, now freed by Tepson, leapt upon the giant's back from a nearby table. Cursing and salivating furiously, he repeatedly smashed the giant with the haft of his axe, right where its neck met its shoulders. It roared out in pain and reached for the man.

Being too caught up in his diatribe, Kolveig continued, "And another thing: calling me 'little' is a sure indication of your attempt at OPPRESSING me!"

Roaring in fury, the giant stretched its arm back, grabbed a hold of the chief, and hurled him at Kolveig. As the large, mulleted man flew through the air at him, the cleric felt a sense of déjà vu.

Knowing that he was about to do something stupid, Tepson tossed a piece of the armoire at the giant's face. It bellowed and turned on the gnome. Tepson shrieked and began sprinting around the pile of boxes, just as Kolveig had done earlier.

"It is time to GO!" yelled the terrified gnome.

Ignoring Tepson, Kolveig examined the barbarian who he had nearly collided with. Luckily, the man had missed him and collided with the wall head-first instead. Helping him to his feet, recognition came to the cleric. He decided to utter a prayer to Karl, even though he knew that this man was not one of the faithful, and doing so in such a rushing and obvious way only added to the risk of having to undergo some sort of Divine Test.

Red light began to knit the barbarian's grievous wounds together and Kolveig hurried him down the passage. Regaining his coherence, the barbarian stared at the cleric in unabashed awe as the latter seemed to be losing his own coherence.

The giant turned its attention to the cleric and the barbarian. Tepson took a chance, ran a short way further, and grabbed something from where the barbarian had been held earlier. The gnome grinned and hurled it at the giant.

Tepson was glad that he had remembered the pruning shears... and that the giant seemed to hate them so much.

Dan Osarchuk

* * *

Elfriede, Kalla, and Gudre were just beginning to dismount when they heard the commotion. The tribal chief, head bloodied but otherwise healed, leapt out of one of the giant shed's windows, followed by a little bearded man and a now obviously delirious man with a big black beard and an olive jacket.

The three men stopped and stared ridiculously at the striking maidens, who blushed in return. Hearing a rumbling inside, Kalla spoke up: "We must flee! *Gross Vertagern* is on his way!"

The men started to scramble towards the now remounting women. The barbarian chief stopped though, furrowed his brow in contemplation, and asked, "On his way to what?"

Ignoring him, Gudre helped him to her horse, who groaned under the added weight.

Kalla kneeled at her horse, offering Tepson a boost.

"I can do it myself!" said the gnome grouchily. Both he and the maiden blushed.

Elfriede reached her fair hand out to Kolveig, who only said, "Kernervan... I like angrily... Bourgeois horse."

She grabbed the disoriented cleric and pushed him onto her saddle as Vertagern burst through his door.

"HOLD STEEL! IMAGONNA SMASH YOU!

The horses neighed in terror, but the Dinglesfuhr maidens were skilled riders and raced away, saving the three men who were double-mounted with them.

They cleared the ridge back to Mohee, who was nearly done chewing yet another rock. Kalla, having some extra room due to

Tepson's smaller size, reached out her hand and helped the man onto her steed.

As the group rode back to the tribe, Gudre put her hand on one of the barbarian's strong thighs provocatively. The man looked back at the curvaceous, lightly-clad, pig-tailed beauty behind him.

"Gorm", she whispered in his ear, "won't you soon wish to join me in bed?"

Gorm giggled. "Oh yes, me very tired. Haircuts are exhausting."

Chapter 12

Into the Woods

The raven alighted upon an ancient pine, its peak pointing far above the surrounding foliage. The bird gazed down on them with knowing eyes. The two men moved closer to the great tree. Oborren breathed a sigh of relief: they had been following the bird for hours.

The hunter stared up at the raven.

"Where to now?"

The bird cawed and flew away.

Fine, thought Oborren angrily, the Gods can lead me on senseless journeys anytime they wish!

He noticed Bjartar moving on and caught up with him- it wouldn't do to have a henchman in the lead, thought the hunter.

The two came to a longpost fence that stood unpainted, spanning in either direction with a fell air about it. Oborren sensed that something was wrong, but couldn't quite place the disturbance. He quickly hopped the fence with Bjartar close behind. They walked on in an effort to find out what was amiss with this place.

They rounded another tree and took in a surreal vista beyond the ridge below. Looking down, a ranch house and adjacent stock pens were visible now, but something was terribly wrong. Instead of animal livestock being kept within, *humans were lolling about in the pens* in a most despicable way!

Oborren's face twisted in outrage; Bjartar readied his bow. It would seem that this place needed cleansing. They moved in.

* * *

It had appeared that the world-walk was not exactly what Halfdan had hoped for.

The cleric wandered through the woods, happy at least to be free of the duplicitous Terrance- or whatever his *real name* was. Still, Halfdan was concerned that he had now become hopelessly lost. And as much as he loved roaming the wild lands, he was no forester. If he did not find a path or protection by nightfall, Halfdan assumed that he might not see the next morn.

How strange it was that humans were unable to survive in the wild without certain supplies and skill. Yes, perhaps the hunter-gatherers of Fjord Vallee might live without most comforts of civilization, but even they required some fire and shelter. Halfdan knew of no *normal humans* that could survive a cold night in the woods without such preparation, nor could they fare very long on collected berry or raw meat. It stood to reason that perhaps humanity itself was not quite part of the world, at least as much as the animals and monsters were. How could humans really be native to a place if they could not survive when it was in its natural form?

Being here amongst the cedars and oaks in the shining sun, it was easy to see the allure of the open wild though. No Lord or Monitor was present to tell one what to do. No gabbard or thief was around to pass judgment or snatch one's livelihood. Here in the woods, Halfdan was no one's slave and no one's master. Death and discomfort were the only penalties that the beasts and elements might bestow in the wild- simple yet costly.

He guessed at why folk would wish to form towns, cities, and other settled lands. True, they might then have to bend knee to some mortal lord or lady, but they would also have less fear of starving to death, dying of hypothermia, or being torn apart by some wild beast. Such sensations could certainly be seen as awful, even moreso than serving a master, but Halfdan also felt like he would rather die than be a work-slave again.

What amazed Halfdan too was how his mind still played tricks on him even after walking alone for hours. It was all he could do to watch the hapless fears that he was being stalked by some forest denizen to arise, or the delusion that he had impossibly ventured back into some familiar place that looked just like the arrangement of forest that he was standing in. Was it delusion or some 'Mysterious Action' of Quant Theo at work? In other words, was his mind mistaken or did Reality actually change and shift? Whatever the case, it helped to remember to keep his faith in Odin, to keep holding I, for like a Sleipnir-trip, he had been carried away from his erstwhile comrade, at least.

The way of Providence could be hard to fathom. The cleric hoped that this walk through the forest would not be his doom, but then again, the presence of Consciousness such surrender provided was its own reward. It was always available and it was always the true sense of happiness, whether he made it out of the woods or not.

* * *

"Damn! If I only had my book. Now it will just rot away in the hands of those closed-minded Tyrians!"

Another gaol-breaker wandered the woods too, muttering to himself, but with far less predilection for mystic insight. What had begun as a steady journey to the Estate with Halfdan had now degenerated into a hopeless tramp through the forest.

It wasn't the end of the world though; he had memorized *most of* the tome. How could he not? From place to place he had wandered before, from world to world. How many years he had traveled, he had lost count. And this wasn't the first time he was temporarily stranded in some God-forsaken world without indoor plumbing or even a *wireless connection*, but he vowed that it would be the last.

"And tonight is the night," he muttered again. "I thought that fool, Halfdan, would at least understand. Maybe he really is from another world, but he has lived in this one for too long and has let himself grow attached..." The man spat.

Tonight was the final night for the Venus/ Mars alignment. *The door* could then be opened at the Estate once again; hopefully there wouldn't be any savage Cultists there this time. That party who had rescued him last year did slay most of them.

"Even if they call it 'Venus' and 'Mars' in this stupid place! I can't wait to be free of this ridiculous Vale! If I see one more idiot-"

The man stopped in mid-sentence. He had heard something. He waited, but heard nothing more. His heart began to beat faster.

Fear was upon him- he knew that there must be something nearby, something that hunted him. He sprinted deeper into the woods, chills running down his spine, goading him to run even faster. The sound was obvious now: hoofbeats- soon they would be upon him!

Try as he might, the short man was overtaken. Riders in white tunics with black crosses emblazoned, like longswords pointed downwards, closed in. One pulled out a bullwhip and knocked the man off his feet. He flopped onto his stomach, hitting the cold earth hard. The scent of soil mingled with that of horse and his own terrified bowels.

The riders circled, four in all. One dismounted, bearing no helm but instead a witch hunter's hat. He stood over the fallen man and paused to savor the moment.

"We have you now, Wilstrin," said Father Farhred. He motioned to his comrades, "secure the witch."

* * *

"Get away from me!" hissed the hunter.

A deranged man, unfortunately unclad and covered in mud and dung kept approaching Oborren to sniff him. When the hunter went to smack him away, he recoiled and simply made a "moo" sound. Oborren winced in disgust.

"Can't you hjelp him?" Bjartar asked cautiously.

"I am no wizard," said the hunter severely. "I think we'll need to find out what's inside first in order to have any chance of 'helping' these... *people.*"

Oborren used the term loosely. The whole pen was populated by unclad, filthy humans who made the sounds of cows, pigs, sheep, and chickens. In an adjacent field, some even galloped around ridiculously on all fours and made the sound of horses. It would seem that the natural order of things had been turned on its head. It was fitting that the Gods would send a hunter here to set things right. Oborren just wondered at why it always seemed that *he was the only hunter available to set things right.*

As the two approached the main building, Oborren also considered the relationship of these people to the beast-heads. They were still in Pentagram Tannery and these humans were certainly *behaving like animals*, and yet they did not have animal heads, other body parts, nor were they ferociously aggressive. What were these people and why were they behaving so?

Hunter and henchman split up as they neared the barn house. The day was growing late and the air was growing colder, thankfully diminishing the stench and hullabaloo of unwashed humans snorting, baying, and clucking. Both readied their weapons, though Oborren knew that Bjartar only had a hand axe for melee. If something moved closer than the effective range of his bow, the hunter doubted that his henchman's smaller weapon would be enough to keep him alive for long. Oborren had to admit that it would be a shame if the man died too quickly.

The hunter moved around a corner, the crude wooden beams beneath his feet doing little to quiet his approach. Crossbow ready, Oborren realized that Bjartar could hug the wall closer thanks to the vertical nature of his longbow's limb when compared to his own crossbow's horizontal lath. As a result, Oborren held his weapon lower, at stomach height, ready to shoot the first creature that jumped out at him.

He cursed himself for not outfitting himself and his henchman with proper bolts and arrows, but since he had little idea what sort of fell creatures might lurk inside, he had no way of knowing which types to make ready; that is, even if he had the right type of bolts and arrows to draw from. The hunter bit his lip and hoped for the best.

As the sun set, Oborren's dark hunter's grab began to blend in with the encroaching shadows upon the structure. Body poised, he advanced carefully, making sure to not step on the middle of any of the boards of the barn house's porch. One more creaking sound could be all it would it take to give himself away.

His henchman was most likely not as careful, because he now heard a commotion on the other side of the building. The sounds of creatures with *actual* cattle, stag, and goat heads erupted in that direction, as well as inhuman screams of pain. At least Bjartar got a few of them, thought Oborren.

Seizing the opportunity, the hunter burst through the barn house door and took in a horrifying scene. Penned in corrals were scores of humans, living in filth as animals. It seemed worse to Oborren than even the humans outside, since that held at least some similarity to the way primitive tribesmen might live. But here, it just smacked of total exploitation.

An obese human woman moved up to Oborren on all fours. She, like the others, was disrobed and feculent. To make matters worse, she began barking at him and even began fuming from the mouth. The hunter was shocked that she also had a crude collar around her neck.

Then he saw it: the reason why the humans were living like such oppressed animals. A horse-headed atavar stood a dozen yards away. He spotted some other bestial-men deeper in the barn, as well. Unlike the humans, they walked upright and wore some measure of clothing and cleanliness. Horse-head looked at the insane dog-woman and whistled for her to heel.

Outraged, Oborren knocked the deranged woman aside and let his crossbow fly. One shaft took horse-head right in the throat, while his second, quickly-loaded shot struck another, a goatman, through its heart. The hunter quickly shifted position to get some cover behind an empty corral's wall.

As he reloaded, it seemed that he had taken the beasts by surprise, for they did not counterattack. Horse-head still didn't move, but goat-head ran away- perhaps the bolt was not of the correct type to truly kill it. Oborren also wasn't sure if he had really broken its morale or if the goatman was just one of the less aggressive ones who had not gone off immediately to kill and eat Bjartar.

The remaining beast-heads howled in their inhuman tongue and fled, while the remaining humans began to bay and whimper, surprisingly upset by the change in circumstance- all except one. A strangely familiar woman's voice could be heard a few stalls off to the right.

"Come at me again, beast-males, and you'll regret it!"

Oborren recognized the voice immediately and dashed over to her.

There he found his former comrade, Brymanah, tied down to iron clamps in the stall. She appeared to have been terribly tortured and abused by the beasts and yet she still lived. Cutting free her bonds, he placed her over his shoulder. She was quite tall and strong, so the hunter struggled, but now determined, he made their escape.

As they extricated themselves from the ranch and back towards the hill, Brymanah awoke enough to walk somewhat with the hunter's support. The terrible howls and roars back in the distance signaled that many atavars remained and that they would soon pick up the trail. The hunter and amazon quickened their pace.

Oborren could only guess at why the beast-heads were treating the humans so. Perhaps they were just evil and twisted? Or was it some sort of ironic fate meted out to humans to live as the livestock that they usually ruled? He could still remember when that horse-head had whistled at that woman who thought she was a dog. The hunter hoped that he had truly killed it with his crossbow bolt, but sometimes monsters were just stunned by an attack or even cleverly feigned death.

It didn't really matter though, there must still be over 50 atavars at the ranch with many more human slaves. What an affront to the natural order of things! Oborren fumed at this outrage and at his current inability to kill them all.

But now, thanks to the Gods, he knew where these monstrosities dwelled and had gotten at least one of his comrades to safety. Oborren could always return to the ranch and... he glanced back at the sound of the howling bestial men and a lone human's scream of pain... avenge his henchman's death.

* * *

The shadows grew long in the southern woods. Van Dwick enjoyed venturing in this region, just beyond the edges of Dinglesfuhr. It made him feel at least somewhat relevant again, like back in the days when being Fieldmarshall *actually meant being entrusted with his land's defense.*

He knew that his land was now in great danger, that the Dinglestor would soon be thrown open wide by maniacs within to allow for its subjugation from without. Mekla, his Dinglesfrau, had fallen into this madness and begun to even sponsor the Glowing Spectral Personhood as the State Cult. Even worse, she had begun to use her Secret Police to remove any who resisted the Cult and its fanaticism for *Underreign.* Most common folk were thereby becoming afraid to even discuss the problems with Dinglesfuhr doing away with itself, let alone challenge it.

So it was to the Old Ways of the land that Van Dwick turned now. Before even the Amaranthine Wizard took power, the area was deemed quite haunted. The Fieldmarshall hoped that those haunting spirits would take pity on Dinglesfuhr in this dangerous time, to save it from the impending calamity which it now faced.

Van Dwick rounded a copse of trees and found the cleft in the earth. Something dark seemed to watch him from the corner of his eye. The hairs on his neck began to stand up on end as he felt the unquiet shade behind him. Apparently, he was at the right place.

Quiet Upon Shenbyrg's Dawning

He knew this to be the grave of the Fallen Watchman, killed by invaders during the early days of Lights Out. For centuries, his family kept the story as tradition. Van Dwick poured an offering of raspberry strudel and Koka tea upon the ground.

"Bring us justice, Ancient One, where you did not receive it."

Chapter 13

Winnonar

Luce laughed as the milkmaid brought in another gooseblood pie. They certainly were tasty, but not as tasty of course as the pear tarts of Calvary. He tugged on his blond ponytail and made a strange face. The milkmaid laughed at him easily, but then quickly gave him a look of suspicion as he ogled her body. The maid flung the pie on the table and strutted away.

My, how different women could be from different places, he thought. Was it simply a discrepancy of location? Or was it more one of culture? This place was more Norse, while the Vale was more Teutonic. But even Norse maidens could vary considerably from place to place, even in the Old Countries, so who could know for sure?

Was it something different in the people or in the land itself that made the women behave differently in Minas-Ninona vs. the Shenbyrg Vale? It was true that the Minas-Ninonan Norse women seemed more direct and outgoing than even their Norse Vale counterparts. Luce guessed at why that was truly the case.

Quiet Upon Shenbyrg's Dawning

The entrance of Ragennar and the *Chosen One* let him put those questions to the test.

Oh, how breathtaking she was to finally behold in person: a smaller blonde maiden from a smaller Midwestern town, so innocent, so pure, so... deadly! Luce couldn't help but chuckle to himself.

"Who are ya?" she asked.

And she's becoming a bit more outgoing too. Good. Luce smiled and brushed some crumbs off of his garish clothing.

"I am Luce. Ragennar was kind enough to bring you to me." He nodded to the grizzled warrior with the rust-colored beard.

The woman's face darkened. It was remarkable.

"I am cursed", she began, "cursed by Hjel hjerself."

"I wouldn't worry about her, my daughter. Hel is the dark truth responding to the shattering light of, as they say, what her father is."

Emhild considered his response. The man seemed confusing.

In a bizarre manner, Luce continued, this time now singing: "You have a great purpose to manifest, my dear. What Hel has given you is a blessing, not a curse, so you need not fear!"

At this, Em broke down in tears, sobbing. Even skalds usually didn't get this bad of a reaction. Luce was shocked that he had even begun to feel her sadness within himself- remarkable!

"All men who would love me... die, you betchya!" she cried. Ragennar handed her a viking handkerchief.

Luce strode forward and embraced the distraught maiden. Em's body shook at the vicissitudes that this life had wrought upon her. The skald patted her on the back and hummed another strange tune.

He looked down at Emhild and smiled. Something about him reminded her of an uncle, but also of a rascal. He reached down and tickled her arms and she couldn't help but laugh.

She pulled back, somewhat embarrassed now. Then he spoke again.

"You are a gifted woman indeed, Emhild, if you can see the mirth in the darkness."

Em's eyes opened wide. Luce continued to be held in awe at this woman's depth. He had to remember to compliment Hel on her work the next time they spoke.

Ragennar shifted uneasily. There had been a look of concern on his face, but when he saw that Em was cheering up, he relaxed. Luce looked at him and smiled, almost as if he could read the grizzled man's mind.

Torsteinn and some other warriors entered the room to lead Emhild away. She bowed her head as she left; she was now resigned to the fate that the Norns had assigned her.

When they were alone, Luce spoke with Ragennar.

"You have done well. Soon she will be the Helan Queen that we hope and dream about."

"Is there no other way, Dróttinn Luce?"

Luce smiled at Ragennar and chewed some more gooseblood pie. He offered another slice to the norseman, but he declined.

"I've traveled eons and spent lifetimes to make this happen, Ragennar." Luce's eyes began to take on a strange light. "The pieces are already in motion. Putting Emhild in the right place at the right time will bring about the final end of it all."

"Of it all?" questioned the warrior.

"Yes," replied the skald.

Ragennar shivered and knelt before his Lord. He bowed his head in reverence, fighting back his fears that this poor woman might suffer greatly before she brought about the end.

* * *

The dream came to her again. Her love by her side, such a connection, not quite felt again in this life- two halves of a whole. Oh, how they loved each other, walking in the woods, he was back from campaign, *hopefully for good*!

Then the shot! The pain! OH. My belly!

Oh and look at him: he'll never let me go... ever... won't he ever be happy without me?

The image shifted again; rarely did she have both dreams occur on the same night. One of her childhood imaginary friends came to mind, but then vanished again.

Where was ma? What did I do? I took a wrong turn, stayed in the wrong place and now... now... I'm lost, lost in this strange world. The clothing rack...

What if I had stayed with her? What if I hadn't died?

Why did so many people that she love have to be lost to her? Her mother and the man who was her lost love from a life past. What did they do to deserve this? The dark presence of Hel, one of fatal ostracism, began to increase all around her.

Why?

* * *

118

Emhild awoke with a start. She took in the dark tapestries and skull imagery placed about her private sanctum. Some girls might go for this sort of arrangement: opulent, guarded, and pampering, but it was really morbid and not her taste.

She stretched her legs and arose to find a fine silk gown of black. She guessed that Ragennar had left it for her. Emhild had to admit that she liked him- he treated her like a daughter, but the not-so-subtle hints as to her great destiny to become some Helan Queen were getting ridiculous.

Emhild strode from her apartment, bare feet being massaged by the luxurious black carpet. Servants bowed low as she passed into the hallway. Being treated like a Queen of Death certainly seemed surprisingly sensual. At least they weren't littering the place with corpses and bones.

She soon passed through another doorway into the temple. Em removed her gown for the morning ceremony. A cool breeze sent a shiver through her, but it wasn't as bad as breezes in her hometown this time of year. There was also the aroma of the river- the Mighty Mississip. The extra touch of moisture in the air seemed to take the edge off the autumn chill.

Em had come to learn that Winnonar was a key base in the Helan Domain in this corner of Minas-Ninona. Its excellent harbor and protective bluffs allowed Luce's followers to raid other settlements, such as Stockholm and the Wicson's Cross. Few would stand against the black-clad vikings that came howling from their ships and those that did were cut down by the Helan's river advantage. Emhild guessed that having *her blessings* at their disposal would make the Helans even stronger now.

As for Winnonar itself, she had taken a liking to the town. Though the folks seemed as Norse and nice as in Bjeiland, there were lots of other differences. There were Kashubian Slavs, amazing stained glass upon buildings in the style of Victoria, not to mention the River, which was much larger than the one near her home in Bjeiland! Em wanted to see the Library and the House of Healing too, but Luce wouldn't hear of it. It seemed that even Helan Queens couldn't do what they wanted when they wanted to.

A number of thralls were led inside, followed by many karls: the free men and women of this Minas-Ninonan town. A great statue of Hel occupied the northern side, her bifurcated nature represented by the stone of alabaster and coal that split her mighty form. Four braziers burned purple red, casting the corners of the temple in a strange light of fatal promise. A palpable sense of divine death lurked in the air.

Emhild sat upon her tripod chair in front of the large statue and placed a cape of black feathers over her fair, dishabille body. A number of the karls opened their mouths in awe at such a stunning visage, but quickly lowered their heads when Ragennar and the other guards stared at them.

Emhild began, "Great Queen of Death and Dismay, we kneel before ya on this day."

The brazier lights went out. All went silent as the presence of the Goddess was fully felt in the room. The only light now shone in from the entrance to the east where the Mighty Mississip could be seen and the orange-hued bluffs beyond. A cloud began to pass over the sun, making the temple grow even darker.

With this signal from Hel, the thralls were led forward to kneel before Em and the statue. The fair blonde woman from Bjeiland looked upon them sadly, knowing what would come next. She caught Ragennar's gaze, who seemed grieved as well, though he hid it as best he could. Em guessed that the warrior felt for her, rather than the thralls. Some of the latter were even smiling, though most looked afraid.

"Great Matron of Final Oblivion, hjave these sacrifices."

The temple grew darker. Emhild removed her cape.

Dan Osarchuk

* * *

The small wagon train lumbered under the clear blue Midwestern sky. Norse riders trotted in a large circle around one wagon in particular that bore a black canopy with a white skull emblem. A blond man with a ponytail drove the wagon, which was part of a train of just two more. A few other warriors and workers walked beside the rear wagons, as well. Light horsemen rode at the boundaries as scouts. It was only a small force of the Helan Domain.

A rust-bearded rider rode up to the blond man who was driving.

"Hjow much further should it be, Dróttinn?" asked Ragennar.

"Oh, not too much further," answered Luce. He looked up at the sun shining and smiled. They had begun to pass within a forested gorge; some brown leaves still clung to the many trees.

"Ya seem very hjappy, master."

"I am. Soon we will be returning to the home that I had for oh so very long!"

Luce smiled at Ragennar, a sinister look in his eye.

"But won't the Gods demand a hjeavy price for allowing us to travel so very far?"

Luce smiled again at the man and motioned back to the wagon he drove. "We have already paid it."

Just then, one of the scouts signaled an alarm.

With a terrifying roar, gangs of monstrous-looking humanoids erupted from the trees. These creatures had hides the color of coal, strong frames, and hideous features with the noses of pigs. Orcs!

Quiet Upon Shenbyrg's Dawning

As the orcs set upon the men, Ragennar immediately moved his mount beside the black wagon and reared his horse back in defense. Luce only laughed. Torstein and Konigsgild moved in with their own mounts, as well.

Five lynx-eyed orcs broke through the line and made it within striking distance of the wagon. Ragennar ran one through with his sword, while Torstein trampled another with his horse. Two more dodged Konigsgild's spear and stabbed his horse with their own meat-cleaver weapons. The poor beast squealed and collapsed, pinning Konigsgild beneath it.

Ragennar charged forward grimly, leapt off his horse onto one of the orcs, and then got up and smashed the other in the skull with his sword's pommel. Though wounded, the orc roared and slashed the grizzled warrior across the chest, but his mail turned the fell blade. Ragennar countered by slicing up into the creature's crotch, slicing clear through it and sending its innards splattering into its approaching fellows. Torstein ran another through with his axe and jumped down to tend to Konigsgild.

Seeing the battle erupt outside the wagon, Emhild opened the door to help Ragennar and his men. More orcs saw the fair, small blonde woman emerging, roared again, and rushed towards her.

Ragennar turned and cursed. "Get back inside the wagon, Em! Ya crazy?!"

She obeyed, but not before a group overwhelmed Torstein and Konigsgild.

Luce simply kept laughing to himself and spurring the wagon on. Orcs would attempt to get in the way, take one look at him, and then flee in terror. He even broke out in song during his mirth: "...take me on up from this gorge!"

Ragennar glanced back and it looked like the two rear wagons had become overwhelmed. The screams of Torstein and Konigsgild could be heard as they became victims of the orcs.

122

"We hjave to go back for them, Luce!"

Luce only stopped singing and laughed harder. The remaining riders closed ranks about the black wagon. The orcs began to thin, as most of their fellows went to pillage and slay the two wagons that were caught behind.

Emhild opened the wagon door again and stared at Luce. She was still crying over the loss of so many of their people.

Luce smiled at her and said, "And now the Gods have been paid."

* * *

The remaining Helans sat in the Cave of Mysteries.

Emhild, adorned again in just her black feather cape, shivered in the dank air. Flowstone formations shimmered in the lantern light, creating a surreal feel. Ragennar and the other warriors sat sternly upon the many shelves within the chamber, strange symbols marked upon their faces. The rust-bearded warrior stared at Luce angrily.

Shadows lurked upon the walls, though Emhild could feel nothing but contempt for Luce herself. She knew she had to follow him, at least for now, how else would she uncover an end to her curse?

The garishly-dressed man only smiled back at her. She's coming along just fine, he thought. He nodded to her to begin.

"Darkest Hjel," Em's light voice made a strange echo with the acoustics of this place as distant water dripped, "we hjave come for ya to take us hjither. Hjither, wither, soil at catch, Niagara to Niagara, furthest stretch."

The Helans waited; the lantern light grew dim.

"To the land of Albanya, from this Saratgo to the other, down where the Springs lie."

A deathly presence moved about the room, and yet no one else fell... for now. It did seem like Hel's price had already been paid.

Em just hoped that it was worth it.

Chapter 14

The Agitation of the Tribes of Fjord Vallee

"Hazel nuts? Taste seventeen and a half. In working class neighborhoods."

Elfriede looked at the deranged cleric with concern.

"How can we help him?" she asked.

Kalla was already back upon her horse. Gudre was just returning from the cave with Gorm. He had a big smile on his face, as did she.

Tepson turned to the Dinglesfuhrian woman. "Being that he's our party healer, he would be the one to help himself!"

Gorm looked perplexed: he pointed his fingers in various directions as he attempted to reason out the conundrum that the gnome proposed.

"Powder doom. Ale is certainly. If you think?"

Kolveig's addition to the conversation did little to clarify matters.

"He must retire to Caelum Mount, for only a wizard can resolve what ails this cleric," suggested Kalla.

Tepson still found the Dinglesfuhrian manner of speech to be strange, even more so than the way other folks spoke in the Vale nowadays. It was especially noticeable in Kalla and Gudre- not as much with Elfriede.

"Caelum Mount? Is it salty?" blubbered the cleric.

As for Kolveig, Tepson had heard that such things could befall the so-called spellcasters of the world in this bizarre Age. Oborren had told him about '*mishap*' befalling wizards and similar types, especially when they pushed the bounds of Reality too far. The gnome imagined that the same might seem to happen to clerics such as Kolveig. And since the magic of clerics was apparently more subtle than that of wizards, so too would the mishap be. For example, rather than being possessed by a demon, the cleric had simply gotten dementia when he had healed Gorm. It seemed that sometimes a heavy sacrifice might be needed to make magic work, at least that's *what people said*!

The gnome shook his head; perhaps this place had finally driven him crazy too.

"Whatever has occurred with him, this Kolveig," said Gudre, "we must make due haste to near Dinglesfuhr. The Fjord has beauty, but perhaps not proper sanative for this Karlist."

"Dinglesfuhr? Fjord? Vampire-like undead labor? Onion?" asked Kolveig.

Elfriede patted the Karlist on the back to comfort him. "We'll take him with us to Dinglesfuhr. Perhaps Onkel Van Dwick might know someone who could lend him assistance?"

A great roar resounded in the distance: was it another dinosaur... or the giant come calling? All waited for a few minutes, but nothing appeared.

Kalla nodded in agreement finally. Tepson sighed: *oh great, we get to visit another bizarre place with eccentric people.*

Gudre kissed Gorm goodbye. Gorm still seemed perplexed. Could it be that Kolveig was some sort of philosopher? The man had saved his life and blessed him with his divine power. His words were certainly very confusing. He had heard that philosophers could be that way.

"Dinglesfuhr. Powder doom. Fjord. Is it salty?"

The others rode away. Gorm pondered recent events for nearly an hour and then finally snapped his fingers in realization. Kolveig wasn't a philosopher- he was a prophet! Where was Mohee? He had to let the rest of the tribe know what *the prophet* had foretold!

* * *

"I HAVE ALREADY SSSTATED MY REASSSON VOR BUSSSINESSS, CUR!" The elaborately dressed wizard, great encircled 'M' upon his chest, had lost his patience with the guards at the Dinglestor.

"Mein Lord, you fail to have the proper papers to pass."

"PAPERSSS! YOU VANT PAPERSSS! I vill turn your whole damn land into papersss and then alight it on VIRE!"

"On what?"

"VIRE!" The wizard pointed his blue gloved finger at the guards for added effect.

The blond boy, who accompanied the wizard, clarified, "Lord Mistro means to say, *'Fire'* ".

Mistro became even more irritated. "That'sss vhat I said, IDIOTSSS!"

Quiet Upon Shenbyrg's Dawning

The Dinglesguards looked at each other nervously. A number of halflings, dressed in black jester's outfits, walked right passed the humans. The guards simply looked at Mistro.

"Vhy are you looking at me, vools!?!?" exclaimed the wizard, "you're letting the stupid halvlingsss in! Vhy don't THEY need papersss?!"

"Because, Mein Lord, they are Special Guests of the Dinglesfrau."

Mistro stared at the halflings as they entered the city. One of them made a rude gesture at him and laughed. If it were possible, the wizard became even angrier. His face turned completely white, nearly apoplectic.

"THAT DINGLESSSVRAU BETTER GET HER HEAD OUT OF HER BACKSSSIDE AND REALIZE THAT *I AM A SPECIAL GUESSST!*"

Luckily for the guards, a dark-haired Dinglesfuhrian walked up at that moment. He was dressed in the same black and purple manner as them, but the cut of his uniform, medallions, and manner suggested that he was of much higher rank.

"Honored Mistro, please let me welcome you to Dinglesfuhr and apologize for," the man glared at the guards, "my subordinates' lack of decorum."

The wizard nodded and stroked his moustache as his anger abated slightly. Some of the color even began to return to his face.

"I am Fieldmarshall Van Dwick, Commander of the Army of Dinglesfuhr." The man clicked his heels together and saluted.

As the wizard and the boy followed the Fieldmarshall, Mistro stopped for a moment and stared into one of the guard's eyes. He then uttered a dark curse, "May your vavorite puppy suffer increasssed vlatulence, CUR!"

The cursed guard turned and looked at the other guard in confusion. The other just shook his head- it was best just to let the wizard pass rather than try to figure out what he was saying.

* * *

Snik Snak laughed as the blinded orc smashed into a tree. The brutish thing's mewling and whining stood in stark contrast to the aggressive posturing that it had shown the yellow goblin only a few minutes before. The other orcs looked on, dark snouts and hides showing unnaturally in the unusually bright sun of the haunted Sylvanian mountains. They seemed impressed that the little monster had stabbed out their chieftain's eyes with a stolen hunter's dagger after he had feigned surrender. Snik Snak was small and a goblin, but they thought he might make a good leader. He certainly was brutal enough.

The goblin snuck up behind the blinded orc. It seemed to smell him, roared and lashed out, but Snik Snak easily got out of its way. With its back now turned, he stabbed the orc repeatedly in the kidneys and it wailed in pain. The other orcs, seeing who the new chieftain now was, rushed in and began beating and kicking their former leader ruthlessly. It screamed in horror as they began tearing off its limbs and eating it as it died. Snik Snak stood back and smiled.

"They not goblins", muttered Snik Snak to himself, "and we got no megajacks, but orcs should help me gain control of other goblins! Then real fun begin!

* * *

Elfriede looked at Kalla and smiled- for some reason the guards at the Dinglestor had let their group pass without needing to show any papers this time. It was a strange, but pleasant turn of events.

Otherwise, the rest of the group did not look as happy. The Karlist cleric continued to babble to himself, the gnome looked quite depressed- perhaps he was worried about Kolveig, and Gudre certainly seemed downtrodden too. She had taken a great liking to a certain someone ever since he came to the Fjord earlier this year. Elfriede and Kalla were afraid that she might move her residence there instead.

For now though, there was other business to attend to. The Dinglesfuhrian maidens took in the sights, sounds, and smells of the Dingleplatz. They did feel more constrained here than when bareback riding of course, having to wear the compensatory dark petticoats and fine hats, but seeing so many people and shopping opportunities made it all better, at least for Elfriede and Kalla.

"I miss Gorm and the Fjord," lamented Gudre.

Kalla patted her on the back, "I know, but we must revisit our home, see to our duties, and..." Kalla winked at Gudre, "wear proper apparel!"

Elfriede knew that Kalla's family had its roots in the Ancient Aristocracy of Dinglesfuhr, to even the Amaranthine Wizard himself. She agreed: "Ladies: why don't you show our gnome guest the best of our land, while I see my Onkel about helping our... friend."

Elfriede paused for a moment when she realized that the cleric was arguing with her horse about the merits of supply-side economics. She soothingly began to guide him and the horse to the Fieldmarshall's Quarters.

* * *

"Dinglesfuhr will soon fall and her people become decimated, if nothing is done about it, Herr Mistro."

"That *could be* a ssshame." The wizard seemed to show only a passing interest in Van Dwick's prediction.

The Fieldmarshall looked insulted, " *'Could be a shame?'* Mein friend, genocide is always a shame!"

The blond boy who assisted Mistro snuck to the other side of the room and began examining the various trophies while the adults spoke.

"Indeed," agreed the wizard. "But iv a people are no longer villing to protect themselvesss vrom extinction, then vhy should I posssibly care about it?"

"Not all Dinglesfuhrians have fallen for this foolish Cult! Not all wish to tear down the walls and be destroyed!"

Mistro smiled cruelly as he looked for something to hurl at his assistant. Van Dwick's insistent gaze brought the wizard's full attention back to the conversation.

"Then I urge you to reconsssider the proposssal I have vor you." Mistro twirled his moustache as he watched the Dinglesfuhrian's reaction.

"It seems that we would only trade one ruination for another, Herr Mistro!"

The wizard only smiled wider and more wickedly.

The Fieldmarshall continued: "Wouldn't it be enough that we allied with you, rather than, say... Caelum Mount?"

At this, Mistro found a small statue to throw at his assistant, who yelped and moved away from the trophy case.

"CAELUM MOUNT?! Vhat a bunch of POSERSSS! My proposssal standsss: take it or leave it!" The wizard grabbed his assistant by his collar and made to leave the room.

"We couldn't possibly pay what you require, Mistro. Dinglesfuhr was a wealthy land, but the Dinglesfrau now squanders that wealth on the search for remaining Mountain Folk and halfling buffets. And with the new 'Visitors' that will arrive, we will become even more pauperized!"

"Isss it my problem how badly the Frau squandersss?" challenged the wizard.

"We cannot pay, Herr Mistro, I wish we had the funds."

"Then I leave you to your vinal doom!" declared Mistro.

At that moment, Elfriede was shown into the room. The wizard stared at her and his assistant took the opportunity to try and look at the trophy case again.

Mistro got a strange look on his face. "Perhapsss there isss a vay for you to pay me after all, Van Dwick..." He stared at Elfriede menacingly.

"No! NO! You will have nothing to do with my niece!" It was now the Fieldmarshall's turn to sound menacing.

"Oh really?" taunted Mistro, "vouldn't she vish to prevent the vall of Dinglesssvuhr herssselv?"

Elfriede looked at her onkel: she couldn't really understand what this stranger was saying!

"What does he mean, Onkel?"

Van Dwick looked at his niece sadly, she was a grown woman now and it looked like Dinglesfuhr was out of options.

Mistro began laughing maniacally.

* * *

"That will be 27,136 gold coins and 6 copper," said the man clad in white. The red lapel with a smiling face showed on his jacket that he was Officially Approved by the Great Shield Ghul to Practice Medicine in Walstock.

132

Dan Osarchuk

"How in the name of Minerva could I possibly pay that much!?" said the village man. "I could give you the 6 copper..." he reached into his pocket.

"Oh don't worry!" said the physician, "you can pay on each new moon to satisfy your debt."

"Pay how? What do you mean?" the village man looked confused. He glanced down at the sling which held his recently tended broken arm.

"First, you need to make sure your children attend the Schoolhouse and then you need to mark these scrolls." The physician pulled out a pile of parchment nearly 3 inches thick.

"I'm not going to send my children to that mad place! And what does that have to do with my paying you?" The village man was beginning to get irritated.

"Oh really?" said the physician seemingly nonplussed. "Just a moment..."

The physician left the room; the village man felt like maybe finally he had come to his senses.

Rather than the physician returning, a knight in chainmail entered the room instead. He too bore the same symbol as the physician, though in the knight's case, it was on his white tabard- he was a Hospitalier! The knight looked grimly at the village man and pointed a strange sort of lance at him. It began quite thick, though it came to a needle-like point on the front. The Hospitalier held an extension of the lance behind the flange with his other hand.

"Dr. Ludwig says that you are refusing to pay your charges," stated the knight.

The village man shook his head in agreement.

"Then we will get our charges from you directly."

Before the village man knew what was happening, the Hospitalier impaled him with the lance. The man's screams of pain soon became shrieks of agony as the knight pulled on the back end of the lance, drawing out the man's vital humors.

After a few minutes, the Hospitalier drew the lance out of the lifeless man's body and looked up at a flickering box mounted on the wall overhead. He spoke to it.

"This is Hospitalier Drenart, we have a collection in the lobby. Oh, and we also need a Seeker of C'ps: some children need to be saved."

Chapter 15

Sojourn to the Yonitarian Church

The feeling of spaciousness began to grow within Halfdan as night fell. Something about the night sky and the woods allowed the stillness within him to remain more profound, his presence of mind to become more clear and resolute, expanding exponentially into the world around him. Such a state made it easier to notice how his consciousness pervaded all that he perceived.

As he watched within, any fears and desires that he had arose and dissipated, and he realized that he was not them. All that remained was the peace, the peace beyond all human understanding.

Amongst others, Halfdan sometimes found it harder to remain aware of this high state. In those cases, he might lose his step with the concerns of their judgments or of his own. On the other hand, when he was alone he might even wonder that perhaps he was all that existed, for it was impossible to prove otherwise. How could one really know what truly was occurring outside of one's own thoughts and perceptions? All else is an inference, as Nissar would say, a guess: any attempt at proving otherwise was simply suspect of being the product of yet more imagining.

Many balked at such notions, calling them 'foolish' or 'irrelevant' or even 'mullock'. But what could be more relevant than a clearer understanding of Reality itself? And could Solipsism ever actually be disproved? Could anything?

The apparent practicalities of life often prevented further exploration of this line of reasoning though. If, for example, his was the only mind that was, then how and why could one feel pain, feel loss? Something *must be* standing in the way of happiness, and that would strongly suggest something *other than* just the existence of one's own limited mind. Ironically enough, that would also be impossible to disprove, as well.

Still, people could seem so strange to Halfdan sometimes. What drove them really? He knew that he had his own self-doubts, even hidden hatreds, but he could at least find some greater understanding and forgiveness of his own self-loathing by simply observing it. But others could be far less reasonable or forgiving: why? It was such a mystery!

Was Halfdan doing this all to himself or was Life acting independently from him? Or was it some sort of esoteric mix between his own subjective intention and the world's objective result? Or did the Laws of Reality themselves change from day to day?

Take all the women that he had attempted to court over the years since he and his wife had parted ways. The vast majority paid Halfdan less than a passing thought. Those few who did decide to take part in Halfdan's life for a time always seemed to do so unbidden and then always departed within a moon's turning or so, often, if not always. Why was that? And was there even a reason to uncover that Halfdan could even comprehend?

Was he running this show without his own knowing? Or was it some unfulfilled price of Fate that forced him to relive the wheel of pain and desire, day after day? There was no shortage of replies to these questions, for Halfdan had asked himself and others over the decades for the answers and yet seemed to always wind up right back where he started.

And perhaps the strangest aspect of all was that he actually found all these limitations to be strange. If this was all there was- a world fraught with challenge, misunderstanding, and difficulty- then why would he find that unusual? And his resulting inability to successfully relate to people not only defeated his courtship, but also most chances of true friendship, success, and even gainful employ.

In the end though, Halfdan found great relief in returning his mind back to I, to becoming one with pure consciousness again. He watched his life as if it were a stage. He was happy even without success with women, in employ, or in finding his way out of these woods.

> When you do let go
> Of the pain of "no"
> It's nearly as good
> As getting the things
> That you should

A raven cawed loudly upon an ancient pine ahead. It was time to refocus upon the current world. It was nearly night now and Halfdan heard the sounds of human animals beyond in the distance. That was usually not a good sign.

* * *

Oborren panted heavily as he helped Brymanah over the final hill. The stars had begun to emerge over the vista below; an orange band of setting sun lit the distance majestically. All seemed so quiet and peaceful, almost as if they had not recently discovered a slave camp of humans that thought themselves to be animals, ruled over by *actual animal-headed* monster masters.

Quiet Upon Shenbyrg's Dawning

The chill started to intensify for the hunter, his sweat and exhaustion even began to make him shake. With a final effort, he helped the amazon to the great tree were he and Bjartar had seen the raven before. The warrior-woman patted him on the head in condescending thanks as he collapsed.

The amazon too began to wobble from her many injuries, but then she felt the presence of someone watching them.

Oborren noticed it as well and immediately looked to take cover in a nearby bush. He spotted a lone figure, smallish for a man and slender; he bore a spear. Something about him seemed familiar too.

The figure still said nothing, but didn't seem hostile for the moment.

Oborren called out: "Ho there! Who goes?"

"I" was the only reply.

Then the realization came to the hunter who it was. Only the Odinnic could be that abstruse.

* * *

Brymanah was not looking well, but she remained strong enough to refuse to let Halfdan attempt to heal her.

"No... man... may... lay... a... hand, *especially... you!*" she huffed.

"You certainly have a way with the fairer gender," Oborren teased. But he soon shook his head, "All jest aside, if she doesn't get help soon, she probably won't last. Those beast-heads harmed her severely."

At the mention of the monsters, Brymanah reached to her side so she could stab something, but her cutlass was gone.

Outraged fury arose in her face. She glared at the men until Oborren explained, "The atavars must have took it." Brymanah relaxed again somewhat.

"How can we save her?" enquired Halfdan.

"By my judgment," began Oborren, "we aren't very far from Stephania, but we won't be very welcome in that land and I doubt that Brymanah could make the trip, even if we were. "

"Wouldn't they wish to help one of their own?" asked Halfdan.

"Yes, but they might not let us leave either. Word has it that the amazons have grown increasingly hostile of late- even moreso than usual. "

Brymanah groaned as she clutched her stomach. Some of the wounds on her back had begun to bleed again.

"I have a route to get her there," offered Halfdan, "and a way of dealing with the amazons."

He looked at Oborren, who finally nodded. Brymanah said nothing, indicating her willingness to not refuse the offer for now at least.

The cleric focused on a nearby copse of trees. They might be taken for ones in Stephania. These things were not always certain though...

* * *

"May the Many Goddesses smile upon you."

The Shell Oracle completed her invocation and passed her hand over Brymanah's stomach once more. She frowned, but continued to attend to the rest of her body. Brymanah was already beginning to look better.

Quiet Upon Shenbyrg's Dawning

The interlocking beams of the Yonitarian Church stood above the assembled amazons. Oborren and Halfdan were there too and, thanks to the Oracle's insistence, were even allowed to remain ungagged and unbound. It didn't stop a number of the Dames from watching them closely though. How far could men be trusted?

Halfdan did notice a change over the amazons since the last time he had visited. It had been a few years, but now some of the amazons seemed *different*. At least half of them had emotionless looks to their eyes and were dressed in yellow and black. He reached out with his consciousness and felt something very disturbing within them.

The cleric glanced at the hunter, who gave a knowing nod. Oborren seemed to have his own suspicions about the changed amazons. Fortunately though, the Oracle seemed to be unaffected, at least for now. As the ceremony ended, the assembled amazons rose and began to chat amongst themselves. There was something off though, because many had an almost buzzing quality to their voices. Halfdan guessed that the sound was coming from the half that looked divergent.

Brymanah rose and stretched her mighty muscles. The other amazons started to swarm around her in interest and congratulation. Her old manservant, Torm, went to greet her, but was pulled back by a Dame that had him on a leash.

Halfdan took this moment to speak with the Oracle. As he approached, a number of Hippolytes moved forward, ready to impale the man for his transgression. The Oracle waved them down though, greeted Halfdan, and even embraced him.

"It's been a long time, cleric," she beamed.

"Too long," Halfdan agreed. "What has been happening in Stephania?"

The Oracle smiled and moved with him a little further away from the crowd.

"A number of the Sisters have begun *to change*," she whispered. "Great Hera has been quiet about this matter so far, but I have been... *concerned*."

"Can I lend any help?" offered the cleric.

The Oracle smiled, "Not at this time. I may need to call upon you later though." She finished quickly, seeing two Dames approaching with Brymanah.

Halfdan noticed that these amazons also wore yellow and black. In fact, based on his limited knowledge of amazon caste dress, nearly all of the Dames were now so outfitted, as well as a lesser percentage of Hippolytes and Matrons. Oborren spotted it too; both men could certainly see the lifelessness in the changed amazons' eyes.

One of the Dames spoke. She was a bit fuller figured, had somewhat angular features, and platinum hair. "We will be taking our Sister back to our quarters to rest." She nodded at Brymanah and stared at the other.

Halfdan sensed that something was wrong.

"And what does Brymanah think of this?" enquired the cleric.

The Dame immediately whipped out her hand and smacked Halfdan in the face. The Oracle made to intervene, but even she was stunned by the inhuman look of hatred in both Dames' eyes.

Brymanah then spoke, "Poy and Jeg are my Sisters. I will return with them." She looked at Oborren and Halfdan and nodded curtly. "Thank you for bringing me here."

The three walked back into the crowd of amazons. Halfdan noticed that his cheek was beginning to burn from where Poy had smacked him. It seemed to be some sort of allergic reaction. He remembered to simply watch the sensations arise and the pain lessened.

The Oracle looked upset and made to say something, but was interrupted by one of her priestesses. They whispered for a moment and then the Oracle waved and departed. A large number of yellow and black-clad *changed amazons* were beginning to surround the two men. Their emotionless glares were even beginning to unsettle Oborren. There were nearly a hundred of them.

"I don't think that I can kill all of them," said the hunter grimly.

"Steady, Oborren, there are worse ways to die."

Oborren stared at the cleric incredulously. "That's it? I thought you had a way of dealing with the amazons?"

"I did, but I don't know if it will work on mutant amazons."

Oborren shook his head: why had he allowed the amazons to take his weapons? And why had he listened to the crazy Odinnic?

Suddenly, most of the changed amazons began to back away. Some even began turning their heads, unable to look at the men. A few remained nearby, but they didn't seem quite as hostile as moments before.

"Let's depart now," said the cleric, "I'm not sure how long they will be held at bay."

The two men moved back from the crowd of yellow and black-clad amazons. Halfdan kept facing them, while Oborren ran and got their weapons from the men's lavatory. When the hunter returned, he noticed that only two amazons of the roughly hundred of the original group were still following. The cleric stared back at them. Oborren handed a makeshift spear to Halfdan- it looked like it had once been a shovel.

"We'll need some mounts too," whispered the cleric. The hunter glanced over at the remaining horde of changed amazons in the Church Sanctum. It looked like they were moving closer and growing angry again. Oborren noticed that Halfdan still had not removed his gaze.

The men dashed for the door. With their backs now turned, the two closest amazons screamed and ran back to their Sisters, slowing the overall advance. Halfdan took the opportunity to slip outside with Oborren. He slammed the main door shut and wedged his spear into the handles in an effort to hold it fast. Furious screams of the many amazons echoed within and their beating fists resounded upon the door.

The two men each grabbed a horse that was confusingly tethered near the side of the Church and made their escape. Mutant amazons began to emerge from the windows. As the riders passed by the main door, even more burst forth and screamed at the escaping men. The buzzing sound they made was incredible.

Halfdan and Oborren rode hard for at least a mile before the hunter ventured a word. The mighty *irontrees* of the Ancients loomed to the north. Halfdan knew that they once held power upon their lines of steel, lines that made that world what it was, but was now no more.

Oborren only saw them as strange relics, the Ancients' pantomime of enormous pines. Did the Ancients have amazons too?

Fairfacts Lordship beckoned to the southwest. "Well, you certainly have a way with women, Halfdan! What in the name of the Gods did you do?"

"I let myself feel attracted to them," said the cleric curtly.

"What?" Oborren clearly didn't understand.

Quiet Upon Shenbyrg's Dawning

"When I let myself be the least bit attracted to a woman, most of the time they are repelled. And even if I'm not attracted to one..."

"What happens then?" asked the hunter.

"They inevitably turn from me too."

PART 2

Chapter 16

Maurian Escort

"Iv thisss doesssn't vork, then ve vill have to try a supposssssitory!"

Kolveig shrieked as the wizard hit him on the head with a golden tack hammer. Elfriede looked on in concern; Tepson just wanted the noise to end.

BINK! Mistro struck the Karlist cleric's head once more. He shrieked even louder. Tepson wasn't sure if his *own head* was going to explode from all the caterwauling. Perhaps the Karlist could be muzzled?

At that, Mistro gesticulated around the cleric's head and then snapped his fingers. Kolveig looked right at him.

"How do you, veel?"

"My head hurts."

Mistro grinned at the Karlist's response. Elfriede looked surprised that the cleric spoke clearly- it had been nearly two days since he had fallen into madness.

Tepson spoke up, "So you're supposed to be some sort of wizard, right?"

Mistro turned and stared at the gnome, too offended by such a question to even respond.

"Isn't it all just some hocus-pocus? I mean, there is no scientific basis for magic..." continued the gnome.

The wizard glared at Tepson. It would seem that Mistro was attempting to bore a hole into the gnome's head with his gaze.

"Come on: isn't all this magic just some delusion?"

Mistro's face turned pale white and his hands began to shake as his eyes went wide. He pointed a finger at the gnome and stuttered, "Vould... vould... vould you like to VIND OUT?!"

Elfriede interrupted the calamity that was about to befall Tepson. "Are you able to heal Kolveig of his other wounds?"

The wizard continued glaring at the gnome and called for his uniformed guards to approach.

After a full minute, he finally spoke, "Vell, he isss a cleric, so he can heal the ressst himssselv! Oh, and Elvriede," Mistro turned and looked at the woman, "Remember our agreement: bring me back the object I desssire- POSSST HASSSTE!"

He then took a step back, motioned to his guards, and said to the three, "You now have your ordersss- now GET OUT!"

As they left, the wizard narrowed his eyes at the gnome and muttered a dark curse.

* * *

The journey from Mistro's tower to the borders of Mauriatown had been uneventful. Cries could be heard to the east as they left, but Elfriede warned them against venturing into Walstock proper.

Dan Osarchuk

There was no telling what sort of reign of terror the new Count was enacting in the name of R'ti and the other Fell Cults. Otherwise, the three enjoyed the pleasant fall afternoon, the rolling hills, and the brisk walk upon the Mighty One trail. Tepson was especially pleased by how silent Kolveig was. He even looked a little thoughtful, something fairly unusual for him.

As per Mistro's instructions, the party now did veer to the east, avoiding the main Maurian checkpoint in the distance. Not that the Maurians would be unaware of this intrusion into their territory, it was just that they were traveling to a place that was more out of the way for the task ahead.

The party rounded a hill and Elfriede took out the wand that Mistro had given them. She showed it to the others: it had a white top and seemed to be fashioned from some sort of hard, paper-like material. Kolveig was quite pleased that the tube portion was red.

Tepson laughed. "That idiot just gave us a road flare."

"Tepson! Mistro was the one who granted Kolveig healing!" said Elfriede.

Kolveig smiled at Tepson and pointed to his head- as if Tepson didn't remember.

"I don't care what he appeared to do. Maybe Kolveig just healed on his own."

Kolveig shook his head in disagreement. "I might not appreciate some Bourgeois Lord in a White Tower attempting to invoke his Wizard's Privilege in order to Corrupt Almighty Karl's Enlightened Redistribution of my Mental Resources, but even I don't doubt his power, no matter how Capitalistic it is."

At least the cleric's sanity was restored, thought the gnome.

Quiet Upon Shenbyrg's Dawning

"Why do you doubt magic so?" asked Elfriede. She pulled the white tip off of the wand and said, "Oooo!"

The cleric nodded in approval too: the bright flame that erupted from the wand was clearly *red*.

Tepson shook his head. "Because I've seen the great works of science: computers, aircraft, marvels far more amazing than what that silly Mistro could ever perform."

"Yes," said Kolveig nodding, "but you did turn me back from being a squirrel..."

Tepson frowned. The cleric might have a point about magic in this world. He wasn't sure if it was just irritation at that realization or also at Kolveig that was causing his sudden headache. Elfriede looked concerned.

"Umm, Tepson..." she started.

"What? I'm fine!" said the gnome grouchily.

"We have a new problem," finished the woman.

Kolveig was starting to growl, but Tepson realized that Elfriede wasn't looking at him, she was looking at some people in uniforms: about seven in gray shirts with caps, three in blue shirts with helms and breastplates, and two that looked like cops in full dress uniform. One of them was a woman with striking blue eyes.

Kolveig seemed to notice her too. He stopped growling.

* * *

The journey through Mauriatown was strange for the party. Tepson, though being much smaller than all the guards and possessing no special abilities as far as Elfriede knew, was still watched closely. And it seemed that the poor gnome did have a headache, but only batted Elfriede away when she tried to assist him.

She had never seen Mauriatown before. All she knew about the place was that they followed some sort of Leader and were constantly ready for war with nearby Helltowne. Elfriede did know that the Glowing Spectral Personhood *hated Mauriatown*, a sentiment possibly shared by Dinglesfrau Mekla, if rumors of her new sympathies were to be believed. Both might consider the Maurians to be *Amaranthine*.

Elfriede also found it odd that their route was one that cut across the countryside. If this was some sort of official escort, then why did they wish to move so secretly? Elfriede caught glimpses of other gnomes working as slaves in the distance. There seemed to be many of them and they worked what looked to be bean fields and other crops. Perhaps the Maurians wished to conceal the presence of Tepson from the other gnomes?

The other strange aspect of the journey was Kolveig. Elfriede was under the impression that Karlists also hated Maurians and yet he was happily chatting with the woman in the black uniform and hat. Such dress indicated that she was high in the Mauriatown hierarchy: why was the cleric so friendly with her? She did have striking blue eyes that reminded Elfriede of her friend Gudre. She wondered how she and Kalla were faring back in Dinglesfuhr.

Seeing that everyone else seemed preoccupied during the walk, Elfriede reviewed Mistro's instructions mentally. Apparently, he had some kind of agreement with the Maurians, otherwise she guessed that they wouldn't let a gnome and a Karlist through this land alive, let alone escorted and guarded. Mistro's current demands for helping Dinglesfuhr were steep, but much less so than the one million Dinglemarks that he had originally demanded to bring the promise of help from Mauriatown to her onkel.

Quiet Upon Shenbyrg's Dawning

Elfriede's agreement with Mistro now seemed a small price to pay. The Vale could be a dangerous place with all manner of competing philosophies. For a century, her own land had lived in peace. But if Mekla was actually supporting the Personhood's strange new policies, it seemed that disaster would soon come to Dinglesfuhr unless something was done about it.

She glanced at her comrades. Tepson was grasping his head, but she didn't know whether it was because he was ill or just irritated at all the Maurians watching him as they walked. On the other hand, Kolveig seemed pleasantly animated and made light banter with the Maurian woman that he walked beside. The cleric kept mentioning the socialistic similarities between his faith and that of Mauriatown, but left out any mention that they were essentially diametrically opposed to each other.

Such things were known to happen when a man was smitten with a woman.

* * *

It appeared that that the group was nearing the northeastern border of Mauriatown, since signs of dire warning could now be spotted pointing in the opposite direction.

One of them read: "ATTENTION: IF YOU ENTER THIS LAND WITHOUT PROPER IDENTIFICATION, YOU WILL BE <u>KILLED</u>!"

At least they are up front about it, thought Tepson.

In fact, despite the Maurians hating him for being a gnome, he had to grudgingly respect them. Their society gave the impression of order and cleanliness and he didn't see any strange folk that claimed to have magical powers. All the uniforms and signs also reminded him somewhat of the old days, or the Time of the Ancients as the people now would call it.

Nevertheless, what Tepson seemed to like most of all about this land was that it got Kolveig to stop his proselytizing.

The group soon stopped in the middle of a field. The woman who was speaking with Kolveig addressed the party, "We hope you have enjoyed your stay here in beautiful Mauriatown, please come again soon!" She smiled and winked at Kolveig.

"ALL HAIL the Leader!" She saluted and the other Maurians echoed her. They then all stared at the party awkwardly. Tepson guessed it was time to go.

As the party ventured into the land of Strass Hill, Elfriede moved closer to Kolveig.

"You certainly seemed to have savored your trip through this land!"

"How could I? They were all just a bunch of FASCISTS!" he insisted.

Elfriede smiled at the cleric; he smiled back. Both knew that one never could choose who they fell in love with. That was a matter for the Gods.

Tepson just tried to ignore them both and keep walking. He hoped his headache would go away soon.

* * *

The land grew more forested as the three journeyed further north. There was some debate over whether they had traveled too far or not, but Tepson insisted that if they hadn't hit 66 yet, then they hadn't gone too far. Elfriede and Kolveig just stared him incredulously: sometimes gnomes said such silly things.

"Let us just ask at a farmhouse for which way the Caverns are?" said Elfriede.

"I wouldn't do that," argued Kolveig, "this area is rife with Pro-Authoritarian Reactionaries."

Elfriede frowned. Perhaps her two companions really were crazy?

After some more haphazard wandering, the party stumbled upon a narrow dirt path. They followed it until they heard the sounds of splashing water and people talking ahead. The party crouched down and approached cautiously.

Despite the increasing chill in the evening air, a number of Norse folk swam in the waters of a moderate-sized lake with a bit of a sandy beach and a large rocky outcrop beyond. Elfriede couldn't help but be impressed by the fortitude of these northern people: riding bareback in Fjord Vallee in the afternoon sun was one thing, but swimming during a fall evening in Strass Hill was another.

And despite their more solid chins and angular cheekbones, they did not fit the stereotype of being hairy norsemen, thought Elfriede provocatively. Yes, both men and women were blond-headed like many Dinglesfuhrians, though larger-boned, but it seemed that all who swam were completely devoid of body hair as far as she could tell. She looked back at her companions to see how they felt, but Kolveig had already begun to stroll to the lake.

"Anyone Who Knows Anything of History Knows that Great Social Changes are Impossible without Clothing Upheaval."

The Norse stared at the Karlist. Elfriede wondered how they would ever get to the Caverns now.

Chapter 17

Fairfacts Lordship

The two riders let their mounts rest at the stable outside the University. The slender, aging man stretched his back and searched the immediate area for something else to be used as a spear.

"It won't do any good," said his companion in black, "they don't allow weapons on the campus."

"What will you do then?" Halfdan gestured at Oborren's crossbow and flail.

"I'll leave them inside," Oborren cocked his head back to the stable. "If you have any other arms with you, you had better do the same."

Hunter and cleric crossed the road, taking special attention to watch for any Stephanians coming from the north. They spied none so far, so they continued on.

Quiet Upon Shenbyrg's Dawning

The men came to a lone guard post, though there was no wall or fence to prevent any real incursion around it. They waited in line, taking note of the folk gathered. Most looked well-dressed, fed, and clean, as well as seeming to lack any particular clear cultural identity, unlike that of most other settlements of the Vale. Being that the two had just escaped from a land of enraged, yellow jacket-mutated amazons, Halfdan and Oborren found the lack of culture in these people to be a welcome change.

They soon entered the ivory walls of the University building. Both found it strange that no guards stood outside: who were these people to protect themselves without magic or steel? A statue of Athena stood over the archway. As patroness of justice, protection, and knowledge, perhaps she might save them from the deranged amazons to the north, tyrannical communists to the east, or belligerent vikings to the south? Oborren hoped that Fairfacts Lordship would at least avoid being conquered until after he was able to gain the information he sought.

It had been a few days since his encounter with the harpy, but he was little closer to uncovering the riddle held in the message of its satchel. The hunter still knew not who the 'Director in WS' was- he had failed to reach his contact in Pentagram Tannery due to the unscheduled rescue of Brymanah. Halfdan might have guessed, but he was unsure. On the other hand, both men certainly had a much better idea of what was meant by 'Bee Queen in HK', especially after the amazons-made-mutant-vespula had nearly cornered them in the church. Luckily, Halfdan's predilection to be repulsive to women had saved their necks, but Oborren wondered at what had happened to Brymanah.

The University building was well-maintained and quite spacious, with large windows, white painted walls, and light paneled wood. It had a pleasant air of comfortable intellectualism, nearly a higher realm of consciousness in its own right. Halfdan found it ironic that the Universities of today were so different than that of the later days of the Ancients. He had heard that Cults had come to rule what should have been places of learning in the final decades before Lights Out, so much so that they eventually became mockeries and even rackets of what they were intended to be.

Wandering deeper into the University Hall, the men were pleasantly surprised to see rows of bound books on display. The space here was darker, mainly lit by lamplight, and a little musty too, though the men didn't mind. Oborren and Halfdan took some time to examine the many volumes, as much to gain greater understanding of questions unanswered as to enjoy simple bibliophilia.

Though one read for a greater understanding of Reality, the other read for a greater understanding of how to Slay the Unnatural. Still, the love of reading can draw in those of any persuasion. Both Halfdan and Oborren were also tired and didn't have a very comfortable rest on the floor of the Yonitarian Church's men's lavatory last night. It was a relief to relax and focus on more pleasant things for a while.

Their literary reverie was unfortunately interrupted by the sound of many university pupils moving to the Auditorium. Intrigued, the hunter and cleric followed. Word was that a great sorceress was going to give a demonstration and lecture of her abilities. Oborren had a strange feeling about who it might be; Halfdan often found such topics fascinating. So the bookworms put away their pleasant tomes for now and followed the university pupil crowd.

Coming to the corridor just outside the Auditorium entrance, the pair noticed another statue of Athena, as well as one of Odin, much to Halfdan's pleasant surprise. There were also a number of portraits on the walls: pictures of the Lord of Fairfacts himself, Beneglushio, who espoused scholarship and sagecraft amongst all his people, even to this day. It was no wonder that Oborren came to the Capitol of this land for answers.

Quiet Upon Shenbyrg's Dawning

Odinnic and hunter entered and took their seats amongst the many assembled pupils and guests. From their high vantage point, the two had a good view of the stage. It too was made of a light-colored wood, laminated pine perhaps. The stage also had a display of a wide variety of footwear upon it, both men's and women's, though all were quite garish in style and reddish in hue.

A bright red-haired woman soon strutted into view. She wore a pinkish-red cape, an elaborate tunic of cinnamon, crimson gloves, cerise tights, and tall, ruby-red leather boots. Oborren grinned as he recognized her, but was very concerned as to what would happen next.

"Hey everyone!" she began. "Magic has been called the *aealae artes*, the *acroamatic path*, but such BIG words are really just silly!"

"If you believe in yourself," she continued, "and have a really stylish outfit," she struck a pose, "then you can do SOME magic!" She pointed a finger at various shoes on display. Suddenly, they began to levitate!

The crowd cheered and applauded.

Both men were shocked: to show such an obvious display of eldritch power, above ground and in the light of day in front of so many, would certainly invite some form of demonic corruption and/ or divine retribution. Halfdan hoped that the audience might just be too naïve to realize this; Oborren knew that the presenter certainly was.

"Would someone like to VOLUNTEER?" said the sorceress triumphantly.

All except the two men raised their hand enthusiastically.

The red-haired woman selected three: an older man, a young woman, and a child. Oborren held his breath; Halfdan remembered to remain conscious during the spectacle.

"Okay, FRIENDS!" declared the sorceress, "...*let me show you just what magic can do!*" Her voice took on a gravelly, almost bizarre quality with that last statement. The audience laughed, thinking she was just jesting. The hunter and the cleric guessed otherwise.

"One extra-special way that magic works," she explained in her normal, pleasant voice, "is to *harness the Elements.*" Again, with the last statement, her voice changed and this time her eyes briefly took on a rufescent, unearthly light.

The sorceress picked up one of the high-heel shoes on display and handed it to the older man. "Don't you think this is COOL, sir?" she said and then looked at the audience expectantly.

"What?" the man appeared confused. Suddenly, he yelped in pain as he dropped the shoe to the floor. It shattered into shards of ice when it landed, hitting a number of audience members in the front row. They laughed as some red-clad pupil assistants ran up and began bandaging their wounds. The old man was still gasping in pain as he was led off stage.

The sorceress bowed; the audience applauded. Oborren and Halfdan wondered when the witch hunters would be arriving.

"And another *extra-special way* that the *aealae artes* work is to move things around!" The sorceress held out her hand to the still-levitating shoes. She then walked up to the young woman and whispered something in her ear. The young woman clapped.

The sorceress began gesticulating and uttering strange words that echoed upon the Auditorium's walls. Suddenly, there was a puff of smoke above the young woman and a shower of gold coins began raining down upon her. She knelt to pick them up, laughing, but soon became buried in the pile along with a number of other audience members in the front row.

"Isn't that NEAT-O?" asked the sorceress.

Quiet Upon Shenbyrg's Dawning

The crowd cheered and clapped wildly.

"And now for my final demonstration," said the sorceress, "I will demonstrate the power of ANIMATION!" She looked at the child on stage- the only remaining volunteer. The sorceress produced a toy animal and began to approach.

Not being able to stand it any longer, Oborren got up and shouted down to the sorceress, "That's enough!"

The startled audience turned in their seats and stared at the black-clad man who was yelling at their presenter. Most looked nervous, as if they had conspired in something unlawful. A few took offense though and got out of their seats to confront Oborren.

"We don't welcome witch hunters coming here to disrupt the lecture!" said one man.

Another shouted out: "Yeah! Why don't you go back to your Tyrian Temple, you Anti-Intellectual Tyrant!"

Seeing that the audience was getting hostile, Halfdan realized that it was time to intervene. He picked out a number of key women in the audience and let himself feel very attracted to them. They quickly picked up on his unseen sentiment and began fleeing the Auditorium. Bedlam ensued as the remaining audience attempted to get out of the way of the women fleeing Halfdan's contrived interest.

The hunter shot a glance at the Odinnic. "That's quite a trick you have."

Halfdan replied, "Sometimes curses can be blessings. Still, now would be a good time to be somewhere else."

"True," replied Oborren, "but first, I have someone I need to talk to."

* * *

Why was it that so many of the inhabitants of all the different worlds I've travelled to were always trying to set me on fire?

Clouds filled the sky, causing a gray light to shine upon the small, country Church of Tyr. Witch hunters stood around a short prisoner with a mustache. An aging man, leader of the rest, shifted in his white robes and armor. The downward-pointing sword symbol of Tyr was marked throughout the place: upon the leader, his men, the church, and even on the prisoner's face.

Wilstrin looked at the many dry boards of timber arranged around him. The pile must have been 10' in diameter and he was buried in it neck deep. So much for being burned at the stake.

"So Witch, do you have any final remarks before we Purge your Unclean Soul forever?" asked Father Farhred.

"Yes," replied Wilstrin, "don't light the pile."

Farhred laughed at his temerity. "And why not, Witch?! We have your Occult Tome. Why shouldn't you be burned for your Heresy?"

"Because I got the book from someone else."

"Oh really?" said Farhred. He looked at the other witch hunters and chuckled. "You wish to Name another?"

"Yes", replied Wilstrin, "a man that I knew from the Gaol."

Farhred smiled grimly. He considered Wilstrin's claim.

"Remove him," said the witch hunter finally, "let's see what other heretics this Witch leads us to. We can always burn him later."

* * *

Quiet Upon Shenbyrg's Dawning

The crowd was still agitated as they passed down the corridor. Some remained thrilled by the performance, others were angry that it was stopped by an apparent witch hunter, and one young woman was relieved that she was rescued from the pile of gold coins. She still held many in her pockets, as did many others leaving the performance, not knowing that they would simply turn into much less valuable candied versions within the hour. The benefits of magic were necessarily meted by their required costs; otherwise their repeated use could destroy Reality itself.

The sorceress speaker seemed quite lucky in avoiding the mishap that inevitably befell those who would use magic for frivolous reasons. But, like in all things, her luck eventually ran out.

As the pupils and guests began to clear out of the corridor, the sorceress started packing up her remaining unsold footwear. She sang a happy song to herself, but was startled when Oborren and Halfdan came out of hiding.

"I will call for the guards, because they don't really seem to be guarding me right now!" she said with a less-than-convincing aura of menace.

"Will they guard the people in this University from your irresponsible antics?" countered the hunter.

The sorceress made like she was going to cry.

Halfdan interrupted, hoping to redirect the woman, "We need your help."

The sorceress perked up again. "Oh really? A Demon Summoning perhaps? Or maybe a Transmogrification? " she said chipperly.

"No, no," clarified Halfdan, "we need an audience with Beneglushio."

"How can I help with that?" she asked. "Oh, you mean TELEPORT you to him?"

The sorceress began to move her hands around and utter words of power. "This may feel a little disorienting and mess up your inner balance for a few hours..."

Oborren grabbed her hands and stopped her. "We need you to *take us to him*," he explained.

"Oh!" she said, "but why?"

"Because you caused us to become a little disliked around here."

The sorceress giggled; Oborren rolled his eyes.

Nodding happily, the sorceress began to skip and sing her happy song again, guiding the men down the hall.

As they tried to keep up with her, Halfdan turned to Oborren. "Could Beneglushio help us make sense of how Walstock might conspire with Stephania?"

"I hope so," said the Oborren. At that, the sorceress looked back at him and smiled.

Oborren gestured to the sorceress and continued, "And if not, at least it will keep Cherries out of trouble for a while."

Chapter 18

The Caverns Crystal

Elfriede wondered at the Cavern entrance and at her companions' strange reaction to it. They had claimed to be seasoned spelunkers, but yet they hesitated here and did not seem to want to enter.

"Who shall go first?" she enquired.

Neither the gnome nor the cleric said anything. They just eyed the yawning cave opening suspiciously.

After all this, Elfriede felt just like walking in by herself. The escorted trip through Mauriatown had been fine enough, but they had only narrowly avoided a battle with the mostly unclad norsefolk at the lake. She didn't know whether the fact that they lacked body hair made it more unpleasant or less. Apparently, the Strass Hillians didn't need their weapons, their ram-horn helms, or even their clothing around to effectively drive off a proselytizing Karlist!

The party had soon left the lake, which they had later learned was called Waxing Moon Cove. Apparently the 'Waxing' title had multiple interpretations: both lunar and depilatory. They had then stumbled into a small village that had been suffering from some attacks by a supernatural entity. Since the villagers didn't seem to be currently oppressed by any earthly masters, Kolveig had urged the party to continue on and Tepson was only too happy to avoid something that was claimed to be 'some kind of demon' by the locals.

Further down the road lay the Norse town of Strass Hill proper, but the party did not digress and had headed straight for the Caverns. So here they now stood. Elfriede wished for this adventure to be over with quickly, so that she could return to Dinglesfuhr and let her onkel know of their success. She also was growing tired of her companions' bickering.

"Well gnome, I grant you the right to enter first," said Kolveig bowing.

"On the contrary," countered Tepson, "a Karlist cleric should lead from the front." The gnome held out his hand in invitation.

"You'd like that, wouldn't you?"

"I would."

"I know you would- that's why I SAID IT!"

"Good!"

"Oh YEAH? Then maybe I WON'T!"

Elfriede sighed at the arguing men. She pulled her dark violet traveling cloak around her tightly, lit her lantern, and stepped inside. The gnome and the cleric, now embarrassed, quickly followed behind.

Her light illumined the initial entrance cave's walls. Their feet crunched on the light gravel inside and they discovered a passage leading downward. The scent of rock and light mildew filled the air. The men readied their weapons as the Dinglesfuhrian lady lead on.

166

Down they wandered, leaving the autumnal Norse land above behind. At times, they had to walk single file, for the passage could become quite narrow in places. It still made Tepson nervous, because the cave walls had many curves and recesses and the ceiling would even become exposed to other passages the further on they went.

Tepson knew how dangerous underground travel could be, especially in this current period. Though he still had his doubts about magic, he knew that goblins were certainly real, as well as certain *biological aberrations*, such as that *thing* that nearly killed the party on the bridge during their last trip below. It was a testament to Elfriede's lack of experience with dungeon delving that she had decided to go first.

Feeling rising concern for the woman, Tepson politely nudged past her into the lead. She smiled and patted him on the shoulder. Unlike what Brymanah might insist, Elfriede made no argument when the small man moved to the fore- it certainly seemed a wise course of action.

The party made their way down a short, natural staircase that curved to the left, opening into a moderate–sized cave, roughly 30' wide and 60' deep. The walls shimmered in Elfriede's lantern light. Tepson gingerly made his way up to the nearest one to examine it.

The formations appeared to have quite a lot of quartz mixed with the usual limestone that one might find in Vale caves. There was an almost energetic hum to it that made the gnome feel unsettled. He hoped he wouldn't experience any more *hallucinations* down here like he did the last time he entered the underworld- hallucinations that others might call 'magic'.

As Tepson moved back to the group, he noticed that Elfriede and Kolveig were staring transfixed at the opposite while. Both their faces had grown quite pale.

Quiet Upon Shenbyrg's Dawning

"Do... do you see that over there?" whispered Elfriede alarmedly.

Kolveig too pointed. He was uncharacteristically at a loss for words. Tepson turned and saw what looked to be something dark standing near one of the stalagmite formations. The gnome shifted his head back and forth, assuming that what he was looking at must just be a stray shadow or some trick of the eye, but it didn't vanish! He was beginning to get nervous too.

"In... in... in the Name of Karl: Oppressor Spirit, I command thee to Stop Trying to Harass the Proletariat!"

At Kolveig's chastisement, the dark form seemed to vanish. He breathed a sigh of relief, as did the others.

"I had hoped that we might uncover more Left-Wing Paradises down here, but we just might be in store for something else!" The cleric did enjoy the two fey realms that he had entered during his last subterranean sojourn.

Tepson and Elfriede considered the Karlist's words for a moment.

"Why did we have to venture down here again?" asked Tepson. The gnome doubted that this Mistro, a whacko who thinks he's a wizard, would have a reasonable excuse for the three to risk their lives in the underworld.

"Like I said, friend Tepson, Mistro promised he would help my land if we retrieved an item for him," replied Elfriede.

"And let me guess," countered the gnome, "this 'item' can only be found on the deepest level of these series of tunnels?"

Elfriede shrugged and only added, "I'm not sure, but he did say to beware of the Cave Beetle. Apparently, it is enormous."

Kolveig shivered at the thought. He remembered another giant beetle that the party had fought within the goblin warrens. It nearly skewered Brymanah with its many legs. Perhaps it was best not to mention that to Elfriede and Tepson just now.

"Not that Material Possessions matter, but what is it that the Wizard Oppressor wants us to retrieve exactly?" asked Kolveig finally.

"Yeah, we all need to know in case *one or more of us di-*" Tepson stopped himself as he noted the increasing look of concern on Elfriede's face.

Seemingly torn between looking for any more lurking dark forms and answering her party's upsetting questions, Elfriede finally explained: "Mistro said only that it was a red box in a room of purple crystals."

"That's it?" asked Kolveig in disbelief. "How in Karl's name are we going to find that down here, *even if it is red*?! This place could stretch for miles! I mean, no offense, but your Overly Capitalistic Dinglesfuhr may not be worth it, Elfriede! Besides, it's only a matter of time before the savages invade it!"

Kolveig was apparently not as skilled at stopping himself from talking as Tepson was.

"The savages are going to invade Dinglesfuhr?" Now all of Elfriede's attention was focused on what one of her upsetting party members was saying.

Kolveig stood wide-eyed. He had accidentally revealed his Secret Mission from Antraxus!

As the cleric stood dumbfounded and the Dinglesfuhrian woman glared back suspiciously, Tepson conceded: "At least we haven't run into the Cave Beetle yet."

* * *

Quiet Upon Shenbyrg's Dawning

The tunnel wound deeper and Elfriede's lantern began to flicker. Luckily, Tepson had reminded her to bring extra flasks of oil for this spelunking expedition- the woman realized that she didn't really know what to expect. Something was certainly *odd* about being underground. She wasn't sure if this was the case in all cave environments or if it was just this cave in particular.

Elfriede was certainly no stranger to creepy places: she was from Dinglesfuhr after all. But the disturbance here was different; it was much more otherworldly and strange than the generally dread terrors that could lurk in the shadows of her homeland. Her people did have a number of legends about the underworld, that it was the home of Hades and that the dead dwelt there when they left the land of the living. She imagined that only the dead *who remained around the living* were the ones she was used to in Dinglesfuhr.

With the lantern now shining more brightly again, the party came to its next challenge: a fork in the passage. The path to the left slanted up slightly and then curved right. The path to the right was much narrower and sloped down rapidly into darkness. The cleric immediately began marching down the left passage.

"What are you doing?" asked Tepson.

"Going the only Rational Way, of course," answered Kolveig as if the gnome had asked a ridiculous question. He stopped to make sure that the rest of the party was ready to follow.

"How about we put it up to a vote?" asked Tepson.

Both Elfriede and Kolveig looked at the gnome in disbelief: voting would never work, not with this party!

Grumbling, Tepson made to follow, when he thought he saw something move in the passage to the right. He tapped Kolveig on the back and pointed in that direction.

Sensing it too, the cleric shrugged and said, "It's probably just something Fascistic."

Suddenly, there was a horrible scream. The two realized that Elfriede was being pulled into the passage by some dark form. The woman struggled as something chill and unsettling grabbed her by the arms with an unholy might. It was all she could do to not drop the lantern.

Acting quickly, Tepson rushed forward to stab the thing with his pickhammer, but his attack only passed through like the dark form wasn't even there.

Kolveig acted quickly too and gingerly took the lantern from Elfriede's hand so that it wouldn't drop. Then he shrugged. Elfriede looked at him in incredulity as the thing continued to drag her down the right-hand tunnel; the cleric just watched.

Realizing that her comrades were either unable or unwilling to help her, Elfriede panicked and made a quick prayer, "Oh Dark Hades, spare me from this horrid shade... and... curse that damnable Karlist!"

Both the gnome and the cleric stared at the poor woman in shock: the former, because she was now beseeching *a supernatural* entity; the latter, because she was beseeching *the wrong supernatural* entity.

Elfriede screamed again as the shade got its arms around her and tugged her off her feet. The sounds of her cries echoed upon the limestone walls, causing a horrific dissonance as if many, varied voices were screaming as well. Kolveig covered his ears at the racket and uttered a prayer to Karl, making sure to not drop the lantern.

Tepson struggled to grab Elfriede's flailing hand, but couldn't get a grip. Something seemed to keep pushing his hand away. He was reminded greatly of that horrible thing that had nearly killed

Halfdan in the Schoolhouse last year. The gnome caught himself hoping that the cleric would do something to save Elfriede, that he might use some–

And then, as the dark entity was right about to pull Elfriede into the midnight tunnel completely, their eyes met. Tepson saw the terror in Elfriede's eyes, but also a look of betrayal too. She had trusted them to keep her safe and now she was being dragged into oblivion. The gnome thrust out his hand in one more superhuman effort to grab hers, but she was gone, leaving one last heartrending cry.

Tepson began shaking and sobbing, staring into the black abyss at his lost friend.

He turned to Kolveig in outrage. "Why didn't you help her?"

"I didn't want to drop the lantern."

The gnome just stared at the cleric in shock.

"So..." said the cleric finally, "should we return to the surface now?"

* * *

"Dinglesfuhr. Powder doom. Fjord. Is it salty?"

All the assembled tribesfolk chanted the words of the prophet. Gorm placed the stylized talismans of the Great Doom-Sayer Kolveig upon of their necks. Each was made of a string of twine and had a flat rock carved with a stick figure caricature of the cleric. The tribesfolk shivered in religious ecstasy as they each received their pendant.

When the work was done, Gorm stood in front of his tribe again, pointed to the west, and said, "Dinglesfuhr."

The people turned to look in that direction.

Next, he pointed to the sky and declared, "Powder doom!"

The tribesfolk shivered in fear.

Then he pointed to the tribe, as well as to the land around them. "Fjord!"

The tribe seemed to regain their confidence somewhat.

Finally, in a great booming voice, the barbarian reached out his arms and asked, "Is it salty?!"

The tribesfolk repeated and roared.

"Is it SALTY?!" he asked again.

They repeated again and roared even louder.

"IS... IT... SALTY?!"

Rage and burning fury were in the tribe's eyes as they looked at Dinglesfuhr.

Mohee began to speak in disagreement, but Gorm knew what he would say already.

"Kolveig is Great Doom Prophet because he made Great Doom Prophecy!"

Seeing that the barbarian's logic was infallible, Mohee sat back down.

Chapter 19

Shenan-dehowa Shenanigans

Dusk was falling upon the many trees in the *Pairc o'
Chomhdháil*, casting soft shadows upon the white roofed platform
on which the assembled people stood. Luce smiled at the Helan
Queen. Here at the seat of local power, the conquering Norse
made ready to decide the fate of the defeated Celts. The crisp
aroma of wood fire burned in the distance- touched by the slight
scent of funeral pyre as well.

"You certainly made short work of McBride, Highness." The
skald smiled impishly, his cheeks becoming rosier in contrast to
his blond locks and brightly-colored clothing. He then began
singing at her in jest, "*We are mighty!*"

Emhild stared at him impassively, her pale blue eyes still
showing red from her recent grief, lips curled in lingering
innocence, pain that was only hidden somewhat by her own long,
flaxen hair.

Ragennar lowered his head in despair. He wished for his queen
to take at least some solace in defeating this Alban tribe, *the
Shenendehowans*. They had foolishly resisted her generous

request for peaceful capitulation. Now many of their leaders rested in Hel like so many others who had fought the Helans: fought and died.

"But we hjave won the battle, my *Dróttning.*"

Emhild looked back at Ragennar and smiled. She was glad that he would never try to caress her. She liked that he still lived.

"And yet the matter still stands," interrupted Luce, "Hel has granted you victory. It's time you made a sacrifice in return!"

As he spoke, the twisted skald looked around at the assembled Shenendehowans murderously. All averted their eyes from so obviously cruel a man. Ragennar hoped that the sacrifice of these Celtic Alban warriors might be enough to appease Hel; the norseman trusted that even she might not demand the life of innocents this time.

Luce focused on one warrior whose courage seemed to return and dared to meet his gaze. Unfortunately for everyone, Luce began to sing with morbid suggestion, *"Everybody needs a little time to slay..."*

The nursemaid in Em then came to the fore.

"No one shall be sacrificed today, Luce, dontchya know."

At this, the skald's face turned an even brighter red, but now triggered by anger rather than joy.

"Hel must be appeased!"

"Then what hjave we to do?" Em's emphatic retort even gave Luce pause.

The man shook his head and smiled, "There is nothing else to be done, nursemaid: the land of Shenendehowa was given and something from Shenendehowa must be taken!"

Dan Osarchuk

Ragennar stared at the doomed Celts. They were men, not too unlike himself- brave warriors all. More had red hair, grey or green eyes, and went barefoot than Norse folk, even though this new land was almost as chill as frozen Minas-Ninona. They also fought differently, most carrying spears or great swords, while some favored bows. The Shenendehowans in particular trusted to their strange Gods and tattoos to turn blades, many eschewing armor altogether. The most bizarre even fought completely bare and leapt with reckless abandon from the horse-drawn chariots that their captains drove. It was a feat that might give even the wildest Minas-Ninonan berserker pause.

Emhild too looked at the men with pity and remembered the conquest of the town in which they now dwelt: the Springs of Saratgo. How did so few Norse conquer so many Celts? Em shook her head in despair. Yes, McBride seemed a tyrant that few might miss, but Luce's scheme of taunting him and his chieftains to force themselves upon Em had caused their deaths and now leaderless, his people were open to conquest. There was also a Saratgo in Minas-Ninona just like in this land of Alban: was there more to the connection between the two places than just the Spell of Travel that had convinced Hel to bring them here?

A man entered the platform where those assembled stood. His hooded head and long beard signified that he was some sort of holy man; his curved engraving pendant and plaid cloak signified that he was yet another Celt.

Even Luce paused before challenging the man. All the captured Celtic warriors bowed their heads immediately upon noticing him and many of the Norse captors felt compelled to do so, as well.

"Oh look, it's a druid," said Luce mockingly.

The man stared back at the skald. His eyes betrayed no emotion, his face showed no apparent age.

Quiet Upon Shenbyrg's Dawning

"Are these the sacrifices for yer Goddess that ye be a-having?" asked the Druid calmly.

Luce stared wickedly at him.

"Will that be a-nough then?"

Luce said nothing but smiled. Emhild cringed: how much more death would be necessary? Ragennar too felt that there was no honor in killing those who were already captured.

"Me people will never follow you a-willingly for long," said the Druid, "Ye are not like us. I doubt even the Frisians would bow a-knee to ye."

"I know," said Luce, "but it will be lots of fun while it lasts."

* * *

"Why did he bring us hjere?" pleaded Emhild.

The rust-bearded Ragennar stared off at the Chariot Track and shrugged.

Em couldn't understand it. Why did the skald have Hel bring her and these other Minas-Ninonans hundreds of miles to some random land to curse its leaders with death and its subjects with conquest? Em was no warlord, but even she knew that so small a force of norseman would have little hope of retaining control of the thousands of Shenendehowan Celts that dwelt here, let alone prevent other nearby clans of Celts or even Teutonic Frisians from conquering this land for their own.

What other scheme might Luce have in coming to Alban?

And where had that trickster gone to? He had only taken two of their party with him, Grimar and Hallvard, leaving the remaining twenty to guard her. Ragennar had guessed that Luce was looking for some item in the ruins of the Ancient Capitol to the north. Em needed to learn more.

A crowd of Celts at the far end of the field cheered as the chariots broke into another race. Emhild found it exciting, but couldn't keep her mind off of what Luce might be up to. It was then that she spotted a familiar looking man sitting cross-legged on the ground apart from the crowd.

She leaned over to Ragennar and said, "The man yonder, bring hjim hjere." She pointed.

"The Druid?" asked Ragennar incredulously.

"Ya," she replied.

The hooded man was led to the Helan Queen and thoroughly checked for any hidden weapons or other objects that might harm her. She was beginning to see her Norse bodyguards as older brothers, because they were so protective, so large, and because any amorous intentions that they might have towards her were out of the question.

Once vetted, the Druid then stood before Emhild, though her guards still stood ready.

"I hjave a question for ya," she began, "why would someone want to conquer this land?"

"That's strange coming from the one who a-conquered it."

"But I still hjave to ask ya, ya know," Em insisted.

The Druid smiled at her wryly. "Perhaps your trickster-skaldy friend decided for some a-conquest along the way?"

The Helan Queen looked at him to continue.

"Great lines o' power run beneath the earth: *the leys.* They a-stretch throughout Amercia and to lands beyond. The wise or the..." the Druid paused as he stared in the direction of the Pairc o' Chomhdháil, where many of the warriors were sacrificed, "...the ruthless may find the way to a-travel quite quickly therein."

"Amercia?" asked Em.

"Ah, you would might a-know it as Vinland, being that ye are Norse" explained the Druid.

Em found the rest of the Druid's speech strange, but she guessed what he was talking about. Performing the ritual at the Cave of Mysteries back in Minas-Ninona had led them to emerge at the Springs of Saratgo here in Alban- it was simply just a matter of walking out a different cave whose exit had changed by a thousand miles. Luce couldn't have just snapped his fingers and brought them here, nor could Emhild- that would have been too risky, too outlandish in the Gods' eyes.

Seeing the nursemaid's reaction, the Druid continued, "Each line has a terminus, a place o' power where two or more lines meet. Ye can a-feel it in the air. We a-call them *nemetons* here; ye probably a-call them something else in yer barbaric tongue. It could be that your Luce is simply on his way to somewhere else and the Springs of Saratgo are just a waypoint, lass."

* * *

"You know, Grimar, this used to be the high seat of power for this land." Luce pointed at the ruins of what was once a great city.

Grimar simply shrugged; he had seen the Appolis Ruins in his homeland- they all looked similar.

"Oh the warlords that followed tried to rebuild it, but failed again and again. War and destruction has made it beautiful. And oh, what is that?" asked Luce rhetorically. "The howls of orcs who have made yet another kill. You know, Grimar, even though we have to get back, I'd love to stay here throughout the night- you know why?"

180

The large Norse bodyguard simply glanced at the trickster to his side.

"That's when the zombies come out."

The skald looked to see what Grimar's reaction was. The bodyguard did not seem moved.

Luce continued, "You have the more recent zombies made, then the ones made years ago, the ones decades ago, and the deeper you go *under the ruins*," he paused again for dramatic effect, "the older the undead are."

He smiled evilly.

"It would be every archaeologist's dream."

Grimar just shook his head; Luce's monologue had now gone past his level of understanding.

Suddenly, a crashing sound up ahead signaled the men that danger might be at hand. Hallvard readied his longsword and Grimar readied his axe. Luce simply smiled and began to sing, "*There is a dwelling...*"

And then they were upon them: not orcs, not zombies, but men. These particular men struck the Norse as closer to their culture than that of the Celts and yet they were still noticeably different. It seemed they were yet another tribe of Albans, different than the Celtic Shenendehowans. They wore leather jacks, had stylized beards, and darker hair. The attackers were also armed with crossbows, something these Minas-Ninonans eschewed as a coward's weapon.

The larger bodyguards scrambled to get the initiative on the attacking Albans. Grimar's axe took one across the chin and Hallvard slew another through the gut.

Quiet Upon Shenbyrg's Dawning

There were too many though. One fired, striking Grimar in his chest. Blood exploded from his mouth as he fell. Hallvard blocked another with his shield, but some other Albans from behind produced long clubs and pummeled the norseman's back.

Hallvard went to swing and have his revenge upon the club-bearers, but was stopped by a woman's voice.

"You won't be a-needing that strike, Blondie." Unlike the others, she did seem like a Celt.

Luce smiled as the Albans slew his remaining bodyguard and gazed upon the woman. She had long red hair and was quite voluptuous in form. Something in her mind spoke to him.

"Oh, you'll do just fine," said the skald.

* * *

The group sat in the longboat, specially made for this outing. Overhead, the rock glowed in reds and yellows as the walls and water below remained dark. There was little need for torch or lantern in this place.

The Druid sat at the front of the assembled Norse. The woman that Luce had found during his journey to the Capitol Ruin sat next to him. She watched the water below with concern.

Luce himself sat next, chewing on some local fare of spiced chicken wings. His mood was inscrutable: whether one of humor or of tension, it was hard to tell. He paid little heed to the strange fey lights above them.

Emhild said nothing, though it was not in the manner of usual Helan grimness. Perhaps she had forestalled the loss of yet more innocent life? It was the least she could do. She wondered what the skald would ask of her next.

Ragennar was also silent. He knew the decision was now even out of the hands of his *Dróttning*. His thoughts went to fallen

Torsteinn and Konigsgild, as well as all the others who had fallen by following Luce.

"Well Dróttinn," began the grizzled warrior, "we hjave traveled to yet another cave."

"Indeed," smiled the trickster. "And now Hel must be appeased! A sacrifice *of Shenan-dehowa for Shenendehowa!*"

He glared cruelly at the red-haired voluptuous woman sitting next to the Druid. Her name was Gaeswyn. She shivered when she saw the trickster produce a dagger and tried to shift her seat away from him.

Suddenly, Luce stopped the boat and stared at the waiting Minas-Ninonans. All held their breath. He gestured to a dry passage that they had arrived at to the right. The group disembarked and began to make their way down it. Some lit torches as the fey light was dimmer here. When a number of the norsemen made to tie up the longboat, Luce shook his head.

"We won't be needing it again," he said.

The passage led to a series of smaller chambers, one of them with an amazing stone set into the floor: it looked to be shaped like a heart.

"This should a-suffice for what ye be a-seekin'," said the Druid.

"I know," mocked Luce. He put his dagger away. Gaeswyn breathed a sigh of relief. Ragennar looked confused.

"I thought that Hjel required a sacrifice from Shenendehowa in return for our victory in Shenendehowa?" he said.

"She does," replied Luce. He giggled. "But there is another land that bears a similar name to slake her morbid thirst."

The other Norse knew not what he meant; they doubted it would be pleasant.

As if in reply to their unasked question, Luce began to sing again: "*I long to see you! Away you rolling river!*"

Emhild closed her eyes and hoped that the Gods would forgive her if more death was done by her presence in this new land. She just couldn't stand to see any more Celts sacrificed. When she opened her eyes again the heart-shaped stone was visible in the other chamber. Em risked another quick prayer to Freya, hoping that love would save her.

In the background, Luce kept singing his strange song. At least the melody was cheerful.

Chapter 20

Upon the Dark Lake

Oborren was still perplexed by Beneglushio's guidance as they approached the small Strass Hillian village. Had it even been a week since he was here last? The hunter wondered about how they would take the news of one of their own, his henchman for only a short time, until his... unfortunate demise.

Halfdan found the area fascinating. Here, the hills were even steeper than in Walstock. He hadn't stopped in this region since he and his former wife had passed this way over a decade ago. It was the first place they had stopped to rest when they had first came to the Vale.

Halfdan wondered too at why Norse dwelt here and not just the usual Teutons. He had heard of lands much further north and west where many Norse dwelt, a land called Minas-Ninona- a place rumored to be linked somehow to his own home in Calvary.

Who knew how the various cultures sprang up in the Vale and in other places after Lights Out? Had the Norse really come to Calvary via some portal or had the people living there simply spontaneously became so? And why were they Norse, while just to the east, Walstock was Teutonic, and yet to the south, Caelum

Mount was Olympian. What was more, back in his *original homeland* of Claw Island, Olympians, Celts, Frisians, Sumerians, and others predominated.

Halfdan himself was only partially Norse, despite his name. His own countenance was more Slav mixed with Celt. It was by living with his adopted family, the Oldsons, the ones who had taken him in after he had traveled *around the bend* at an early age, that he took a Norse name. Ironically, he had eventually ended up in a mainly Norse settlement: Calvary.

Cherries, for her part, was probably unaware of the cultures and ethnicities of people in the Vale, apart from their style of dress. The sorceress cared little for Strass Hill or what had happened after Lights Out. Instead, she had decided to follow the hunter and cleric from Fairfacts Lordship, because she was worried that Oborren would be angry at her if she didn't. She also found something dark and mysterious about Halfdan, which reminded her of her master Mistro. Serious men could be such silly-willies, even if they were repellant.

Mistro had told her to take a break from magic and try a different profession. So she had *sort of obeyed* and just begun *showing magic off to others*, as well as selling Stylish Footwear. That was why she had given her demonstration at the University at Fairfacts Lordship. She guessed that she couldn't do that anymore though! Perhaps by traveling with these men for a while she would become inspired to take up some New Neat-o Project! Traveling with Oborren before certainly gave her some inspiration, even if it had also led to *demonic possession.*

It was at this juncture that the travelers encountered the local folk. It looked like some sort of meeting was occurring in the village square.

As the three strolled into the village, a number of the women there spotted Halfdan and began to immediately withdraw within their longhouses. The menfolk took notice of the travelers too and moved towards Cherries. Her skintight erubescent garb over her supple form did little to dissuade them.

Seeing that things were already beginning to devolve, Oborren spoke up, "People of Strass Hill, we've come here to honor Bjartar."

At the mention of one of their own, the norsemen recognized the hunter and focused their attention on him. Some of the norsewomen even rose above their repulsion of Halfdan enough to listen as well.

"What hjappened to him?" asked one Norse maid.

"He fell", Oborren paused as many of the villagers sighed in dismay, "in battle with the beast-heads."

Seeing the people's concern, Halfdan spoke, "He feasts in Valhalla now."

The people glanced at the Odinnic for a moment; the darkness in his eyes stopped them from looking very long. A deep presence began to fill the area at the mention of a Norse afterlife.

"So how's everybody doing?!" said Cherries as she tried to change the subject.

"We've captured an Agitator from Hjelltowne..." said one of the men, "hjee wished to bring 'Social Justice' to Strass Hjill".

Oborren recognized the man as one of Bjartar's and Sven's friends from the barn battle with the harpy. He couldn't place his name, which was probably good, because both men whose names he knew were now dead and Oborren didn't necessarily wish for him to die too.

"An Agitator, you say?" asked Halfdan. Something grim was around the cleric. The townsfolk were beginning to get nervous again as the aging man stared at them, waiting for their reply.

"Yes, silly-willes! That's what they said!" explained the sorceress. She put her red-polish nailed hand on Halfdan's shoulder. The grim presence diminished enough for the villagers to speak.

"Y...ya," said the Norse maid finally. "Hjee be over hjere..."

The party was led into the town square. They weren't surprised when they discovered who was tied to a witch's pyre.

* * *

"So you abandoned your party members in the Caverns?" Oborren found such an act to be extremely disloyal and selfish, but then again, the one who did it was a Karlist.

"You make it sound *so terrible!*" Kolveig insisted. "The Bourgeois Dinglesfuhrian lady was dragged away screaming into the underworld by some non-Karlist specter and the Capitalist-whipped gnome didn't want to return to the surface with me. *What else could I do?*"

The hunter, the Odinnic, and the sorceress all stared at the Karlist.

"We should hurry," said Halfdan, "we might still be able to save them."

Oborren shook his head. It was a valiant idea, but he assumed that the dark entity had either slain or done something even worse to the poor woman from Dinglesfuhr by now. And the gnome, well, he was short...

"Hurray!" said Cherries, "another dungeon adventure! And I have *just the shoes* for it!"

Kolveig rolled his eyes at such Rampant Consumerism: didn't Cherries know that people were lacking for shoes in Fjord Vallee?

The men hurried Cherries to get ready quickly and the four of them set off. The sun was beginning to set behind them as they travelled east to the Caverns. Dark clouds rolled in from the north and south, like some gargantuan aerial leviathan preparing to devour the dying golden orb. A cold wind blew from town. It brought an aroma of food and wood fire as the Norse there tried to keep out the night, as well as any horrors that might come with it.

The group soon came to the cave entrance and Oborren lit two lanterns. He gave one to Cherries and one to Halfdan, who had just made another spear from a nearby tree. Kolveig readied his stylized hammer and sickle. The Odinnic and he stared at each other suspiciously as both trusted to separate Gods. Cherries glared at them both, still irritated that they had rushed her in putting on her scarlet-highlighted caving boots. Oborren wondered at how long it would take for the party to come to blows and die horribly.

* * *

"Oh, look at all the pretty crystals!"

Oborren had to smack Cherries's hand away again as she tried to touch the walls.

"Do you know how dangerous that is? Who knows what sort of booby traps or curses you might get by randomly touching such things in a cave!"

Cherries snickered at the hunter: "You said '*booby*'!"

Oborren shook his head in irritation.

Even Halfdan and Kolveig had to snicker too; it was the least they could do in this dark place.

The Odinnic certainly could feel the energy emanating from the walls. He guessed that the many crystals present here indicated that this area was a nexus for ley lines. He sensed the spirits in this place too, but he kept their disturbing influence on him at bay by remaining firm in the I sense.

Kolveig was still at a loss as to why the rest had wanted to come back underground to search for Elfriede and Tepson. Neither were especially good Workers or Agitators. He also felt the spirits move about this place and made ready to Expose Them for the Tyrannical Landlords that they Were. The spirits avoided him too.

Another intersection stood before the party. Oborren made to speak when suddenly, a blood-curdling scream could be heard in the distance down one of the passages to the left. It sounded like a woman whose soul was being ripped asunder.

"I guess we know which way to go now," he said forebodingly.

* * *

The party moved deeper into the Caverns, passing through a number of other chambers, when they entered one that held a small lake. This cavern must have been huge, for neither Halfdan's nor Cherries's lanterns could see any walls on the other side. The passage continued passed the dark subterranean water, much to Oborren's concern.

Everyone's attention was drawn back to the lake, which stood perfectly still and perfectly reflected the cavern ceiling above. It was almost as if the illusory stalagmites in the lake were part of a real cave floor itself. Such a setting could be a doorway to other places, other lands and worlds entirely: but who would dare venture into them?

> *Oh the worlds, my friend*
> *To come back around upon you*
> *Again*

Dan Osarchuk

Something stirred in the dark recesses of the cavern, though the party stood transfixed watching the otherworldliness of the water.

Halfdan, being used to the ensnarements of the mind, snapped out of the mesmerism first and tapped the other party members to bring them back to awareness again.

A strange, slurping sound could be heard now. To the party's horror, it appeared as if a large piece of cave formation had detached itself from the very wall and was oozing towards them. Despite its rocky visage, it moved and shifted as if it were some form of heinous jelly, having a mass of nearly 15' in diameter!

"A *cave nodulation!*" whispered Oborren in bated terror.

The rest of the party had no idea what he was talking about, but knew it wasn't good, because the hunter seemed so afraid.

Cherries immediately began to utter strange words and a ball of flame started to appear in one of her hands, but Oborren stopped her.

He shook his head, "Cave gas!"

Halfdan had to admit that the fire the sorceress produced was amazing, a sight only seen in the underworld when magic was wrought, but yes, it was not a good idea for her to throw large amounts of fire around if there was a chance of unintentional explosion.

In response to the party's increasing terror, the cave nodulation began to rear up and opened what seemed to be a large maw. The stench from its growing orifice was awful, something akin to rotten milk and blueberries. And though the protrusions from the nodulation looked quite fearsome, the flailing worm-like tongue that erupted from inside its mouth nearly made Kolveig faint.

Quiet Upon Shenbyrg's Dawning

The stinking abomination lumbered forward as Oborren and the rest looked for the best means of escape. He began to lead the party a little further down the passage, deeper into the caverns.

"We may have to face that thing when we come back again," said Halfdan.

"I know," said the hunter, "but we certainly cannot defeat it now!"

As they made ready to race down the rapidly narrowing tunnel, Halfdan, Oborren, and Cherries glanced back as they heard Kolveig scream.

"Ow! Ow! OWWWW!!!!"

They now saw in the flittering lantern light that the nodulation had wrapped its worm tongue around one of Kolveig's legs. It was beginning to drag him towards its stinking, deadly maw. The Karlist wailed and cried as he desperately tried to saw the tongue from him with his sickle. He retched as the uniquely awful stench of rotten dairy and berry grew stronger.

Cherries stared at Oborren with a crazy look in her eye. He started to shake his head again, but she just grimaced.

"Swamp gas is just another PAIN IN THE ASS!"

Her voice sounded uncharacteristically gravely and demented when she spoke. The others ducked for cover, knowing how reckless the sorceress was being. Cherries launched a jet of flame right into the beast's gaping maw, causing it to make a horrific squealing sound. The stench intensified. It withdrew its tongue from the Karlist too, leaving only a puncture wound where its sphincter mouth had attached to his leg.

Kolveig vomited; Halfdan ran up and pulled him back to the party.

192

Oborren glared at Cherries like a father would at a naughty daughter.

"I thought I told you NOT TO USE FIRE!"

She lowered her head and gave a hurt look. "I thought you said to not throw a ball of fire- *I threw a jet of flame!*"

* * *

Kalla broke down crying again as the Glowing Spectral Speaker related the tale of the Mountain Folk and the Wicked Amaranthine Wizard. And she was not alone: many other Dinglesfuhrian people, young and old, male and female were gathered around the man in the Dingleplatz. They listened in rapt attention as he spoke of the many evils of the Dinglesfuhrians and how they could make amends by engaging in Underreign and other concessions. By the end of his story, the people were lining up to give this man and his cause, the Glowing Spectral Personhood, as much coin as they could. It was the least they could do.

The blonde woman was especially distraught, because of her family's ties with the Wizard himself. The man seemed to notice her guilt and strolled over to her after the crowd had expended their money and departed. He was tall and his hair bluish in color, indicating that he had the Mountain Folk blood that he claimed. He looked down at the woman and stroked her head as she bowed at his knees.

A crooked smile appeared on Hymnir's face as he forced her head down closer to the pavement.

"How low can you bow?" said he.

"As much as I am made able, sir" she sobbed and she pressed her head against the ground. Her shapely body shook, framed by the well-made Dinglesfuhrian paving stones around her.

Quiet Upon Shenbyrg's Dawning

"Is that all you can do to cleanse your name? To cleanse Dinglesfuhr?" he asked.

She looked up at him in confusion. "If there is something more," she pleaded, "I would DO anything!"

The tall man made another crooked smile at her. He took her by the hand and helped her up.

"I am YOURS!" she declared.

The man smiled more deeply.

"Good. There is much work to be done." Hymnir watched her reaction; the Dinglesfuhrian was subjugated.

He continued. "There is *a little man* I wish you to visit just passed the Fjord. But first, let us go to the Temple for your Initiation. Soon *you will be cleansed*, as will all of Dinglesfuhr."

Chapter 21

The Throne of Hel

The stench of burnt milk and fetid blueberry still clung to their sinuses as the party ventured down to yet another cave gallery. Halfdan could certainly see how the Ancients might have enjoyed traveling through these Caverns, but he doubted that they were even remotely as dangerous then as they were now.

Cherries gave a sheepish look while Oborren glared back at her occasionally. The hunter wasn't sure if she had killed the cave nodulation, but she had certainly harmed it. He was beginning to become concerned by her great power, compounded by her almost child-like naivety at how dangerous it could be.

Kolveig wondered too at the sorceress's might, but was thankful that the party had saved him. Moreso though, his mind kept focusing on the puncture wound on his leg. Halfdan had offered to take a look at it, but the Karlist wouldn't give that Odinnic Heretic The Satisfaction. Kolveig had, of course, beseeched Karl to help his leg Redouble Its Socialistic Efforts to mend and heal, but it was to no avail. That a strange purple rash had begun to form around it didn't help matters either.

The group soon came to what looked like a chasm in the middle of the passage. Oborren gingerly moved up to it and glanced down, but could not see the bottom. Taking a torch from Halfdan, he tossed it below, but its light went out before any bottom could be seen. Both shook their heads in concern.

"Is there any way around?" asked Kolveig.

"Only a narrow ledge on each side," replied Oborren.

The Karlist shrugged. "Oh well, guess we should venture back to the surface..."

Oborren glared at him.

"Perhaps we could just JUMP across!" said Cherries enthusiastically. She made ready to go first.

Halfdan stopped her and shook his head, "It's at least 10 feet!"

"I can do it!" announced the sorceress confidently. "I just need to summon some elemental wind..."

"NO YOU WON'T," growled Oborren, "we don't want to risk any side-effects!"

"Side-effects?" scoffed Cherries, "don't be a Silly-Willy!"

"I *will be a Silly-Willy*. And you're not using magic now!" scolded the hunter.

Cherries put her hand to her face and snickered mischievously.

"So what shall we do then?" asked Kolveig impatiently. The pain in his leg had begun to flare-up again.

Halfdan tested the ledge with his spear. "We'll have to walk carefully; I'll try it first."

After the hunter secured a rope to him, the Odinnic made his way slowly over to the yawning abyss, cleared his mind, and stepped on to the ledge lightly. Cherries and Oborren grasped the other end of the rope tightly, but the ledge held for now.

Nodding, Halfdan made his way to the other side, found a stone outcrop to brace the rope, and took hold of it himself. Soon Cherries was across and Oborren was waiting for Kolveig to go. The Karlist collapsed to the ground in pain; the hunter could see that his face was turning purple.

"The other healer is already across the chasm, so you better pull yourself together," said Oborren sternly.

The Karlist cursed the hunter and tried a final prayer to Karl, promising him anything in return if the God saved his faithful cleric... and punished the hunter!

After a moment, the sound of left-wing patriotic music could be heard in the distance and the cleric got up. His face looked a little better and Oborren was able to help him across the abyss.

"Did your fake god save you?" asked the hunter sarcastically.

"We'll see if he saves YOU if you get stung by some Fascist cave monster!" muttered the cleric back.

"*Fascist cave nodulation*," corrected Oborren.

"Whatever!"

* * *

The dark cavern was quite enormous here, far larger than the four had seen yet. Up above, the many quartz crystals twinkled in the lantern light like stars over some mysterious benighted land. Something stirred in the distance, a scuttling sound.

At Oborren's suggestion, the party spread out, but not before attaching lengths of rope to each other's backpacks. He had originally thought to have them break off into pairs, so that none would get lost, but he could think of no combinations that wouldn't end up catastrophically for one group, if not both.

Kolveig, being the main potential partner who really couldn't be paired with anyone, had even resisted having a rope attached to his pack, but eventually acquiesced. Apparently, his desire to leave the Caverns as quickly as possible outweighed his outrage over Being Tethered Like Some Bourgeois' Slave, at least for the time being. Oborren had considered just letting the Karlist wander back alone, but he was the last one to see Tepson and this Elfriede woman; he needed to remain, no matter how irritating he was.

So in the dim light, the party fanned out. Kolveig insisted on taking the far left, Cherries came next, then Oborren, then Halfdan on the far right.

Suddenly, Cherries screamed. The rest of the party whipped out their weapons, ready for an attack.

After a few seconds of waiting with no more cries from Cherries, the hunter asked her, "What happened?"

The sorceress, still upset, could only mutter, "I... I... think that something *touched me.* "

Oborren looked at Kolveig accusingly, but the Karlist just held up his hands and shook his head in denial.

Halfdan stared into the darkness, "There is *something else* in here. I can feel it."

"Thanks- that's very helpful," said Oborren impatiently. "Cherries: what touched you?"

It seemed now like she was hyperventilating. The hunter grabbed a flask out of his pack and made her take a swig. Finally, she was able to speak.

"I... I... I... think it was.... *a midget!*" She sat down and began scratching at her clothes as if she were covered in ants.

"Oh!" said Kolveig in relieved understanding, "that's just-"

"MWHAFEKJWHGXDWTUE!!"

A deranged gnome came blundering out of the darkness. Kolveig recognized it to be Tepson, but the man's eyes were wide and he looked very disheveled. He flopped around and dove into the sorceress's lap, screaming in gibberish.

Cherries was so upset, she couldn't say a word, let alone blast him with flame. She just sat there mortified; face ashen white as the maddened gnome dissolved what little was left of her own sanity.

"Do something!" implored the hunter to the two clerics.

Kolveig shook his head, "That's just how gnomes can get sometimes."

Halfdan pulled the small man off the sorceress and smacked him across the face. That seemed to bring him back to his senses. The gnome shook his head and his eyes settled on the hunter.

"Oborren?" asked Tepson in disbelief. "Is it you?"

"It is. You must have been down here for a long time to become so demented."

"Ye... yes," stammered the gnome, "I lost my torch when..." he looked at the Karlist in rising anger, "when Kolveig RAN BACK TO THE SURFACE WITH MY PACK!"

The Karlist made a guilty look and tried to slip away. The others glared at him angrily.

Quiet Upon Shenbyrg's Dawning

"I was just making sure that the party possessions were Redistributed Fairly."

" 'Redistributed fairly'? 'Redistributed fairly'?" said the gnome as his fury boiled over. "I'll GIVE YOU 'REDISTRIBUTED FAIRLY'!

The short man took a swing at the Karlist; Kolveig avoided the blow, being a few feet taller than him.

"Maybe you need a stool?" teased the Karlist.

"RRRRAAAARRRR!" growled the gnome as he lit into the cleric.

It took both the Odinnic and the hunter to pull him off Kolveig.

"Now's not the time! We can't beat up the Karlist yet!" insisted Oborren.

Eventually Tepson calmed down and Kolveig nursed his many small-handed fist wounds. Oborren gave Tepson some rations and water, while Halfdan tended to some of the gnome's injuries.

Even Cherries had begun to calm down. Midgets really freaked her out!

"So was Tepson that 'something else' you felt in this cave?" asked the hunter jokingly.

"No," said Halfdan, "there's still something down here."

"MORE MIDGETS?" shrieked Cherries. She leaped up and landed in Halfdan's arms. The aging man struggled to hold her, but her terror of gnomes seemed to outweigh his repellant curse for now.

Something scurried closer to the party and Oborren readied his crossbow. Climbing up the rock, the party spied a foot-long beetle. Cherries spotted it and buried her face in Halfdan's chest to hide from it.

Tepson strolled up and shooed the thing away. "So much for there being a massive cave beetle!"

* * *

Oborren kept noticing dark shapes lurking in the corners of his eyes. The rest of the party seemed to notice them too: the two clerics, the sorceress, and the gnome were more on edge than normal. Not that spelunking wasn't usually enough of a concern, but the palpable feeling of being watched at least made the party move quietly and without protest.

One shadow in particular loomed near Tepson. In the flickering lantern light, it appeared as some massive two-headed turkey fiend. The shade had a potent presence, so much so that the rest of the party members felt its ominousness. Halfdan took a moment to walk up to it, stare at it clearly, and its presence receded.

The Caverns here had begun to break off into smaller chambers, some of which might have even been hard for Tepson to stand up in fully. Something moved out of the corner of Cherries's eyes.

"Jeepers Creepers!" she turned to the nearest party member for solace, but it turned out to be Tepson. The sorceress looked at him cautiously and ventured a smile. The gnome just shook his head. He wondered why everyone in the Vale seemed mad.

"Ho there," whispered Halfdan to the rest, it looked like some sort of alcove lay ahead.

Oborren prepared to tell the party to fan out, but thought better of it. They didn't fare very well when they did that last.

So, as a tight group, they examined the alcove that Halfdan had noticed. An amethyst light shown from the purple crystals upon the walls within. There was a dais of what looked to be natural limestone upon which stood a throne of alabaster and coal carved with images of skulls and leering faces. Also upon the walls and about the place were strange, very life-like pictures of evil masked men and women, horrific display, and vile acts of murder. It all glowed in the strange, macabre purple light.

"I'm sure you're brave enough to sit on the throne," teased Kolveig as he glanced at Tepson, "that is, if you're tall enough to reach it!"

The gnome made a fist and held it up to the Karlist threateningly. Kolveig winced and turned away.

Halfdan and Tepson especially realized that the life-like pictures were actually *posters*, relics of the Ancient days. Tepson even recognized some of the pictures as death metal bands that he had read about before his long nap, centuries ago.

Oborren examined the throne carefully, though he didn't dare touch it. He warned the others to not get too close to it either and he didn't have to ask twice. The hunter got out his trusty pendulum, incense, and mirror and began examining the throne for any supernal qualities.

Cherries found the area to be very dull, creepy, and lacking in any bright red colors. The gratuitous blood on some of the pictures did not count for her. Kolveig also found the red to be lacking any Left-Wing Significance and yawned while the others searched.

The party's attention soon turned to the sound of movement in an adjacent chamber. Unlike the ephemeral dark forms that had been stalking the party earlier, this one seemed more real. The men readied their weapons and Cherries readied a ball of fire.

Lumbering into the alcove was a human-shaped form, moving as if a zombie. Oborren advanced with his flail and Cherries pulled back to throw her fire. Kolveig and Halfdan readied their holy weapons.

"Make sure you destroy the brain!" yelled the hunter.

Just as the party made ready to attack, Tepson yelled out, "Wait! That's Elfriede!"

"Elfriede's a zombie? KILL HER!"

No one obeyed Kolveig's command. The hunter shuddered at the Karlist's utter lack of loyalty.

Oborren turned to Kolveig accusingly, who eventually grudgingly nodded in agreement.

"Fine, *we probably shouldn't kill her...*"

The dazed woman wandered into the alcove room and bowed on the floor before the throne. Her tattered clothes gave the party pause: the men due to its suggestiveness; Cherries due to the lack of any red color in Elfriede's apparel.

Tepson moved up to the woman, but she still didn't acknowledge his presence. She kept muttering something under her breath and had a wild look in her eyes. The gnome himself had been in a similar state only a few hours earlier. He wondered if having Elfriede bury her head in Cherries's lap would help her too. Tepson glanced back at the sorceress, but she only eyed the gnome with suspicion.

As the hunter continued to glare at the Karlist, Halfdan sighed and approached Elfriede. Remembering to remain present, he carefully placed his hand on her shoulder. He assumed that his presence would be enough to upset the woman and snap her out of her delusion.

To his surprise, the woman stood up and embraced the Odinnic in an unguarded hug. Halfdan allowed his body to relax and hug her in return. He was glad that this woman had come to her senses, but remained concerned that his continued proximity to her would make her upset- especially since he found her attractive. Halfdan gently removed her arms from him and placed them around Tepson instead.

The gnome had just tucked a red box and some other souvenirs into his pack and smiled. He enjoyed the hug, knowing he would be allowed to finally beat up the Karlist once they returned to the surface.

* * *

Puffy gray clouds floated in the deep blue sky. A cold breeze set the dried leaves that still clung to the majestic oaks rattling. A sibilant zephyr within the branches conjured a more serpentine air, causing a strange counter-vibration within the eaves of the farmhouse.

Three young children played outside. Their distraught mother watched from the kitchen window. Where had their father gone? It'd been days since he went into town to mend his broken arm-what had happened to him?

She was soon startled to see two strangers come over the hill. She yelled to her children to come inside and grabbed the longbow from over the mantle. After some arguing, she shooed her kids back into their room and told them to lock their door. Then she realized to her horror that her youngest son was still outside!

Looking around frantically, the mother got a better look at the two strangers out the window. One was a woman with a serpent lapel on her jacket. Her sterile ways showed that she had never had children of her own. The other was a white-clad Hospitalier knight, syringe-like lance in hand.

The woman with the serpent lapel ran up and grabbed the young son.

"We should take this child with us so that he won't get stolen!"

The mother had heard the stories of such evil Cultists. She took cover and took aim at the knight. She'd die before she let them take her children from her.

Chapter 22

The Side Way Inn

Very late night greeted the six spelunkers as they finally emerged from the Caverns. The dark shades had continued to watch and the stench of the cave thing at the lake lingered, but the party emerged relieved to be out in the wider world again, where things were not so contained. All who had originally entered were now leaving alive, so the expedition was considered a success.

A star shone shimmering on the horizon. Elfriede and Cherries shut off their lanterns, they were nearly out of oil anyway. Oborren and Halfdan sniffed the fresh air and looked for any changes in the surrounding environs. Tepson and Kolveig glared at each other, still sour over their fight in the underworld below. Oborren walked next to Elfriede.

"You were a scrivener at the County Castle in Walstock?" he asked.

"Yes."

Oborren nodded to Elfriede and rechecked his pack. He decided to show her the message that he had intercepted from the harpy-perhaps tomorrow. He hoped that the riddle of who the 'Director is WS' would then be solved. Ironically, the village where he had first acquired the scroll was less than a mile away.

Halfdan was still amazed at how Elfriede was not repelled by him, but in fact had not even shied away when they ended up walking near each other. He mused that it was best to shift away from her anyway. Cherries seemed to take a liking to the Dinglesfuhrian lady as well: she could hardly wait to take her shopping for some new clothes and shoes.

The party paused as light began to shine in the east. Sunlight motes shown brilliant upon the clouds near the mountains. Soft shades of yellows and pinks mingled in the expectant air. Something golden and true was arising, inspiring and free, and yet still hidden by the Nuttens, the blue-purple wall in the distance.

The quiet of the early dawn moved through them all. The light grew brighter as they left the dark cave entrance behind. The promise of another day in the Shenbyrg Vale was upon them. The peace of glowing illumination beckoned them to join with the surface world, beyond that of any deep dungeon return.

* * *

"Hjow do you know that we've arrived in the right land?"

The woman's innocent face still gave Luce pause, despite him knowing her for a time now.

"Because, my dear Emhild, the writing is on the wall!" Luce pointed to the life-like pictures in the alcove. The macabre-looking stone throne also caught her eye. It seemed fitting for Hel, and was even made of the same types of stone as in Winnonar. Was that to be her throne?

Guessing her thoughts, the skald replied, "Not yet, my dear. But don't worry- soon you will be seated in all your glory. And then the fun will really begin!"

Ragennar and the others fanned out to explore these new caves in which they had arrived. They were still wet from passing through the underground lake and the cavern they were in stunk of berry and rancid milk. Some strange remains of mud-like rock lay upon the floor. Just like the Cave of Mysteries in Minas-Ninona and the river cave with the heart-shaped rock in Alban, Hel had granted them travel to these new caves... this time to a Vale.

* * *

Kolveig recoiled at the pretty barmaid's question. Perhaps he *didn't want to order anything*! Just what type of a Fascist did she think he was? To continue this stupid Capitalist Charade; to Make a Proletarian Maiden his Lackey- PAH! Even if it was in a tavern!

The Karlist was shaken from his internal rant by yet another death stare from the gnome. Kolveig wasn't sure if Tepson had been more hostile lately simply because of what had happened in the Caverns Crystal or if he was only grumpy that he hadn't eaten yet. Kolveig decided that he didn't care: who could blame the Karlist for abandoning their failed initial expedition underground and the gnome along with it?

Oborren scanned the room. Had he just seen some movement out of the corner of his eye? He had of course heard many tales of this place from his other hunter contacts. Knowing that it was rumored to be haunted only heightened his usual sense of professional paranoia. After returning from the Caverns, Beneglushio had advised him and the party to stay here until the next day. He wondered what the night would have in store. And, as he glanced at his party members, he wondered what terrible things might befall them... and who he might miss.

Quiet Upon Shenbyrg's Dawning

The heady brew that the barmaid set before him brought back many memories for Tepson. He was shocked at how little this place had changed over the centuries. True, there were no longer any electric lights, but what else was different? He shook his head in frustration. It was getting to the point where he couldn't even remember what *electric lights were like* anymore! He hoped that it was just the effects of the ale.

Halfdan attempted to shift in his chair as another wave of pain-sensation washed over his body. Whoever had designed such seating was most certainly a sadist. How a straight-backed chair with hard woven supports at irregular intervals could be seen as any attempt at comfort mystified him. As he watched the I-sense and then the resulting sensations in his body, he became aware of something else. Something in the pattern of the adjoining rooms reminded him greatly of his earlier life. Perhaps this place held the pathways to different worlds *around the bend*? He wasn't sure. His eyes drifted to Elfriede again.

The Dinglesfuhrian Lady couldn't remember much of her first adventure spelunking. She did remember entering the Caverns with the gnome and cleric of course, but otherwise the rest was a blur. Elfriede was glad to meet the hunter, the sorceress, and the Odinnic. And she certainly was indebted to them for saving her—there was no telling what would have happened if she had been lost in the underworld for much longer. Still, she longed to return to Mistro soon, give him the box that Tepson had grabbed, and save her land.

Cherries sat in her seat, quite excited. Beneglushio had mentioned that a *special visitor* was supposed to be meeting the party here at the Inn! She couldn't wait to see who it was!

The pretty barmaid returned with a platter of food and drink. Most thanked her and maintained some measure of decorum, though Kolveig maintained his disdain that such Wage Slavery was occurring and Tepson maintained his disdain for having to sit at a table with Kolveig.

Suddenly, Oborren tensed himself and made for his crossbow. Even Halfdan, normally calm and meditative, methodically moved to react.

The others turned confused and looked to see what had alarmed them. A tall, muscular woman had just stridden into the tavern; a composite bow on her back, a well-used cutlass at her side. She had the bearing and Olympian armor of an amazon.

Oborren stared at her, weapon ready, though he hesitated to fire. A number of other patrons began to move their chairs away to avoid getting hit during the impending battle.

"Is that how males greet friends nowadays?" asked the amazon sardonically.

"Friends?" mocked the hunter. "Thought you would want us to just *buzz off*!" He stared at her suspiciously.

Brymanah smiled, grabbed a chair from another male patron before he sat down and joined the rest of the party at the table.

"You think I've *been changed*?" she asked amusedly.

Halfdan forced his body to relax. Though the sensations from the chair distracted him somewhat, he reached out to sense the tapestry of Consciousness around them all to see if the amazon spoke true.

"Oh goodie!" exclaimed Cherries. "I just knew the *special guest* would be someone fun! Hi Brymanah!"

"You knew that we were getting a special guest?! And you didn't TELL US!?" yelled Oborren accusingly.

Cherries quickly started sobbing; Brymanah glared at the hunter.

Quiet Upon Shenbyrg's Dawning

Kolveig spoke up: "Look at all the Gender Oppression, Oborren. Isn't it awful?"

Brymanah lunged across the table and punched the Karlist right in the face.

Tepson was glad to have the amazon back.

* * *

The evening grew late and the party was thankful to have a nice place to rest. Some had not seen a bed in days, which was normal for Oborren, but not the others. That the Inn was supposedly haunted did not bother them so much now: most had to deal with the shades of the Caverns Crystal only a day ago.

Oborren had purchased just four rooms for the group, since he did not know that Brymanah would be joining them. He was very surprised to see her at all- he assumed that she had been turned into some sort of yellow jacket mutant amazon like the rest at the Yonitarian church. Brymanah claimed that she had escaped, sought them out at Fairfacts Lordship, and that Beneglushio had sent her here. Oborren knew better than to trust someone with such a flimsy excuse.

"Cherries: your room will be with Brymanah."

The amazon nodded; the sorceress clapped her hands together and cheered.

"Tepson: you're with me."

The gnome looked at the hunter and wondered if he snored.

"Kolveig: you get *your very own room*, since you're *Such a Good Agitator.*"

The Karlist shook his head in certain agreement.

"And Elfriede: you're with-"

"Probably not wise," interrupted Halfdan.

Oborren made to protest, but then remembered the Odinnic's repellant effect on women. The hunter found it strange though that Elfriede was not repelled by Halfdan- maybe she was still possessed by some shade from the Caverns?

"Yes, right, well Elfriede: you can room with-"

Halfdan interrupted again: "I'll sleep outside." The Odinnic couldn't bear to subject the poor woman to a night with Kolveig.

* * *

The cold came over Halfdan and he shivered in the stable. Pinpricks of icy air percolated into his hands and feet as he huddled in the hay. Knowing that he was no longer a tutor and that finding suitable employ would now be difficult at best, he guessed that he might need to get used to a life of poverty after this adventure. Eschewing a bed tonight seemed like a wise idea, since he had failed at making a living of his life.

The cleric shuddered and tried to ball up his body to find some warmth. He watched the mixing of the fear of dying of hypothermia combine with the heaviness of chill and exhaustion. Tonight might be the night he finally left this strange world. He was alright with that- he would witness whatever came next in any case.

Death did not come, but he did feel a different presence though, one quite familiar and yet thus far not experienced in this life, except in dreams. Halfdan's soulmate felt closer than ever before. He wondered if it was indeed Elfriede or was something else that triggered this feeling. Perhaps he was connecting with her in this half-living state, for she dwelled in Valhalla? The sense of her kept his heart warm at least as his body struggled in the dropping temperature. He still might join her soon.

Quiet Upon Shenbyrg's Dawning

Suddenly, the sound of horses outside the stable signaled that *something* was amiss. A number of riders approached and were heading towards the Inn.

* * *

"So! Why don't you tell me again what you LIKE!"

The sorceress was giddy: it was quite exciting for her to sleep in the same room as another lady, especially one as interesting as an amazon!

Brymanah stared at the ceiling as she tried to fall asleep again. She had thought that humoring Cherries by describing her favorite color and shoe style would get her to stop talking. She was wrong.

The sorceress had also annoyingly stared at the amazon while she got changed for bed. Brymanah wondered what the hunter had put this woman up to; she doubted that Cherries had the brains to come up with such a scheme on her own.

Brymanah had to give the hunter credit for not firing upon her in the tavern earlier. Most Womyn of Stephania had now fallen to the Kernazons and hunters weren't known for their mercy to abominations. If it were possible, the Kernazons were even more hostile to males than normal amazons were. Amazons like Brymanah still needed males around for labor, doing the cooking and cleaning, as well as for breeding; the Kernazons didn't.

The amazon smiled slyly as she realized the best way to deal with the sorceress. Though intensely irritating, she felt bad for the young Womyn: if Brymanah had indeed been changed, then Oborren had sent this sorceress to her doom. The amazon figured she owed the hunter an underhanded response to his underhanded ploy.

"You know who really likes to talk?"

"Who?" asked Cherries innocently.

214

"Oborren. Why don't you go away to his room and talk to him?"

"GREAT IDEA!" exclaimed the sorceress.

And as she began to leave, Brymanah added: "Oh, and don't forget-" The amazon whispered something else in her ear.

* * *

The hunter was startled by light knocking at his door. With his crossbow out, he made to open it, but then heard a strange buzzing sound.

He whispered to Tepson across the room, but the city-slicker gnome would not awaken.

Wracking his brain for ways to kill a vespula mutant, Oborren grabbed the door handle and made ready to fire.

Throwing open the door, he was mostly glad to see it was Cherries on the other side and that he didn't shoot her. Apparently, the amazon was more clever than he had suspected, because of course, he had thought she had turned Cherries into a mutant yellow jacket amazon when she came buzzing into his room.

"*Kernazon!*" Cherries corrected.

The hunter guessed that perhaps Brymanah had not been changed after all; he doubted that Kernazons had any sense of humor. The sorceress jumped up and down on his bed.

Tepson buried his head under the pillow, but could not muffle the noise. He got up and, only in his undergarments, stared at the woman. Cherries's face turned bright red and she began backing away from the gnome. Satisfied that she was now scared into silence, Tepson went back to sleep.

To his dismay, the sound of crows could be heard outside.

Quiet Upon Shenbyrg's Dawning

"Sleeping in haunted caverns was more quiet than this!" he exclaimed.

Oborren grabbed his weapons and told the rest to do the same. He beat on the walls to alert the other party members.

* * *

The Inn was dark at this late hour. The multitude of rooms spanned in all directions, some at a slightly higher elevation, some slightly lower. The various doorways and room styles that made up the place gave it an air of otherworldly possibility. So much to be experienced in so quiet an area: no wonder some thought it was haunted.

The grim men stalked through the place. Their black and white tabards glided quietly over the floorboards, as if they were ghosts themselves. Even the short, whimpering man that they led ahead of them made little noise, as much due to the manner by which he was gagged as the secret purpose for which these dour witch hunters moved.

A dark-clad man emerged from one of the many doorways to meet their approach. His countenance and manner was not unlike them, though hunters of different specialty, they were all hunters nonetheless.

His crossbow held ready and the resolute look in his eye made any need for discussion unnecessary. Farhred knew that this lone hunter wanted to know why eight heavily-armed witch hunters were leading a condemned heretic into the Side Way Inn in the middle of the night. And Farhred knew that this hunter was either a master crossbowmen or had a number of allies hidden about the place, for he showed no fear.

The haunts of this Inn might give pause tonight for quite a show. With so many weapons and those willing to use them at hand, it would be a performance of blood. And as the life dripped from the dying, those without noble purpose might remain as well, forsaken by the Gods and trapped in this Inn.

And become ghosts themselves.

Chapter 23

Tribute to Goblins

The moon rose over the darkened Fjord. Mists flowed amongst the scattered woodlands, leaving cool blankets over whatever sleeping savage or huge beast that dwelled within. The moist scent mingled with the aroma of the wilds here, reminding the lone female traveler of sunnier times before.

Part of her wished to ride bareback and free in this land once again, but how could she? Such Horrible Atrocities committed in the name of her own land of Dinglesfuhr! She had to make Amends; no sacrifice could be too great.

Kalla did miss Gudre... and Elfriede... whatever had become of her? It wasn't the same without her friends. The former must be upset over the change that had come over Gorm and his tribe; the latter had been gone for days with Tepson and Kolveig now. And yet Kalla took solace in her *new friends*. Perhaps the Glowing Spectral Personhood would provide her Salvation and a New Family? She did have a Special Duty that could help them and help to *cleanse Dinglesfuhr forever.*

Quiet Upon Shenbyrg's Dawning

She climbed another hill. The muscles in her arms and legs ached and grew taught, though she was energized in the night air. Finally at the hilltop, she could now see their camp. Kalla remembered her instructions from Hymnir: *avoid the savage men, find the goblins. Provide them Happy Service with the Hand of Friendship so as to better Invite Them Into Our Lands.*

The Dinglesfuhrian woman had to admit that the aroma arising from below stunk. The little green-skinned humanoids with long, crooked noses danced and shouted around a large fire. It smelled of burnt mullock. Kalla realized that she probably wasn't being Sensitive enough with her assessment. A number of hulking, darker-skinned humanoids were near the center too, surrounding a bright yellow-skinned goblin. He must be their leader. She smiled at the honor of being the First Spectral Person to Offer Her Hand in Friendship.

The lone woman climbing down the hill was soon noticed by the goblins and orcs. They hooted and laughed wickedly as they closed in around her with their brutal spears drawn. She tried to remain calm and Understand Things from Their Point-of-View. The creatures noticed her rising fear and only laughed more cruelly.

The yellow goblin chieftain yelled a command and the others backed down from attacking the woman right away. He strode up and looked at her lasciviously.

"What you give us? Bring!" it ordered.

Kalla's hand shook as she removed the parchment from her pack that Hymnir had given her. The goblin snatched it from her hand and read it quickly, his eyes growing wide with greedy pleasure.

He then said something in the goblin tongue to the rest and they all began laughing inhumanly. They moved in on the woman with evil looks on their beady eyes.

220

Dan Osarchuk

As Kalla screamed in terror, she realized what 'Offering Her Hand in Friendship' to the goblins really meant.

* * *

Van Dwick rested his feet on his fine *smalltable*. He marveled at the piece of fuhrniture: finely carved from a cherry tree from somewhere in the north- Blue Mountain perhaps? He sipped his excellent Amaranthine Schnapps and looked at his neatly pressed officer's uniform that lay upon a target dummy that he had requisitioned from the Dinglesguard.

He often marveled at the greatness of Dinglesfuhr. Despite its past mistakes, it brought so many beautiful and useful things into the world.

Suddenly, he heard a heavy beating on his door. Being a trained military man, his eyes went immediately to the window and he spotted a shadow lurking by. He put down his whisky glass quickly and reached for his sabre. Thinking fast, he also pushed the uniformed dummy into the center of the room and extinguished the lantern light.

No sooner had he done so when the door burst open. Two large men entered, both dressed as nobles, but their manner and the truncheons they bore marked them as members of Mekla's Secret Police. They immediately went for the dummy, so Van Dwick moved in behind and knocked one out with the pommel of his sabre. The other turned to face him, but the Fieldmarshall was quicker and pushed the man into the window. An archer, the shadow Van Dwick had seen lurking by his window only moments before, lost his shot with the Secret Policeman now in the way.

With his enemies in disarray, Van Dwick raced out the door into the Dingleplatz. The night was late; no one else walked the streets. The Fieldmarshall, still in his nightwear, started to run to the Dinglesguard barracks. He soon heard the sound of pursuers though and looked for a shop to hide in.

Spotting the storefront of a clockmaker, the old man tried the door, but it wouldn't budge. Sprinting out of a nearby alley were three more Secret Policemen.

Van Dwick tried the door again, but the Policemen were upon him. He yelled in struggle, but they were too many and they were too strong. Restrained, the Fieldmarshall watched as Eind strode up with a smug look on his face.

"In the name of Dinglesfuhrian Security, I am placing you under Political Arrest," said the black haired man. Van Dwick glared at him.

Eind continued: "Seditious acts with a known Enemy of Underreign."

Van Dwick wished that he could warn Elfriede somehow as the men led him away. He doubted that he would ever see his niece again.

Something dark watched as the man was taken. Something dark and old and vengeful. It followed.

* * *

The great carnosaur roared when the large man leapt upon its back. With nothing but a rock in hand, the barbarian smashed the beast in the head repeatedly. The carnosaur twisted its neck to and fro, but the man was quicker and dodged away from its over-telegraphed movements.

Its roars terrified the assembled tribesfolk. Burning campfires lit their worried faces as they watched the epic battle unfold. Some bore the holy symbols of the Great Prophet Kolveig, while most didn't. Those who did, those of the Deer Watchers tribe, muttered to themselves the Mantra in support of their great leader.

222

Dan Osarchuk

"Dinglesfuhr. Powder doom. Fjord. Is it salty?"

The others belonged to other tribes, each with their own tribal totem. None seemed to have the destined faith, mantra, and fearless leader that the Deer Watchers had though- nor did they have as impressive haircuts.

Suddenly, the beast flung its head forward and then back again, hurtling the hulking barbarian onto the ground. It immediately turned and made to bite him with its massive mouth of sharp teeth.

But the barbarian was faster and held the carnosaur's bite back with his own muscular legs. Its enormous jaws pushed against him as he tensed his muscles, pinning open its mouth and sabre-like teeth from coming in contact with his exposed flesh. Then, with a quick motion, he tossed the rock down its throat. The carnosaur choked and the barbarian got up and started punching it in the muzzle.

"Good fight!" said the barbarian to the carnosaur. "I name you: 'Bitey'!"

Bitey soon collapsed and the large man lifted open its jaw in triumph. The tribesfolk cheered. Some of the children from the Deer Watchers began handing Great Prophet Kolveig pendants to the rest.

The barbarian then *crawled into the carnosaur's mouth* and the crowd grew terrified. They could see that the beast was still breathing, even if its eyes were closed. Were there no limits to this man's bravery? They waited for what seemed like eternity to see what would happen next.

Soon the barbarian reemerged, wiping Bitey's saliva off of his stylized mullet. He stood before them triumphant as he posed on top of the beast's head.

Quiet Upon Shenbyrg's Dawning

Gorm had shown the other tribes the True Path to Salvation.

He uttered the mantra: "Dinglesfuhr. Powder doom. Fjord. Is it salty?"

All those assembled repeated it with great reverence.

And then Gorm held up the rock in triumph. Just like the mantra asked, it was probably salty now. He would taste it, but he needed to give it back; he had borrowed it from Mohee.

* * *

Mekla pored over the document, even at such a late hour. For nearly a week, she had been driven to do what was necessary to have Dinglesfuhr finally make amends, once and for all. Helka and Esmerre looked on as their Frau vigorously read through the Official Changes that she felt were necessary.

Helka tried to hold back a yawn and pulled back her dark hair to see the document more clearly.

"Are you sure that these actions are fully warranted, Mein Frau?" she asked.

Mekla looked at the younger woman and smiled. "Indeed. This is just what we need to remove the Stain from our Honor!"

"But Mein Frau," said Esmerre, "won't Underreign destroy Dinglesfuhr?"

It looked now like Mekla was beginning to grow impatient. She liked Esmerre; the blonde woman looked as if she could have been her daughter. But Mekla had never had any children of her own, so she brushed aside the mental association- there was no room for Insubordination here!

"Such sentiment you express would seem quite... *Amaranthine.* Anything less than letting any number of foreign people, no matter their character, dwell in one's home and use one's possessions is the *Ultimate Evil*, of course!"

At mention of such an accusation of treason, Esmerre's face turned pale and she immediately shook her head, indicating that she was willing to go along with whatever Mekla wished.

Mekla smiled grimly as she dismissed the women and called for Eind. In a way, she felt bad for the woman and for Dinglesfuhr. Allowing in *thousands of Permanent* Visitors would certainly change her land beyond all recognition. But it had to be done, Dinglesfuhr deserved it... it *needed to be cleansed.*

She took the shiny shard that Eind had given her earlier in the week out of her desk. There was a new Traitor that he had discovered and she pondered how to best punish him. A feeling of elation came over her. All the pretty colors looked so very nice.

* * *

Cherries tried to maintain her concentration, but kept getting distracted by the ornate display in the parlor.

"There are SO MANY cool rooms here!" she whispered to Elfriede.

The Dinglesfuhrian lady rolled her eyes and glanced around the corner, broken table leg in hand. It was late and she was tired. Why had Oborren told them to come downstairs ready for trouble?

Suddenly, Tepson came peeling into the entranceway followed by two well-armed and armored witch hunters.

Elfriede stuck the table leg out and tripped one of the men. Cherries grabbed a vase, but lacked the heart to throw it at the man closer to her. The gnome looked back in dismay as the witch hunter that the sorceress had spared caught up to him and lifted him up by the scruff of his neck.

Quiet Upon Shenbyrg's Dawning

Elfriede yelled in challenge, ran at the witch hunter, but was easily knocked aside by the larger man. His companion too was getting up.

"Looks like we've caught the little runt after all!" he exclaimed.

"No way!" yelled Cherries. "He may be an icky little midget, but he's still not a runt!"

The sorceress let a blast of flame erupt from her fingers. Elfriede found it strange that the woman hadn't the heart to hit the witch hunter with a vase, but happily tried to light him on fire. She was also relieved that Cherries had the wherewithal to target the one *who wasn't holding* Tepson. To their horror though, the flame stopped within a foot of the witch hunter.

He laughed. "We are well-prepared for dealing with witches! Now it's time to die!"

The armored man thrust with his tyrsword and took Cherries in the gut. He laughed again as the red haired woman screamed in pain and doubled over, her blood dripping onto the carpeted floor.

With the other witch hunter's attention distracted by his friend's cruel act, Tepson punched him in the groin and launched himself at the one who had stabbed Cherries. Both men and even Elfriede were startled by the little man's ferocious rage, especially when he began biting off the fallen witch hunter's ear and strangling him.

The witch hunter that was still standing dropped his sword and reached for some holy water, thinking that the gnome was some sort of demon, or at least possessed by one.

Seeing an opportunity, Elfriede called for Minerva's mercy and began to help the sorely wounded Cherries out of the room. Just then, Oborren ran in and shot the standing witch hunter in the throat. The man gurgled as he fell. The hunter rushed to get bandages out of his pack. He checked the sorceress's wound and it looked grave. Oborren wondered where those confounded clerics were.

He turned as Tepson got up from the witch hunter. Not only had he strangled the man to death, but the gnome's face was covered in the witch hunter's blood and his ear was still in his mouth.

"I thought we agreed to take the witch hunters alive?" asked Oborren accusingly.

The gnome just shrugged and went over to check on Cherries. He turned his head for a moment and spit out the witch hunter's ear.

Perhaps the gnome really was a demon.

* * *

"Which way...?" Farhred's voice trailed off as Wilstrin looked at him mockingly.

"What were you going to say: 'Which way, witch?' " The prisoner laughed at his own joke. He knew the witch hunter captain might smack him again, but it felt so good to have the gag off and to make a pun.

Farhred glared at the heretic in frustration. The witch hunter captain would love to beat the witch again, but he had wasted enough time here already. Plus, he was low on men. This inn must certainly be haunted, or cursed at least, for all the many rooms were like a labyrinth, with no entrance nor exit from the building itself to be found. Farhred vowed to burn this place to the ground at his next opportunity.

How fitting, he thought, that a heretic would say that another witch would be found at this heretical place. Was this just where heretics dwelled or did Wilstrin intend for this to be a trap?

One of his remaining witch hunters spotted movement in the other room. Farhred signaled for his men to move in carefully, but when they noticed the symbols of clerics of rival Gods, they drew their tyrswords to attack.

Before their captain could give them warning, they tripped over the well-hidden rope spanned across the doorway. Both remaining witch hunters fell flat on their faces. A barbigerous cleric of Karl advanced first and smashed one of the fallen men across the back with his stylized hammer.

The other cleric, a grim, slender man bearing an Odinnic cross, hurled his spear, not at the fallen witch hunters or at their captain, but at Wilstrin. It struck the prisoner in the leg and he screamed in pain.

Farhred recognized the Odinnic from days ago in the Gaol. He stared as the man motioned for his Karlist companion to stop stabbing the fallen witch hunters with his sickle.

The Odinnic spoke: "Tend to your fallen, witch hunter; we will tend to ours."

The Karlist looked at the slender man incredulously.

"But they're Tyrants!"

It was now Halfdan's turn to stare.

"No!" insisted Kolveig, "They actually call themselves Tyr-ants!"

The Odinnic ignored the Karlist's inadvertent pun and continued, "Stop stabbing them, Kolveig, or else someone dear to us will die."

The grim cleric then turned to Farhred. "I would have a word with Wilstrin."

Chapter 24

Through the Clothing Rack

Dawn shone through the tall windows of the Side Way Inn. A pink and orange sky greeted the diners at the breakfast table. The scent of fried egg, sausage, and biscuit filled the air. Those who had made it through the night understood the moniker of the place far better now: it was certainly odd here... *and sideways.*

For all the vicious melee that had ensued the night before, neither the management nor any of the other patrons had apparently heard the ruckus or, if they did, said nothing of it. If one had told the party this fact the day before, they might have found it to be strange, but not after spending a night in this Inn. What was even stranger was that none were able to find a way out of the place during the battle. Tepson had certainly tried; he claimed the place went on for miles, simply room after room after room.

And yet the whole party had found their way back to their own guestrooms, one way or another, in the fashion that one would assume in a normal building. Cherries had been sorely wounded, but Kolveig had helped her to see that her wounds were not as bad as previously thought. The two claimed that they then spent the rest of the night discussing the wonders of the color red. That they were now sitting quite close to each other and smiling caused the others to raise their eyebrows in suspicion as to how they really spent the night.

For her part, Brymanah was still irritated that she had missed all the fighting- none of the witch hunters had come into the room where she was positioned. Still, she took some solace in discussing the battle with Elfriede. But for some reason, the Dinglesfuhrian lady was still upset over the fighting that she had experienced: Brymanah could not understand why.

Tepson also seemed troubled, though more so because his actions were *actually upsetting* in of themselves. Oborren assuaged him with the fact that adventurers often did upsetting things, even including biting off someone's ear and then strangling them to death.

Halfdan was noticeably absent from breakfast. The Odinnic had insisted that they spare the remaining witch hunters and even help tend to their wounds. It made sense to the party in the end: Cherries seemed fine now, or as much as Cherries *would seem to be fine,* and it wouldn't do to make worse enemies of the Church of Tyr than they already were.

Oborren, took this opportunity to show Elfriede the coded message that he had intercepted in Strass Hill nearly a week ago. The former scrivener confirmed for him that the 'Director in WS' was in fact the new Count, Remus.

"There are also fell things afoot in Dinglesfuhr, Oborren," she added. "We had only entered the Caverns Crystal to help save my land. A Glowing Spectral Personhood Cult is rising to power."

The hunter mused over the woman's tale. It would seem that not only the amazon lands were being corrupted by some fell influence, but Walstock and Dinglesfuhr were in danger of falling, as well. If Oborren didn't know better, it seemed that the bizarre forces of the Insolitus Novus that they had dealt with last year in the underworld and in the Schoolhouse had metastasized to other parts of the Vale. How had such a thing happened?

Oborren glanced at the assembled party. Tepson played with his food, apparently biting off the witch hunter's ear last night had ruined his appetite. Halfdan had just returned and sat next to Tepson. The group's mood lowered at the slender man's return; Cherries and Elfriede even adjusted their seats away from him. Oborren knew that those who walked the path of Odin often did so alone, but to see it occur before him, amongst those that would otherwise be considered comrades, was remarkable.

As the rest enjoyed their breakfast and chatted quietly, the hunter pondered the next course of action. Halfdan, Kolveig, and Cherries seemed almost as caricatures to him: an abstruse mystic, an anti-social socialist, and a potent sorceress with the mind of a child.

On the other hand, Elfriede, Tepson, and Brymanah seemed to be more reasonable people, after their own fashion of course, and yet had been subject to supernatural forces either recently or in the past and could not fully be trusted.

The first three could be counted on to do or say something strange, but they could also be trusted to not secretly be possessed by some underworldly shade, chromatic power to float and summon elementals, or to have some hidden Kernazon alteration. The latter could not be said for the others. How long before the party fell apart due to infighting or even some sort of nefarious betrayal?

"It appears that we have two lands that are under great threat to go with the one that has already fallen," said Oborren finally. "We might venture into Stephania to save it-". He paused and looked at Brymanah, but she shook her head: the amazon would insist that a group containing so few women would be incapable of saving her land.

"So that leaves Walstock and Dinglesfuhr," he continued. "I'd guess too that time is of the essence for with each passing day the situation in both places grows more dire. At some point, we will need to split into two groups."

"Oh I see! And what will your Enlightened Pronouncement be, oh Oppressive Party Figurehead- something Reactionary perhaps?" Kolveig grinned at his own insolence.

Cherries giggled and rubbed Kolveig's shoulders in encouragement. "Yeah! And how are people going to be able to split *into two parts*, Oborren? Even I can't do that with magic! DUH!" The sorceress smiled at the rest of the party as she pointed out what she thought was an obvious error in Oborren's statement.

Oborren sighed: he doubted that few would wish to be in Kolveig and Cherries's group anyway.

"Well," chimed in Elfriede, "I would of course wish to return to my home in Dinglesfuhr. I'm sure that I wouldn't be welcome back in Walstock anyway."

"But your knowledge of the County Castle would be invaluable for our infiltration of-"

"I will go with the Dinglesfuhrian and the gnome male," interrupted the amazon. "I would insist on being in a group of only Womyn, but in this case," she glanced at Cherries who was now making googly eyes at Kolveig, "the gnome is less man enough to be acceptable."

At this the gnome smashed his fist onto the table and his face turned bright red.

"Now let's remain calm..." Oborren reminded.

"Oh yes," said Kolveig, "and let's make sure not to *bite anyone else's ear off!*"

Dan Osarchuk

Tepson turned his fury on the Karlist and flung a fork at him. It missed by a few inches and imbedded itself in the wall.

"That could have hit SOMEONE... LIKE ME!" yelled Cherries.

"And your aim is off, little man" scoffed Brymanah, "leave the missile weapons to the Womyn."

"Yeah! Stick to using your teeth!" mocked the Karlist.

Tepson had enough. He stood up and prepared to *use his teeth on Kolveig*.

A clicking sound brought the assembled party members' attention back to Oborren. The hunter had his crossbow out and pointed directly at Tepson. The gnome turned pale and sat down. Cherries and Kolveig made to make another obvious observation and cruel jest, but then Oborren pointed his weapon at them. They sat down too.

Now that he had the party's full attention, Oborren decided how they would be split. He had hoped to make the most tactically prudent assignments, but he settled on ones that might just prevent those within each group from killing each other before they even got to the land that they were supposed to save.

* * *

Dazzling light shown through the shopping mall windows. New clothing and shoes were laid in straight, shiny rows and smelled of impending purchase. Little Em danced between the clothing racks, smiling and playing hide-and-go-seek with her imaginary friends, straying from her Ma a little while she was shopping, but always returning back to keep her just in sight. The sanitized department store music played from somewhere in the ceiling firmament above, keeping both adult shoppers and child tag-alongs cheery and enlivened.

Quiet Upon Shenbyrg's Dawning

The spirited joy of young Em was hard to assuage. She remained full of energy and one with life- even a trip to a *boring clothing store* could be such fun! All the clerks smiled at her antics and she couldn't wait to return to her loving family in Rochester. She even had begun to have dreams of some gentle boy that she knew she would marry one day, when they both became grown up! All seemed perfect, easy, and free.

Sometimes little Em would notice scary things in the dark- but not today: the brilliant sunlight outside made even the shadows of this place seem harmless, muted, and even a little entertaining. Where could she crawl into next? What would the look be on Ma's face when she jumped out at her from the $1.99 sale rack?

And this time would be *something special.* She usually only counted to *three potatoes* before surprising her smiling mom. But what if she waited until *five potatoes* or went even higher? That would really be a surprise!

So she found one rack up ahead of where Ma was shopping and dove in. *This should be great!* She crouched down in the dark clothes and got ready to count. Something felt strange though, like the fears she had in the dark in the closet of her room. Em was just about to leave and find her mom right away, but one of her imaginary friends, Snaffles, insisted that surprising her mom would be more fun.

So Em started to count to herself quietly in happy anticipation: "One potato, two potato, three potato...."

Even though the rack was full of clothes, the young girl noticed that things were becoming even darker. Getting a little scared now, she began to count even faster, "... seven potato, eight potato, nine potato..."

But it had become almost pitch black in the rack! She was getting really spooked! So young Em finished up and pushed through the clothing, nearly in tears. The store was much darker now and no one was there. She ran around, screaming for her mommy, but she couldn't find her. Even the clerks were gone. The place felt *icky too*, all dirty, and there was even this little black flying thing buzzing against the window. She had never seen anything like it before.

What happened?

Sobbing and terrified that she had done something terribly wrong, Em leapt back into the clothing rack and asked her imaginary friends what to do.

Snaffles said that *he had gone on* and Luna, her other imaginary friend, said that *Em should go on too*. Not understanding what they meant, she began hysterically counting again: "fourteen potato, fifteen potato, sixteen potato..."

Something was happening outside the clothing rack again. This time, it was getting lighter, but also colder too. After about thirty potatoes, she crawled out again to see that the entire store was gone. The clothing rack she thought she was in looked just like a bush now. Em couldn't believe her eyes. She gazed back at the city of Rochester in the distance and it looked all smashed and ruined.

Too stunned to cry, the young girl wandered towards the distant ruins. She heard strange howls in the distance, but luckily they remained far away. It was getting cold. Eventually, a kind couple spotted the blonde girl wandering and brought her back to their home with them.

There she grew up in a small village. It was strange: no electric lights, no TV shows, and no nice clothes from the mall. The people lived by farming and herding. Raiders, both man and orc, would come out of the ruins of Rochester to pillage the village or fight each other- but the villagers didn't call it Rochester; they had no idea what it used to be like. And they called this land 'Minas-Ninona', which was part of something called 'Vinland'. It certainly was different. How long had she been in the clothing rack? And why did this world seem so hard?

Em missed her mom and dad terribly. All that remained were her imaginary friends and she spoke to them often. They would tell her all sorts of strange things- that she had even traveled to another world by accident, to a time in the future even! This world was certainly darker. Perhaps not as dark as when she had first emerged from the clothing rack, but certainly darker than the world that she knew with her parents, the world where she belonged.

This world had a *sense of magic* though, which made things exciting, if not scary. Her imaginary friends were louder and more real than ever before and it made the other villagers talk about her in whispers. Em also had trouble fitting in, because she was certainly *different* than the other children, being from another world and another time and all, whether she let them know her beliefs about it or not.

* * *

An older Emhild allowed herself to readjust to the change in place. All places had a feeling to them, a sense. Something far and over and beyond what could be described by their constituent parts. At least this trip was not as jarring as when she had first entered this world as a young girl.

Anyone could feel that difference if they just took the time to notice. But most folk were too occupied by their family or their friendships or their happiness to really become aware of it. Em had lacked most of those things for most of her life here in Vinland, so it was easy for her to notice. But she could remember the wonderful feeling she had as a child *in her real home-* she longed to feel it again.

Strangely though, Em did feel some of that joyful feeling in this new place. The caverns here looked just as dark and foreboding as in Alban or in Minas-Ninona for that matter. Luce had told her to say 'Hjalf moon to hjalf moon' in her prayer this time. Em wasn't sure why that would take her any closer to the world where she had lost her mother, but she felt it nevertheless.

Luce smiled as he took in the view of the underground lake. He nudged the strange remains of something warped and dead that littered the cave floor.

"It's good to be home again!" the skald declared.

Ragennar, the druid, and Gaeswyn looked at him as if he were mad.

"My Dróttinn, hjow could ya say that: this is not Minas Ninona!" said the rust-bearded warrior.

"The a-leys took us a-far," commented the Druid.

Ragennar stared at the Celt to decipher the riddle he spoke. Luce only smiled wider and turned his attention to Gaeswyn.

"Did you enjoy your trip, my lady?"

"Didn't even know we a-took one," said the voluptuous redhead bluntly. "Just thought we were taking a-dip in t'river."

"Indeed," said the skald, "but your unique abilities will be an immense help to us nonetheless."

Some of the Norse warriors began to yell out in alarm, something about dark spirits floating upon the walls. Luce feigned surprise, but Emhild saw that the skald was up to something.

"Another sacrifice to Hjel? Do ya hjave ta?" asked the Helan queen bitterly.

"Not this time," said Luce with a surprising degree of mercy. "*We don't have* someone blessed by a chthonic Dinglesfuhrian deity, but *we do have* the next best thing."

Luce smiled at Gaeswyn. She sighed and closed her eyes.

A strange sense fell over those assembled. Even the shades seemed affected and they parted for the Norse group to pass.

* * *

The Nuttens loomed larger as the *snoollab* fleet decreased its altitude. Commissar Navi smiled gruesomely at the display of hot air balloons, envelopes colored crimson red, each marked with a golden hammer and sickle symbol within a black inverted pentagram shape. The red dwarf spat upon the trees below, his spittle dark and full of bile from his rotten teeth. He adjusted his black captain's hat marked in the same fashion as the balloons. The dwarf then inspected a small cannon that was mounted to his snoollab's gondola.

"We are nearly to our destination, Commissar," said one of the other dwarves. He had a red breastplate, unlike Navi's olive drab trench coat, and also wore a red barbute helm. His armor and bearing marked him as a warrior and an officer.

"That is Currently Acceptable, Comrade Iruy."

The commissar didn't even glance at the other dwarf, even though Iruy must have been of high rank. Instead, Navi's attention was focused entirely on the bends of the Shenbyrg River in the distance and the large town that lay just beyond it.

Chapter 25

Hospitalia

The great tower of Mistro gleamed white in the distance. Gathering clouds played upon the wind, swirling together, bringing the promise of impending rain. The three travelers tramped down High Street; three travelers that did not seem to be like that of the normal local folk. Their footfalls echoed slightly upon the walls of the decorated homes that lined the road. Oktoberfest was approaching.

"Swilling beer and decorating pumpkins?! How on earth would that help in Redistributing Wealth?" said Kolveig.

He glared at the villagers. The villagers stared back at the obviously armed and insignia-bearing Karlist as the party passed by on their way into downtown Walstock. Halfdan doubted that the villagers would be accepting of *this Diogenes,* even if this were an Olympian town.

The Odinnic said nothing. What was the use in arguing with a Karlist about the merits of Oktoberfest? The slender man simply pulled his own cloak tighter. He readied himself to ward off any impending precipitation or notice from the Watch.

Quiet Upon Shenbyrg's Dawning

"Oh, don't be SILLY- pumpkins are PRETTY! Ha hah ah hah HA!" said the sorceress.

Halfdan would sometimes wonder at what sort of sacrifice Cherries made for having such great and obvious magical powers. No magic came easy, otherwise all would perform it. The sorceress seemed to bear no disfigurement, ill luck, or disturbing presence. He might be baffled that she suffered no mishap for her brazen use of sorcery. Then she would open her mouth.

The sorceress's skintight red uniform did as little to distract notice as her loud laughter. A number of local older youths began to move into the street.

Recognizing that a few could be former pupils, Halfdan drew his hood well over his face, leaving only his whiskered mouth to be seen. Some of the youths were even larger than him; such a run-in might be worse than that with the Watch.

"Hey pretty lady," said one of the youths. The young man wore overalls but no shirt or shoes even on such a cold day as this. Halfdan counted seven of them. Cherries and Kolveig seemed to be oblivious to the impending threat.

"I said, 'HEY PRETTY LADY'!" The youth was beginning to show more open hostility. Halfdan readied his spear, the head of which was cleverly hidden beneath a rag so that it appeared as a simple walking stick.

"Having 'Pretty Pumpkins' is no excuse! How could decorative gourds possibly Counteract the Devastating Effects of Bourgeois Privilege?!" Kolveig looked at one of the youths as he spoke, as if what the Karlist said was obvious to any passer-by.

"But they are PRETTY! How could you say anything else?" Cherries seemed to be getting upset at Kolveig's insinuations regarding the matter.

"I SAID, 'HEY-"

240

Halfdan cut the youth short by pointing his now exposed spear right at the young man's chest.

"We heard what you said," whispered the Odinnic grimly, "now it's time you were on your way."

The youths looked at the slender man and sized-up the situation. He seemed physically weak, but mentally resolute. Kolveig and Cherries were still arguing, but were also beginning to gaze at each other amorously in the midst of it.

"*YOU are* a Silly Willy anyway!" she said teasingly.

"Why would you say that?" said Kolveig in reply as he stared deeper into her eyes. He strode towards her, almost as if under a spell.

Suddenly, they embraced and began kissing intensely and groping each other in most affectionate ways.

The youths rolled their eyes and moved away, snickering.

Halfdan hoped that Kolveig and Cherries wouldn't take too long: they all had a mission to complete.

* * *

The cell door slammed shut. And as much as Sister Aelstad tried to comfort her, Carsanna began crying. Both priestesses had their frocks torn, though unlike Carsanna, Aelstad's didn't reveal any bare flesh, no matter how many times the 'new guards' had attacked her. Having the quality of never being able to be unclad was one of the many benefits of being blessed by Minerva.

"You must turn from your lusty ways." Aelstad's sympathy for Carsanna was genuine, even if her tone was condescending.

"They're coming back!" hissed Sigismund from the cell across from them. Apparently, the new management of the Gaol, now renamed 'the Gaolag', saw fit to have male and females housed in the same area, though they remained in separate cages.

Ms. Candun was still busy trying to fashion a makeshift knife from the materials that she had lifted from their gruel breakfast. She hurried as the guards approached.

"It's no use!" warned Freundel from the male cage. "They'll check our cells after they're done abusing us again!"

Ms. Candun looked back at the deposed witch hunter and glared. She realized though that he was probably right. The Hounds of Vigilance had thrown all of them in the Gaol for simply refusing to attend a Mandatory Required Townhall Meeting in the name of R'ti. Their captors could apparently get away with whatever they wanted!

Deep laughter resounded from outside the cells. A large, unpleasant man, accompanied by two others that were nearly as large and unpleasant, cracked his knuckles and licked his lips. Carsanna, Aelstad, and Sigismund averted their eyes in terror. Freundel and Candun stared at the new guards defiantly.

Brotus, Burb, and Ivnok stared back at the new inmates.

"Remember that one?" Brotus pointed out Freundel to his friends. "He used to come around here, *all high and mighty*, when WE were locked up!"

Burb and Ivnok laughed wickedly and spun their billie blubs.

"Kill 'em now?" spat Ivnok.

"Not yet," conceded Brotus, "Count says: 'no killing until after trial', but he never said we can't have some more fun!"

All the prisoners felt their fear rise with the brutes entering the cells, though some let it show more than others.

* * *

Dan Osarchuk

"Someone will be right with you."

Kolveig glared at the nursemaid; he and the others had already been waiting for over an hour. Even those who sought the healing of Karl didn't have to wait this long: either they were a *good Karlist* and were healed, or they weren't- there was no waiting to find out!

The Karlist rang the nursemaid's bell repeatedly again. She strode over, stared at him, and then snatched the bell away. Intensely irritated, Kolveig returned to his seat.

Cherries was raptly interested in a child's play toy; Halfdan looked to be meditating. Kolveig couldn't decide what was more irritating: the sorceress's giggling or the Odinnic's silence.

"We need to *do something,*" Kolveig whispered as he noticed another Hospitalier walking by the area.

Halfdan opened his eyes; Cherries put down her toy.

"We're supposed to get inside first," reminded Halfdan.

"Obviously, Opiate of the Masses, but it's taking too long," countered the Karlist.

Halfdan wondered at the state of medicine in the current era. As a boy, before his final trip *around the bend*, in what could now be called the Time of the Ancients, people went to the doctor to get better. It apparently involved receiving some sort of lollypop after a man in a white jacket checked one's ears, throat, and heartbeat. In the current day, healing was usually the province of Asclepius or of his father Apollo, at least amongst the Olympians. The Norse didn't have Gods as specialized in healing, though the love of Freya and the clear inspiration of Odin, as well as other divinities, could certainly be effective.

But the Cult of the Shield Ghul that had set up in Walstock was entirely a different matter. They seemed to care not for the patient's overall well-being like Asclepians or Freyans did, nor did they guide the patient towards a greater sense of awareness like Odinnics, such as he. In fact, even though the Shield Ghul was apparently some sort of supernatural being, who would help the worthy rip out, burn away, or simply ignore that which was unwell in a person, the Hospitalia seemed to lack any sense of spirituality at all.

To Halfdan, it was obvious that the Shield Ghul was really a Demon Lord, similar in manner and purpose to R'ti. The 'worthy' had something called 'Assurance', which came from some Byzantine arrangement of payments that were only less inordinate than those who didn't have it. That its servants would provide so little to its patients for so high a price, especially those without 'Assurance', and only after so long a wait made that fact as obviously as the lack of spiritual presence in this apparent house of healing.

There was a New Initiative made lately by the Count so that all townsfolk could get Assurance. Of course, to do so, the Count simply *forced them to buy it*. Such demonic arrangements often destroyed not only the financial well-being of those forced to live under their control, but their spiritual well-being, as well.

Becoming impatient with both the musing Odinnic and the tardy nursemaid, Kolveig then said quite unsecretively, "The next guard should be by *in less than 10 minutes! We need to get INSIDE THE SURGEON'S ANNEX NOW!*"

With that last statement, the Karlist's whisper nearly turned into a yell. The other patients looked at him confused.

To assuage their fears, Cherries spoke up. "Oh don't mind him: he's *just a Sly Talker!*" she said playfully, turning her eyes back at Kolveig.

"How dare you!" He smiled in return.

The other patients rolled their eyes as the Karlist and the sorceress leapt into each other's arms. They then averted their eyes and covered their ears while the two became very romantic.

Halfdan realized that the guards had the perfect distraction now.

* * *

"Oh!" said the village woman passing by on Main Street, "can I see *the adorable child*?"

The tall, strong-looking mother bit her lip, shook her head, and stared at the woman.

After a moment of awkward silence, she finally explained, "The... young... male is unconscious."

"Oh! But just one little peak?"

Before the mother could respond, the village woman rushed over and looked beneath the cover of the *kinderwagon* in which the apparent child lay.

She gasped. "That certainly is a large baby!" She looked at the mother for a reply.

Finally, the mother said, "Yes."

After a few more moments, the village woman moved away and nodded to the mother. She seemed uncomfortable, but the mother simply ignored her and pushed the buggy towards the County Castle. In the distance, the sound of an alarm could be heard. Watchmen and Hounds of Vigilance stopped and stared at a strange, flickering box mounted outside the Castle walls for a moment and then began running in that direction.

Undeterred, the mother continued pushing the buggy through the Castle Gate; the guards seemed too distracted to notice. The wheels of the kinderwagon groaned a little, hinting at the weight of the baby inside.

* * *

Drenart looked down at the couple and was unsure what to do next. There were still a few patients remaining- not all of them had fled outright upon seeing so obviously amatory a situation, but all were disturbed. To make matters worse, the Hospitalier couldn't easily lance just one of the two love-birds, because their bodies were too closely enrapt around each other.

"The Hospitalia is only for patients with *actual afflictions!*" he ordered finally.

The sorceress and the Karlist did not seem intimidated by the reminder. In fact, they only began kissing and caressing each other more passionately. The remaining patients groaned in despair as the Karlist began to remove his jacket. The Hospitalier continued to glare at them.

The sorceress said finally, "We do have an affliction- our hearts have *merged into one!*"

At this, the patients groaned even louder: as if seeing Kolveig in his undershirt was bad enough, the sappiness of Cherries was unbearable. Despite having what looked like serious injuries and virulent diseases, the remaining patients got up and hobbled out of the waiting room.

Drenart's face was visibly growing red, despite the barbute helm that he wore. Sighing in resignation, he unslung his lance from his back and pondered which direction to stab the couple. It was an unusual situation for him; he had only lanced one victim at a time thus far. As the Hospitalier readied the section behind his lance's vamplate, he hoped that he would be able to stab and exsanguinate them both before the Karlist had a chance to take his pants off.

The lovers kept shifting around though, so the Hospitalier had to readjust the angle of his impending lance strike. Halfdan felt an impulse to warn his friends, but he knew that they barely listened to him even when they were not so romantically distracted.

Thinking quickly, he grabbed a chair and smashed Drenart across the back, knocking him out before he was able to pierce Kolveig through the backside. The two love-birds didn't even seem to notice. Halfdan was also pleased that the Karlist's pants still remained on.

The Odinnic then strolled into the Surgeon's Annex and yelled for reinforcements- that the waiting room was under attack. A guard responded and Halfdan reentered the room. He braced himself against the wall.

More guards and Hospitaliers rushed into the waiting room. Their attention was fully taken by the dazed body of Drenart and the inappropriately amorous bodies of Kolveig and Cherries on the floor.

Seeing that the Surgeon's annex was now unguarded, Halfdan held a clear mind for his friends and slipped inside.

A long, sterile hallway greeted the cleric. Quiet groaning sounds of the ill and the wounded behind the many doors suggested further that this was not a true place of healing. Halfdan could hear yelling coming back from the waiting room: he guessed that Cherries and Kolveig didn't have much time before they were overwhelmed.

Suddenly, Halfdan noticed a serpent symbol upon a door to the left. He recognized it as the mark of C'ps, Demon Lord of Child Snatching. If only I had my spear, he thought. Taking the initiative, he burst open the door to find a gaggle of children, from very young to nearly adolescent inside. No adults were in the room, only a picture of a C'ps Cultist reminding them to 'Be Free In The Liberation From Your Parents!'

Growling, the Odinnic broke open the window, instructed the older children to see the others home, and helped them escape. No sooner had he passed the last child through the window, when a very stern and sterile woman entered the room, clad in C'ps dress.

"Child-stealer!" she screamed.

The Odinnic stared at her; she hesitated, but then hissed and charged him with a dagger. He nearly challenged the woman over her hypocrisy, but remembered it was usually pointless to engage Cultists in debate. Instead, Halfdan knocked the weapon out of her hand and flung her into the wall. He grabbed a R'ti long-ruler on his way out, hand bleeding freely now from the woman's attack.

"Stop and face My Fell Lord's Wrath, or Else Your Own Children Shall Be Taken From You!" she screamed.

Ignoring her curse, Halfdan rushed back into the waiting room, only to bump into a guard. Cherries, barely clad now, had just lit a Hospitalier on fire and was cackling madly about how they would all burn bright cherry red.

"You're all just PAINS IN THE ASS!" she giggled.

Kolveig was in worse shape. He was being held fast by two Hounds of Vigilance with another Hospitalier ready to lance him through the heart.

The Odinnic leapt forward and batted the lance aside with his long-ruler at the last moment, causing the Karlist to only be struck through the shoulder. Kolveig screamed in pain, but the Hound of Vigilance directly behind him sputtered and moaned as the lance struck him through the heart instead. Halfdan twirled around and pushed the stunned Hospitalier onto his back, ducking out of the way just before Cherries ignited the remaining Hound behind Kolveig.

Halfdan wondered how much of her mind Cherries had lost to turn her into a semi-clad pyromaniac. Using her powers moreso certainly wouldn't help.

Chapter 26

The Disruption of Towns

The humans were particularly foolish here. Even their females failed to create any sort of protection for their hive. They simply walked in and out of the great white structure without even a guard posted to sting interlopers.

Poy received the telepathic signal of her Queen and watched as her Sisters received it too. Some remnant resistance to her lack of specialness might have stirred, but that element of the former amazon simply melted away. Yes, Poy and Jeg were the ones who had brought the colony into Stephania. First they had brought the blessing to the other Dames, then to the amazons as a whole. The old Poy might have felt famous and self-important for such an amazing change to her homeland, but she was simply part of the hive now. She did her duty; it was for the Hive's collective good, and it was glorious.

Gwyre stood next to her in the same attack group. The formerly chatty Matron now buzzed instead; her eyes showed alien and her stinger stood ready. Poy was pleased that her transformation was nearly complete.

Quiet Upon Shenbyrg's Dawning

The Queen then signaled it was time to attack. Her Sisters released their scent and moved in to strike the humans. Some were even specially blessed with flight now. Poy glanced up as Jeg soared by, part of wing of Sisters to spearhead the attack from above. Poy was not so blessed by her queen with that ability yet, but she knew it was all part of the Queen's perfect plan for the overall benefit of the Hive.

As the humans began to run and scream inside their 'University', something from her former life began to arise within Poy. But unlike her sense of self-importance, this feeling was now encouraged by the Queen's telepathic presence. Dim memories arose of her former life as a Dame, one where she had harmed males for one reason or another, where she had enjoyed it greatly. That old self charged her with greater power now. She and her group buzzed and rushed in, a frenzied assault in the name of the Queen and the Hive.

What could be called 'fervent glee' intensified as her multi-faceted eyes selected multiple targets to attack at once. Though the old Poy might be startled at the physical changes that she had undergone, she would have also marveled at her new capability to inflict pain and single-minded purpose to win.

A group of humans screamed when they spotted her group. The aroma of their terror made her heart beat faster in increasing expectancy. Vital fluids rushed to her lower abdomen, readying her stinger.

She leapt up in expectation and planted it in one human who had stumbled. The feeling was ecstatic. Her sting would give males painful death and give females the honor of becoming her Sisters too: Sisters of the Hive. The woman below her began to foam at the mouth and turn various shades of yellow and black. Poy smiled at her new Sister-to-be as she stung her again and again.

The other Kernazons had found their marks too. Humans were falling in droves: attacked from both on the ground and above.

Dan Osarchuk

Some had made it into the building to hide behind their false-human goddess. The fallen lay screaming; for the males, it would be their last. For the females, their screams would soon become buzzes, buzzes that would grow into perfect harmony with the shimmering colorful light that led Poy and the others- the scintillating light of the Queen.

* * *

Luce smiled as yet another warlord stumbled into Emhild's room. The stench of that good old *Maurian Whiskey* and *Strassmen's Beast* on his breath brought a sense of nostalgia to the skald. The burly warlord could barely find his way inside he was so inebriated. What was his name: Egelbert? Luce knew that he wouldn't be inebriated for much longer.

The minstrels at the bar below continued to play their joyous tune. Luce had bribed them to play especially loudly and only the Ancient Classics, so as to drown out the gurgling and screaming sounds of the warlords when they perished above. And hearing such songs as *Visuals Killed the Banjo Star* only made it better.

The skald had to admit that the Strass Hotel was still a fine establishment for the current Age. The well-carved wood railings, delicious food, pretty hostesses, and strong drink were quite exceptional. It had remained so even after Lights Out. Of course, being now populated by vikings, it had a sort of barbaric feel to it- maybe something akin to the Old West, but with nasal helms and axes, rather than cowboy hats and firearms.

The skald adjusted his yellow hat and looked at his own glass of bourbon. He smiled as he swirled the liquid around gently, showing orange and amber in the lantern light. The deep aroma of fine liquor arose. Luce listened for perhaps another fight or grievance to break out: such Norse places of alcohol consumption were notorious for such things- but he could hear no specific brawls occurring at the moment. All of the local warlords had been invited to partake of the new lady in town and nearly all of them had responded. Those who arrived were now either dead or patiently waiting their turn.

What a wonderful blessing Em was, thought Luce. First Winnonar, then Alban, and now here: the wanton lust of those men who were in power proved to be their own undoing. One little snuggle with the cute blonde nursemaid from Minas-Ninona and that would be their last!

Part of him worried slightly for the poor woman who had been made to lower herself to the role of inadvertent courtesan-assassin. Luce wondered that all this death might make Em want to die, as well. He quickly laughed it off with yet another song: "*Like a low-cost diversion for a new matinee...*"

He stopped his Ancient melody when he heard a manly shriek and then a thud. Another victim- marvelous!

And yet, not all the warlords had responded to the skald's generous invitation. A few followed Tyr and were barred from gratuitous intercourse. Others had wives who were fearsome enough to prevent such dalliances even when the Gods didn't.

It didn't really matter though, conceded Luce. With most of the Strass warriors now leaderless, they would be compelled to flock to the Helan banner. The Minas-Ninonans might look and sound somewhat different than the Strass Hillians, but they were all Norse in the end and they respected a powerful leader. The remaining warlords would fall by their axes and swords, if they didn't fall in line.

And having the new allies from Shenendehowa, Gaeswyn and the Druid, would allow him to deal with any unforeseen circumstances that might arise.

Then the end would come soon. Luce could hardly wait.

* * *

Dan Osarchuk

Gottschalk and the other Dinglesfuhrians rested outside the mine entrance. The sun had grown high in the sky, bringing much needed warmth and light to the tired miners. Granted, work in this salt mine was not as bad as in others: they simply brought up the salty water from far below for it to dry here on the *sunledge*. And it helped that it was so beautiful today: a clear blue sky over the rusted orange and green woodlands below.

Gottschalk had heard of other places where salt miners were *actually slaves* who had to work with solid blocks of salt. The effect of that much salt on one's vital humors must have been devastating. Not so here. Still, it was tiring work, no matter how well they were paid. He had heard the mine's owner grumble about how much it had cost him on more than one occasion. Apparently, he would have preferred to use slaves, but few Dinglesfuhrians would allow themselves to be lowered so.

The appearance of a hand on the ledge drew the miners' attention. They rushed over and saw that it belonged to a lightly clad woman. Her fairly tanned skin, primitive garb, and sinewy muscles showed her to be one of the savages of Fjord Vallee. The Dinglesfuhrians hurried to put a blanket over her after she climbed upon the sunledge- as much to keep her warm as to maintain the Dinglesfuhrian decorum that her land lacked.

The woman's smile at the gesture filled Gottschalk with joy, but he soon noticed more hands appearing around the ledge. Rumors were that *the Krampus* haunted this area, he might have human-looking hands, one could never be too careful! Whether it was some stag-headed monster or not, Gottschalk knew how valuable the salt mine was to any sort of adversary. He notified his men to retreat back into the mine when he saw that it was yet more human savages moving onto the sunledge. They didn't seem nearly as peaceful as the first female one that had arrived.

Though the miners attempted to retreat, the savages were quicker. They howled and shook their hands at the

Dinglesfuhrians. Gottschalk noticed that they all bore strange pendants around their necks and had mullet haircuts. Perhaps they were some kind of fanatics?

"Arm yourselves!" he shouted to his men.

The savages began to back up as the Dinglesfuhrians grabbed their picks and shovels. Seeing that they were now gaining the upper hand, the miners lunged at the Fjord Vallee folk menacingly and the savages continued their retreat.

Suddenly, a huge savage leapt up from below the ledge. Unlike the others, he was solidly built and bore a great axe. One of the miners charged him with a pick, but the large savage was faster and whacked him with the flat side of his weapon. The other savages cheered and rushed the miners in increased vigor, as well.

Gottschalk and two others made it to the mine entrance before the rest were overwhelmed. He prayed to Hades that they could hold off the savages at the narrow entrance until help arrived. The savages rushed forward with reckless abandon regardless; one nearly got his teeth knocked out by one of the miner's shovels.

With almost a religious fervor, the savages dragged the other two miners out of the entrance screaming, but Gottschalk kicked and pummeled the rest. He had never seen the local savages act this aggressively before: what had come over them?

Standing alone now, Gottschalk tried to decide whether to take his chances deeper in the mine without a lantern or to make his stand here. He held his shovel out like a spear to keep the savages at bay, but the large one with the axe strode in and knocked his shovel aside with ease.

He grabbed the miner by the shirt, pulled him closer, and said conspiratorially, "Me not want to hurt you. But this mine: is it SALTY!?"

Dan Osarchuk

* * *

"I Love Ye Too Much to Argue!" said the scrivener. She shut the door on the irate townsfolk.

Remus smiled; the new scrivener seemed skilled with using R'ti Terminology and how to Correctly Handle Pupils' Parents. She also seemed to be a good replacement for Elfriede.

"Hope they didn't give you too much trouble," joked the Count. "Those parents can sometimes get a little emotional when we make their progeny Swear Obeisance to the Holy Ways of R'ti in Cult Class each morning. "

The receptionist smiled back. "It was easy," she beamed, "and don't worry, I kept track of who they were so the Order of C'ps can Rescue their Progeny from Them."

"Good," agreed Remus, "those Pupils shouldn't have to Grow-Up So Unenriched by Their Own Families." He strode off to the lavatory- the day was starting to look good.

The Count nodded to a female guard as he entered. He found it strange, he hadn't noticed her before: she must be new. He shrugged and strode inside.

Gentle harp music played while a very short, uniformed servant took his jacket. He looked new too- must be all the extra tax revenue that allowed for these new hires. The Count was glad that they at least got someone who was a Powerful Female and another who was Height Impaired.

A fine aroma of potpourri mingled with the cleansing flow of air provided by the servant's fan. The Lavatory of the Count's Quarters was a more pleasant place than even the best room in most townsfolk's homes. Remus smiled at Progress At Work.

Quiet Upon Shenbyrg's Dawning

The Count entered a stall marked with his noble seal and shut the privy door. As he sat down for his Countly relief, he heard the sound of footsteps entering the lavatory.

"I hope that's not one of our Most Precious Pupils!" he said trying to adjust his view to see past the crack in the privy door, while still sounding pleasant. "There is a Pupil Lavatory downstairs!"

No response came from the mysterious lavatory intruder. Remus craned his neck to see if the uniformed servant would do something about it, but it looked like he was now using the stall adjacent to his! Then the Count realized who had entered the lavatory: the new female guard!

Rising confusion and anger caused the Count to ready himself for trouble. It dawned on him that he knew neither of these two and this could be an attempt on his life by Anti-Schoolhouse Forces! He leaned down to pull an ornate dagger from out of his boot.

Suddenly, he got the distinct feeling that he was being watched. Remus turned his head and noticed that the very short uniformed servant was leaning over the stall wall next to him!

Before the Count could react, the gnome hit him on the head with a pickhammer.

* * *

"That Count is getting too big for his britches!"

Out in the County Castle courtyard, the townsfolk gathered. They were furious.

"The nerve of that R'ti Cult! They force us to pay for the Schoolhouse, then they force us to send our children there!" said another.

258

"And even they threaten to take our children away if we don't let them take that Glory of R'ti and Its Enlightened Perfection Cult class! Is this education or is it indoctrination?"

The townsfolk were becoming even more irate. Apparently having their children spend the night at the Schoolhouse yesterday without their parents' permission had been the final straw. Since most of the Count's guards and Hounds of Vigilance were still away dealing with a disturbance at the Hospitalia, only a handful of watchmen approached the impending riot.

In the near distance, a number of bright red hot-air balloons could be seen floating in the sky. Their large envelopes showed in contrast to the scenic purple-blue Nutten Mountains behind.

The balloons approached upon the breeze; the people began to forget their anger and started to smile. Some even clapped their hands in excitement. That the balloons clearly bore the mark of Helltowne did not seem to disturb the townsfolk, strangely enough.

One of the nearer ones soon drifted low and smashed into a house upon a hill. The roof was torn asunder and those inside screamed in terror. Some ran out to confront the pilots, but an explosion rang out from one of the mounted cannons onboard, slaying the survivors.

More balloons neared the Castle now. The townsfolk could see the armored Helltowne dwarves and men in the gondolas. A Watchman strode up and waved at them. The Helltowners laughed and chatted to each other in their backyard-sounding language. They trained their cannons on the assembled Walstockers, who simply smiled back and waved.

"It's very hard to control those balloons, you know," commented the Watchman. "Even though they smashed a house- it can't be helped right now. I'm sure they'll pay for it later."

Quiet Upon Shenbyrg's Dawning

Now clear of the Castle walls, the hot-air balloons began their descent. Some dropped faster than the dumbfounded and beaming townsfolk could get out of the way. And, as some of their friends were crushed beneath, the Walstockers finally began to realize that something was wrong.

The dismounting squads of Helltowne red dwarves and human soldiers pulled out firearms, an oddity in this time and day. They began firing indiscriminately at the townsfolk, laughing as any who were still standing broke and ran. Many were stomped beneath the iron nailed boots of the soldiers or had their brains dashed out by the iron stocks of their ruthless firearms. Even the Watchman fell in the smoke and chaos before he could make more excuses for their reckless flying.

Some huge balloons began to descend also, though these released chains that the already disembarked Helltowners caught and guided in directly to land. One held a large, armored bear in a cage; another, some sort of wheeled train loaded with coal.

Yet more hot-air balloons continued to descend on the east side of town, smashing into house, field, and smiling gawker alike. The Helltowners had no idea that the Walstockers would be so naïve to the threat they posed.

Any concerns over effective resistance by the townsfolk were obviously over-inflated. Most of these people had already been Disrupted by R'ti and the other Cults.

* * *

Snik Snak shoved the note in Kalla's face. "Tell me what it says! What it SAYS!"

The weeping, battered woman read it over grimly and handed it back to the yellow goblin chief.

"All Visitors will be welcomed tomorrow. Prepare your people. Dinglesfuhr will be cleansed."

260

The yellow goblin chieftain beamed and readied his orcs and goblins. They were now officially invited guests. It was time to take advantage of the stupid humans- by killing them!

Kalla looked at Snik Snak and wondered at what she had done. She knew she would be going with them, but her hand would be remaining behind.

Chapter 27

Upon a Silvered Star

"Have you brought me the box that I had you ssseek?"

"Yes, Herr Mistro."

"Good. NOW GIVE IT TO ME!"

Elfriede handed the impatient wizard the red box from the Caverns Crystal. Oborren stood at her side.

"Tepson was the one who recovered it," she added.

Mistro grimaced at the mention of the insolent gnome's name. He was surprised that the cur still lived after the dark curse he had placed on him!

The wizard examined the box carefully. "Good," he explained. "I can't ssstand all those sssilly sssp... sssp... all those sssilly... ghostsss in that cavern!"

Oborren shifted and backed away uncomfortably; the hunter was starting to get a saliva-spray from all of Mistro's talking. The wizard stared at him.

Quiet Upon Shenbyrg's Dawning

"AND VHAT DO YOU HAVE TO SSSAY ABOUT IT?" challenged Mistro.

The hunter shrugged: he knew it was useless to argue with a wizard.

"So what shall we do now?" asked Elfriede.

Mistro smiled wickedly. "Vhatever I sssay."

"We have friends in Walstock who might need our help! And what of Dinglesfuhr?" Elfriede was growing concerned.

The wizard's countenance softened somewhat at the woman's innocent entreaties.

"Your vriendsss vill need a lot more than your help. And Dinglesssvuhr is nearly ready to vall."

Elfriede's mind raced as she struggled to grasp what Mistro was saying. He was quite difficult to understand.

"Then we will go immediately!" she exclaimed finally. Elfriede took Oborren by the arm and began to lead him out of Mistro's tower.

"Vait, vait, silly voman! You vill need sssome asssissstance. I don't vant to lose my invessstment!"

* * *

Father Farhred examined the repurposed Gaol with his spyglass. It looked like the R'ti Heretics had finally made their move- Isolation of the Undesirables and then Execution after Confession. He smarted at the nature of such an approach. The Church of Tyr might do precisely the same thing, except they would not leave out the most important part: *burning the heretics!*

Wilstrin crouched next to the witch hunter and Farhred winced. The man remained a reminder that he was delaying his

Dan Osarchuk

Duty to Incinerate Apostates. Wilstrin obviously was a warlock, or at least dabbled as such. Farhred couldn't wait to *burn him*! But Wilstrin still had his uses to serve the greater Law of Tyr, so he would have to wait to purge him with cleansing flame later.

Returning his attention to the Gaol, Farhred wondered at what sort of Infernalism would follow. As with most left-wing Cult conquests, the idealistic revolutionaries would soon be replaced with repressive reactionaries. Then the killing would occur in earnest! Even many of the original revolutionaries would be executed by their own allies; it rarely helped to have the idealistic around after the actual nature of the conquest was known.

Wilstrin continued to stare off into space, attempting to contact some Demon Lord no doubt, Farhred assumed. He looked forward to when he would get to purge him too, but by *real inferno*, not some Heretical left-wing-*non-fire-based execution*!

A number of prisoners were brought out in front of the Gaol, which the R'ti Cult had renamed the *Gaolag*. The male and female prisoners were mixed together as they were lined up to give their Confessions. At least the Church of Tyr had the decency to have *separate execution areas* for witches and warlocks!

The witch hunter could barely contain himself, but he realized that he must for now. Too many of his associates had fallen in the fight at that infernal Side Way Inn yesterday that he had to stick to a careful plan. Oh, how he longed to just stab every one of those Heretics who crossed his path! But no, Tyr would not approve of such recklessness: one must sometimes exercise patience in order to exorcize the cancerous darkness that was Heresy.

Farhred gritted his teeth when some of the prisoners began to speak amongst themselves. He hated it when the Condemned did that! Better to just burn them right away! How could these R'ti executioners tolerate anything other than just prisoner Confessions?

Quiet Upon Shenbyrg's Dawning

"What are they going to do to us now?" said a chestnut-haired woman. Farhred was appalled that he could hear her clearly even though he stood a good dozen yards from the Condemned. Why didn't the guards silence her? Still, she and the older one next to her both seemed to be priestesses: one of Freya and one of Minerva. Even Farhred would hesitate before condemning one of them, let alone both. These R'ti had some gall!

The older woman began to cry and embraced the younger one as a red faced man was led to the podium. Hounds of Vigilance stood around him, billie clubs in hand, and the man winced at their gaze. Since he was dressed as a tutor, Farhred gathered that the man knew of the ruthlessness of the Hounds even before they had taken over the town at the new Count's behest.

A number of hulking Gaolag guards took up their positions to the side of the podium and aimed heavy crossbows at the man. It was unclear whether they were either going to execute him during the Confession or be more polite and wait for him to finish first.

The tutor began: "You can't fight the County Castle!"

Farhred's eyes finally landed on the one he was looking for. Freundel nodded, seeing his captain, who discreetly nodded back at him too. The rest of the crowd's attention remained focused on the tutor who was about to be shot.

The witch hunter had to grudgingly admit that the Cult had a fairly good system of purging what they called 'heresy'. Of course, since they were Heretics themselves, it was no excuse.

* * *

"Why should we go now? WE NEED TO LIGHT MORE PAINS IN THE ASS ON FIRE! Ha HA ah HA ha ha HAAAAA!!!!"

Halfdan wasn't sure who was in worse shape: Kolveig or Cherries.

266

The Karlist still had the Hospitalier's lance embedded in his shoulder and looked like he was nearly ready to pass out. The cleric would seem almost comical with the large, syringe-like weapon sticking out from him if his situation didn't appear so dire.

Cherries, on the other hand, seemed to be untouched physically, but unfortunately also seemed to have lost what little sense she had before. Apparently, the thrill of using too much magical fire had fully infiltrated her mind, finally turning her into a complete firebug.

"Let me heal you," insisted the Odinnic.

"As if that would even work!" scoffed Kolveig. "You, like all the other Purveyors of Delusional Faith in the Vale, would do better to surrender to the True Red Light of Karl!"

Halfdan had to admire Kolveig's tenacity even as close as he was to death's door. He decided to change his approach.

"You need to be back on your feet; we need to leave this place and rendezvous with the others as per the plan!"

The Karlist continued to glare at him defiantly.

"Can you heal your wounds?"

Kolveig shook his head. "Karl does not seem fit to Bless Me with His Redistribution of My Vital Humors at this Particular Juncture."

"Well then," said Halfdan quietly. He turned and looked at the barely-clad sorceress whose hair appeared aflame. She continued cackling maniacally as she let loose yet another burst of fire and ignited the chair that they had been sitting on only moments before. The stink of its burning mattress mingled with the crackling of its wooden frame.

Quiet Upon Shenbyrg's Dawning

An idea came to the Odinnic and he conveyed it to the Karlist: "We could have Cherries cauterize your wounds?"

* * *

"Did you kill the male?" Brymanah raised her eyebrow hopefully, but Tepson shook his head.

"He's just unconscious."

The amazon looked disappointed. "We were supposed to *assassinate him*."

"I know," explained the gnome, "but I just have this little problem with bashing some guy's brains out with a pickhammer while he's sitting on the can, even if he is behind the takeover of the town by yet another evil Cult."

Brymanah shook her head in resignation: Tepson's speech certainly was strange, but it wasn't nearly as irritating as Kolveig's.

"Then we bring him with us," she decided, "we'll just need to-"

Brymanah stopped when the Count's scrivener strolled into the room. She showed shock and concern on her face at first, but then seemed to pull herself together.

"OK," said the woman, "Let's Try and Talk This Out: I see that you've bashed Count Remus on the head. What is your Motivation here?"

Brymanah glared at her; she wasn't acting normally for a Womyn. Tepson nearly broke out in laughter. The amazon reasoned that this Womyn too was in a Cult: most Cultists tried to ignore their true feelings with shields of rhetoric. It was rarely convincing.

Receiving no reply, the receptionist continued, "I Feel That You're Interrupting This Learning Environment with Your Unsanctioned Actional Approach..."

The amazon and the gnome remained at a loss for words. Brymanah was finding this Womyn so annoying that she was beginning to consider challenging her to a duel. Luckily for the scrivener, a commotion outside one of the Castle's eastern windows drew their attention.

Below, Tepson and Brymanah saw an incredible scene: a multitude of crimson red hot-air balloons had landed within the courtyard. Scores of red dwarves and fell men moved about and began to fire upon a crowd of townsfolk. They bore stout armor, firearms, and even larger balloons could be seen landing that held siege engines and vicious giant beasts. The gnome and amazon could not fathom why the crowd had not run sooner, since the balloons so clearly bore the mark of Helltowne.

The receptionist too stood dumbfounded, lacking any possible R'ti prattle to articulate the atrocity that was occurring. Her Cult, like so many others, lived in such a fragile and dependent world that any real calamity was unthinkable. Brymanah was glad that she had stopped talking at least.

* * *

Van Dwick stirred in his chains. He brushed off the halfling scraps that covered him. Perhaps the now-corrupted Secret Police thought that the little scoundrels would consume him along with the food? That would please the Glowing Spectral Personhood, since he was now deemed 'Amaranthine', would it not?

The darkness was comforting. The deposed Fieldmarshall wished it would never end. For in the light, he would be forced to see the disaster that was befalling Dinglesfuhr. Tomorrow the invasion would begin. Oh, they thought he couldn't hear them when they talked about it, but he could! What madness had fallen upon Mekla and the rest of his once-great nation?

Anger over that injustice arose in him even more now, causing red to interplay with the dark cell to cast all in a brown light. In the distance, he could hear some strange howl, but it was not the mad calls of a Cultist, or of goblin raiders, or of halflings coming for yet another dinner. This chilling call reminded Van Dwick of the Valkyrie of legend, of righteous fury coming for purgation.

Startled, he suddenly saw the face of a man staring in through the prison window. His presence seemed altogether familiar. The power of the man was what struck Van Dwick the most, but before the Fieldmarshall could say a word, he was gone. A chill ran down his spine.

All that was left was a single silver star upon the night sky.

* * *

"Look at all the pretty RED balloons! AH HA hah ha! Ha ha HA!"

Halfdan and Kolveig hurried the still deranged Cherries down the streets of Walstock. Townsfolk ignored them and cheered at the crimson red dirigibles that were landing all around. Halfdan couldn't decide if the situation was to their benefit or not: they were still being chased by the Hospitaliers, but the local folk were obviously ill-prepared for so obvious an infernal invasion.

As if to punctuate that point, one hot-air balloon landed squarely on a house a few dozen yards away from them. Those inside only managed to escape at the last moment; perhaps they had heard the sound of the burner that made it fly. Before Kolveig could react with an invective against the Bolshevik-types flying it, Halfdan hurried him around the corner. Cherries stared at the fire that broke out from within the house and clapped.

A harpy, a female flying-thing watched them from a nearby rooftop. She was looking for her master, but she also remembered Halfdan.

Chapter 28

The Cleansing of Dinglesfuhr

Frau Mekla gazed upon the assembled Visitor ranks below in the Dingleplatz: orcs, goblins, halflings, Fjord Vallee savages, and many others. So many New Friends! She smiled to herself, knowing that finally the stains upon her people's honor would be lifted. The Amaranthine Wizard, the Tyrant Himself, may have killed many in his Dark Crusades, but now her people of Dinglesfuhr, guided by her own wise hand of course, would make amends.

The Glowing Spectral Personhood, now fully empowered thanks to Mekla's recent Reforms, came to greet the masses of permanent Visitors to their land. What was once only a handful of halfling *food-seekers* a few, short months ago had become a deluge of so many people from Sylvania and beyond.

Esservassa beamed that her Cult was the first in Dinglesfuhr to greet the Visitors. She and her Siblings leapt and sang praises to the Great Multicult and to the Visitors, ringing their thumb cymbals and allowing their many-colored ribbons and blue-dyed hair to unfurl as they danced. Esservassa shuddered when some of the orcs and goblins stared at her, but quickly regained her composure: she had a New Name Now in return for Her Valuable

Service to Hymnir. *She just knew that it would help her forget what they had done to her.* Her only hope was that she could keep dancing as well with only one hand.

Up above upon the Darkastle walls, tears came to the Dinglesfrau's eyes. Her dark-haired minister, Eind, looked on and smiled. It was truly a beautiful sight to Mekla- such Acceptance of New Friends; such a Liberation from the Old Ways. As the people of Dinglesfuhr moved in to join them, the Glowing Spectral Persons sang their *Lovingnest Song.*

> *Welcome to Dinglesfuhr!*
> *Welcome, New Friends!*
> *What Once Was Ours Is Now Yours!*
> *Cleanse the Stain from our Lands!*

Many Dinglesfuhrians, quite elated now, began screaming "Welcome!" and unfurled banners to signal their hospitality.

Some did not cheer though. One daughter of Dinglesfuhr, one who had seen much during the last week, realized what was truly happening. Elfriede wasn't sure whether the people had become so wrapped in Underreign of their own accord or whether Mekla's Secret Police had finally terrorized enough of them to stifle any outright resistance.

The Visitors watched the Dinglesfuhrians continue their stirring tribute and heartfelt surrender of their national sovereignty. Strangely, they did not seem very impressed. The halflings rubbed their bellies in boredom, the orcs and goblins snickered wickedly, and the savages stared in disbelief at the lack of mullet haircuts.

The Dinglesfrau was perplexed. But Mekla reminded herself that the Visitors were *her Children now*- sometimes Children might need more coaxing to truly be happy.

As the singing abated, Eind signaled for carts of food, supplies, and gold coins to be rolled in. At this, *all* of the Visitors' eyes finally lit up. They immediately rushed forward *en masse*, knocking over the Dinglesfuhrians who seemed confused that the New Friends had not arrived to simply enjoy the company of the Dinglesfuhrians themselves. Some constables went to intervene, but stopped when they remembered the dire warnings from the Secret Police to not Infringe on Any Visitors' Rights.

Seeing the panic beginning to arise from her fellow Dinglesfuhrians, Mekla called for Encouragement and Calm, but the Visitors began to become more unruly. Soon halflings were stuffing breads and cheeses into their mouths and pants, staring at the Dinglesfuhrians unpleasantly as they devoured the fare. The Fjord Vallee savages began looting the supply carts, looking for any salt. Orcs even began to stomp upon some of the fallen Dinglesfuhrians, quite intentionally now. And the goblins, ignoring the gold carts for the time being, began to position themselves and started groping some of the Dinglesfuhrian dancers.

Frau Mekla was shocked: how could the Visitors not be happy when she and her people had shown them such Love?

"Wait, Mein Friends! We have many Fine Dingleshauses for you to dwell within!" The Dinglesfrau pointed to a brightly painted avenue that led to many homes that some of the local folk had 'volunteered' to donate to the Visitors.

At this, the savages stopped their looting, the goblins lowered their hands, and even the halflings stopped eating for a moment. All the Dinglesfuhrians who had welcomed the New Friends hoped that they had finally given them enough.

A call from the Dinglestor broke the silence. Dinglesfuhrian, savage, goblin, orc, and even halfling looked back and saw the many thousands more that had now arrived at the gates.

Quiet Upon Shenbyrg's Dawning

Mekla could barely believe her eyes. It seemed as if a sea of bodies had walked from the Fjord and would immediately flood into her land, if the gates had only been wider... Gladness began to mix with apprehension. She certainly welcomed All Who Would Change Dinglesfuhr Beyond All Recognition, but she doubted that even a prosperous land such as hers could house and feed so many!

The Glowing Spectral Persons simply danced more intensively, invigorated by so many New Friends arriving. Many of the other Dinglesfuhrians cheered too, holding the welcome banners even higher, in order that all could see. Those Visitors who had already entered though were not so naïve.

Elfriede knew all too well what was about to happen. She took one last look at her leader, her Dinglesfrau. Who was she meaning to help by allowing so many others in to destroy her land? What treason could be greater than orchestrating an end to one's own people? Why had she destroyed Dinglesfuhr?

Before the constables could intervene, it began. Screams arose throughout the courtyard that only minutes earlier held the sounds of dancing and friendly welcome. Most of the Dinglesfuhrians fell over each other to either assist the Visitors or flee from their stabbings, bloodied and confused. The goblins lit into all they could: stabbing man, woman, halfling, and savage alike. Some cackled in glee and leapt upon dancers who could not escape in time. The orcs smashed all within their grasp. They laughed ruthlessly at the humans' stupidity. Though the halflings and savage men fought back, the Dinglesfuhrians did nothing. The guards broke and fled the gates, overwhelmed by countless more Visitors pushing in to receive the Free Hospitality of Dinglesfuhr.

As she fled, Elfriede couldn't help but look back and stare at the slaughter of her people, heartbroken. The fight had been completely taken out of them. Those who would have resisted this invasion had already been put in the Stockade; all the rest had been deluded and terrorized into acquiescence. Perhaps it was good to love others, for that was the way of happiness, but the 'Love' demanded by Frau Mekla and the Glowing Spectral Personhood was one contrived, rather than true. It only led to a single logical result: the death of Dinglesfuhr.

Mekla too stared at the slaughter, aghast. Had the Chromatic Voice lied to her? It *had* claimed that if she did this, if she let all the Visitors in, *then Dinglesfuhr would be cleansed*! Eind looked down at the disaster too and smiled.

Her people fell and fled to escape the Visitors. The fires began to break out and grow, igniting the ancient Dingleplatz. It occurred to her then that Dinglesfuhr *was being cleansed*, just not in the way she had thought.

Perhaps she should send some of the Visitors back?

* * *

Oborren shifted out of the way of yet another terrified Dinglesfuhrian. He wondered if perhaps he had taken the wrong profession: one would think that killing unnatural things would be the best way to protect humanity, but Cults could be even more dangerous. Ironically, harnessing that very power might be what saves this strange land.

Elfriede came running around the corner, nearly knocking the black-clad hunter over. She was distraught. Two halflings, also dressed in black, caught up with her and began going through her pack.

"There's no food in there, you scoundrels!" shouted Oborren.

The halflings ignored the hunter and began to pry the pack off of Elfriede's shoulder. Only after he pointed his crossbow at them to prove his point did they flee, screaming and shouting harsh profanities that belied their small size.

Quiet Upon Shenbyrg's Dawning

Oborren helped the fallen woman up. Her blond hair had fallen over her tear-stained face. He brushed it away and felt a wave of sympathy for her. Their eyes met and she smiled back at him.

Changing the mood, Oborren spoke, "We must keep moving, we have that new ... ally... to recruit."

Elfriede nodded and pulled herself together. She checked to see if the wand that Mistro had given them was still there. It was- the halflings hadn't stolen it, though they did get her ration bag.

* * *

Farhred was a little disappointed that the Gaol-break had been so easy.

Yes, Freundel had died heroically in the resulting melee. But thanks to Tyr's mighty guidance of his sword arm, Farhred had felled many a heretic and only lost about half of the prisoners in the process. All in all, it was a success, but the witch hunter would have preferred more slaughter on both sides.

True, the others that now trailed behind him probably did not agree that the escape was easy. And Farhred certainly could guess the warlock Wilstrin's intentions as he fluttered around the Freyan priestess Carsanna. Farhred couldn't wait until he had the time to finally burn the Witch to death. At least the Minervan matron Aelstad walked beside the witch hunter now; little chance of conjuring any impure thoughts in that case.

Farhred missed the days when both his church and hers dominated Walstock with their righteous Law. Look what had become of the town! Infernalist hot-air balloons were landing everywhere, smashing homes and gawking villagers under their foul iron baskets.

"See what happens!" yelled Farhred in fury at the fleeing townsfolk. "You turn to false gods and now it IS YOUR DOOM!"

The people fled again, even more terrified than before after the Tyrian railed against them. Farhred hoped that it was now a more righteous terror at least.

Aelstad put a comforting arm on Farhred's back. He looked at her in shock for a moment, but then realized that she was getting him to refocus his attention on their mission. It wouldn't do to have Freundel's sacrifice be in vain.

Once he was redirected, Aelstad of course removed her hand. It also wouldn't do to have the Tyrian become distracted with any sinful ideas.

The group pushed further through the burning homes, but had to stop and take cover. The sound of some backward-talking Helltowners approached. Farhred and the others were doubly cautious, having seen that the red dwarves and fell men bore many firearms.

They narrowly avoided a collapsing house and rushed to a small grassy area that remained untouched. The heat and stench of burning subsumed the place. Wilstrin took another moment to 'check Carsanna's wounds' as they waited; she giggled. Farhred pondered tossing the vile Heretic right into the inferno then and there, but he then saw a strange box flickering on the road. One of the invading dwarves had left a key in it and it was giving a message.

* * *

Brymanah pushed the shuddering kinderwagon, now certainly overloaded, down the side alleys of Walstock. Tepson had tried knocking the large man out again, but apparently Cultists had the capacity to keep talking even when their brains should have been deactivated from repeated pickhammer blows to the head.

If it were possible, the amazon found the man to be almost as annoying as Kolveig.

Quiet Upon Shenbyrg's Dawning

"This is a Glorious Day for Walstock! Look at all those Beautiful Snoollabs in the sky! They remind me of what Good Pupils could give to their tutors..."

"By throwing them at them?" challenged Tepson. "I thought you Monitor-types hated tutors."

"Oh no!" insisted Remus. "We Love Our Tutors! It's just that they might Need Some Extra Guidance on How to be Better via Improvement!"

"And the villagers whose homes are being destroyed by the Red Dwarves?" mocked Brymanah. "How is that 'Glorious'?"

"They just aren't Being Positive Enough! If they put their Minds in the Right Place, then Everything Would be Wonderful for them too!"

Tepson scoffed: "You're telling us that all they have to do is think good thoughts and they *won't be crushed by the thousands of pounds of hot-air balloon coming down upon them*?"

"Of course," said the Count, "it's THEIR OWN FAULT for not getting the Lives that They Want! They're just Lazy Defeatists!"

Tepson stopped the kinderwagon. It groaned under the weight of the Count. He leaned up to look out the bonnet at the gnome.

"What's the difference between what you're describing and simple delusion? Maybe if I believed that my pickhammer wouldn't kill you if I bashed your brains in, then it wouldn't?"

The Count was finally silent. Brymanah was relieved. All amazons knew that once you got two men talking, it would be nearly impossible to get them to shut up.

She had come very close to decapitating them both.

* * *

Dan Osarchuk

The alleys here grew strangely darker. Terrified Dinglesfuhrian townsfolk ran passed the hunter and lady. The two stopped at an intersection to try to get their bearings.

Suddenly, a group of orcs rushed the area and overwhelmed Oborren. Elfriede became too terrified to speak. They slashed her hunter friend ruthlessly and then turned on her. The monsters ripped her blouse and held her tightly with their filthy hands. She would scream again, but an orc stuck one of its stinking, dirty fingers into her mouth and laughed. The silver stag pendant, the one she had bought that night in Walstock days ago, now shone exposed from her neck.

The beasts dragged her to the ground and laughed as she struggled. What had Mekla done to her land? How could enabling such atrocity possibly set things right?

Suddenly, something vengeful erupted into the alleyway. Startled, the orcs let Elfriede go. With a rush of air, one of the larger orcs was thrust against a building wall with such telekinetic force that its head shattered. The others backed away, unsure as to what had stopped them from their sick game.

"Zweimal falsch ergibt nicht einmal richtig!" Elfriede finished the incantation and pointed the wand at the remaining orcs. In the night air, she could almost see the fiery tendrils boring into their skulls. They would shriek, but their tongues and throats had already been seared- they simply made dry moaning sounds as they collapsed lifeless onto the fine Dinglesfuhrian street.

Elfriede brushed her hair from her face and thought she saw a strangely-dressed constable standing there. She looked again, but he was gone.

Oborren groaned in congratulation; his many orc-wounds preventing him from rising. The path to meet with the new ally had not been as easy as they had hoped. A large contingent of orcs had arrived with the second wave of Visitors, making travel through the side alleys quite hazardous, even though the center of the town was now actually on fire. The howls of the pillaged and dying Dinglesfuhrians were awful, even to so hardened a hunter as he.

Elfriede helped her friend to his feet and worried over his wounds. She had no craft by which to heal them and she sorely missed the talents of the clerics.

"Where can we find this new ally after we free the others?" she asked.

"To the northeast," replied Oborren amidst gasps of pain. He too missed the clerics' talents, but was more upset over the orcs' attack on Elfriede.

"What is there?" insisted the woman.

"It's a mine that has drawn most of our potential allies to it; something to do with their new religion- at least, that's what Mistro claimed. He said you were even present when the new faith was founded."

Elfriede pondered for a time as she helped Oborren down the street with one arm; in her other she held the wand ready against any further attacks.

"Do you think that will be enough to stop any more trouble along the way?" he said finally. Oborren knew less about the wand than Elfriede.

"It should," she replied as they approached the prisoner stockade. "Its power is supposed be ironic."

That realization did not fill the hunter with a great deal of confidence. He spat on the lifeless orcs as they left and tried to ignore the shade that was watching them.

Chapter 29

The Battle of Tower Forest

Perhaps if she slayed the Karlist, then she could return to Stephania and let the Kernazons try to mutate her again?

The welts on Brymanah's hips and back flared up in memory of the traumatic incident from a few days ago. Though both Poy and Jeg had tried to change her, they had been unsuccessful. Brymanah knew not why, nor why they had spared the Shell Oracle.

The same could not be said for her other sisters though. Brymanah was a veteran warrior and Hippolyte, but she still shuddered at the memory of the screaming transformations that the amazons underwent. The buzzing sound the new Kernazons, the loss of humanity of her once-great sisters, was absolutely awful, but she would even prefer it now to having to hear Kolveig utter *one more word*.

"Granted, it's not the best Form of Revolution, on a Stalinist-Trotsky scale of course, but we would be Counter-Revolutionary in not joining forces with the Helltowners at this point."

"And you want to work with these tyrants and murderers- why?" Tepson was also considering killing the Karlist. Here he was suggesting collaboration with the very people that had invaded Walstock, destroyed homes, and shot innocent townsfolk! And he had even stolen his backpack and deserted him in the Caverns Crystal a few days ago!

"Because they're More Revolutionary than R'ti and the other Cults that have taken over so far!" Kolveig motioned to Count Remus who was bound and thankfully gagged, though the Monitor-Director did try to mumble a response.

"Do you mean that their shoes are more revolutionary than this Stalin-Trotsky whatever?" Cherries tried to support her lover as best she could.

The others shook their heads in dismay. Brymanah was glad that a Womyn was in the conversation at least, even if the sorceress's mind had been nearly completely ruined by magic.

"You're just making excuses! These Helltowners are whackos just like YOU!" Tepson pointed a small, accusing finger at the Karlist. The scent of burning homes from the recent Helltowne snoollab landings and assault was still strong in the air; cries of pain emanated from the adjacent street.

"Oh yeah? At least I don't MISAPPROPRIATE PEOPLE'S EARS BY BITING THEM OFF!"

At the Karlist's insult, Tepson turned pale and a furious scowl appeared on his face. Brymanah was glad that the group was nearly coming to blows: perhaps she would not have to be the one to kill the Karlist after all?

"Yes, but he *did try* to give the ear back to the witch hunter..." added Cherries. She did not want to see a fight: she even shook her head for added emphasis and put her hands on her hips to appear more knowledgeable.

"Quite true, my Sexy Comrade," nodded Kolveig. He then turned and looked at the gnome with a cruel smile, "... by spitting it out on him!"

Tepson roared and launched his small body at the Karlist. Halfdan was shocked at the gnome's speed and was barely able to keep him from strangling Kolveig outright. As the Odinnic held the gnome back, his clear presence caused some of Tepson's rage to dissipate, allowing the gnome to feel somewhat less murderous.

"Now we won't be biting off anyone else's ear," scolded Halfdan. "We need to decide what to do with the Count and how to fight this invasion."

"Hah!" scoffed Brymanah. "There are too many of them and the only females we have here are the sorceress and myself!"

"And their outfits *are just awful!*" added Cherries, who was attempting to agree with the amazon.

Halfdan shook his head. "Though the Multiple Cults may all ultimately serve the cause of suffering and tyranny, they don't cooperate well with each other when they do gain power. I doubt that the Kernazons in the north would take kindly to the male-dominated goblins and orcs in the south."

"So what?" said Brymanah curtly. There was something about Halfdan that especially repulsed her, even for a male.

"We have a chance," stated the Odinnic. "Their power isn't monolithic."

"But what about the Helltowners?" queried Tepson.

Halfdan looked at the gnome and nodded. "They are just another Cult."

* * *

Quiet Upon Shenbyrg's Dawning

The Ancient white building stood in stark contrast to the darkening sky. The town had begun to settle into the grip of yet one more False Cult, though the Gods did not appear so acquiescent. Farhred wondered at what the Ancients actually did at the Walstock Town Hall- Wilstrin certainly seemed to have some heretical ideas about the town's distant past- but the witch hunter himself knew that in the current age, little was accomplished.

Oh yes, the Town Council: the competing clans and parties in the town would wrangle over issues before sending them to the Count, but in the end, they never worked for the greater good. Perhaps they couldn't? The perspectives of rich vs. poor, one family vs. another may have just been too different. Farhred would have loved to burn them all in a pyre and let the Cleansing Flames of Tyr sort them out, but now he would have to settle for fighting back against the Helltowners.

The aging witch hunter glanced back at his small group. Farhred was mildly impressed that the warlock Wilstrin, the Freyan priestess Carsanna, and the Minervan nun Aelstad had survived the initial red dwarf attack. He wondered how quickly they would die in this final assault. The Helltowners began to unfurl their Satanic banners from the upper-story Town Hall windows.

"Perhaps we should wait, Father Farhred," said the nun. "We do not hail from a militant order, such as yours."

Farhred reviewed the Minervan's statement for any Heresy, but found none- it seemed simply that the woman was suffering some trepidation over their Imminent and Glorious Death.

"I understand, Sister, but we must enact Immediate Vengeance upon these Apostates nonetheless. Remember the plan: you distract some of the guards by stabbing Wilstrin repeatedly, while the Freyan shows the other guards her bare ankle. I will stride in and set fire to the Town Hall."

Dan Osarchuk

"But... but... didn't you hear that they were going to attack the Tower..." began Wilstrin. Farhred's glare silenced the short, mustached man who was looking extremely nervous. The accused warlock wondered if the Church of Minerva was as harsh as that of Tyr.

"We could fight them another way..." interrupted Carsanna. Her smile and fluttering eyelashes immediately banished any thoughts of violence from the air.

Farhred whispered a Tyrian chant to counteract any charms that the attractive priestess might be using on him. The Freyan smiled and pointed to another alleyway opposite the Town Hall. Standing there were some others that all except Aelstad had met before. It looked like they too were ready to enact Immediate Vengeance upon the Helltowners.

* * *

The light fog lifted as the assembled ranks marched up the Tower Road. Red helms shown as dim fire upon the heads of the marching dwarves and men; their dark moustaches did little to cover their toothy smirks. Well-armored and bearing devastating firearms, this Helltowne battalion was still riding the feeling of invincibility from their recent success in Walstock.

Their commissar leader, Navi, led from the center. His black captain's hat and lack of armor would mark him as an easy target for any Counter-Revolutionaries that might attack if he were at the edge of his troops. Spies had reported that *elves* might even dwell in these woods. Navi brushed the idea off: it was Just another Delusion of the Masses, most likely.

Iruy, the red dwarf commander, had even said he thought he had spotted *something* when the battalion had crossed the River Shenbyrg an hour ago, but nothing had come of it. Navi wasn't sure what to believe. All of his skirmishing forces were still deployed in Walstock- the former Capitalist Populace and

Quiet Upon Shenbyrg's Dawning

Convenient Allies could not be trusted yet- too few Undesirables had been Purged. In fact, Navi did not like the idea of taking his battalion into the wilds at all: dwarves were not fond of woods and red dwarves were not fond of woods that were not on fire.

And that this narrow, winding switchback trail prevented them from bringing neither their special war machines nor their fell beasts continued to concern him. But Orders Were Orders and Navi did not wish to get shot himself for disobeying. So with some struggle, the red dwarf put his Disobedient Thoughts out of his mind.

Their 'Allies' also seemed ill-equipped for a mission such as this. Such Cults were generally only good for destabilizing and terrorizing a local populace in preparation for Official Helltowne invasion. Still, those who helped to take the fight out of Walstock would need to be appeased; that is, until he and the other red dwarves had a firmer grasp on that town and that puppet Count Remus was recovered. The commissar glared at the Hospitaliers, Hounds of Vigilance, and Seekers of C'ps that flanked the battalion- he hoped that any Counter-Revolutionaries would attack them first.

Navi reaffirmed his Oath of Allegiance to Uncle Steel Dwarf and mentally reviewed his Orders: capture the Tower before the Fjord Vallee Rebels did. It was the main route through which snoollab reinforcements could be intercepted. It needed to be secured by nightfall and his was the only battalion that could be spared.

So for now, Navi must root out the Counter- Revolutionaries in this damnable forest and work with the damnable Cults of R'ti, Shield Ghul, and C'ps. Once more reinforcements arrived from Helltowne, Walstock and the surrounding towns could be conquered more easily.

Then all the Dissidents, Current and Future, would be purged.

* * *

The battalion reached the apex of the route and the fell men let out a sigh of relief. The stouter and wider dwarves snarled at their human Comrades: they lacked the True Red Endurance. Navi smiled at the mild animosity running within the ranks of his own troops- if they distrusted each other, then they were less likely to turn on him.

One of the Convenient Allies, a Hospitalier named Drenart approached the commissar. The Helltowners immediately closed ranks and pointed their firearms at him.

Navi grinned at his troops' Required Loyalty and shouted out to the Hospitalier, "What do you want, Comrade?"

"The Hounds of Vigilance are requesting that we have a R'ti Meeting now."

"A what?"

"A R'ti Meeting- such that tutors are mandatorily required to attend at their Schoolhouses. "

"Yes," said Navi in false approval, "*that is an excellent idea. Why don't they have it in the woods over there...*"

Drenart nodded and walked back to notify the Hounds; Navi ordered his men to form up into a defensive square.

A roar from the northeast shook the group. The Hounds made to return to the battalion, but the Helltowners pointed their firearms at them.

"Go into the forest!" commanded Navi.

The Hounds seemed unsure what to do; the Hospitaliers and Seekers eyed the Helltowners warily. Iruy, who was supervising the soldiers on the southwest side of the defensive square, shouted a warning to the commissar. There was some disturbance back in the direction of Walstock.

Ignoring the commander, Navi continued shouting to Drenart: "The Cult of R'ti will have their meeting in the forest now, OR THE CULT OF THE SHIELD GHUL WILL!"

Drenart ordered his Hospitaliers to press the Hounds into the forest.

Just then, all those assembled heard whispering amongst the trees. It sounded like: "Dinglesfuhr."

Snapping back to the matter at hand, Navi ordered his men to make ready. Drenart had his men unsling their syringe lances and do the same. The Hounds and the Seekers started to panic.

"Powder doom."

All froze. They watched the autumn woods surrounding them. Dusk was approaching. A number of Hounds began to run back down the trail to Walstock. Navi had his soldiers hold their fire.

"FJORD!"

The forest erupted with lightly-clad human savages, all with stylized mullet haircuts. A Dinglesfuhrian lady pointed a wand and a group of Seekers fell gasping. A massively muscled barbarian crashed into the Hospitaliers with his great axe.

A dark-clad hunter fired at Navi from a treetop position. Narrowly avoiding the kill-shot from the hunter, Navi uttered his command in the backwards language of Helltowne: "ERIF!"

The area exploded in a cacophony of noise and smoke. Fjord Vallee savages fell and fled at the onslaught. The hunter, lady, and barbarian ducked for cover. The red dwarves and fell men readied their bayonets, but Navi forbid a charge- he knew these Counter-Revolutionaries could be crafty. The remaining Hounds and Seekers were not as wise and chased the savages into the woods. The Hospitaliers formed their own defensive line parallel to the Helltowners. They waited, but nothing came.

Dan Osarchuk

* * *

The night grew dark and cold as dawn approached. Though the red dwarves could point their firearms for hours, the men of Helltowne were not as strong. Grudgingly giving into practicality, Navi allowed his soldiers to rest in shifts at the center of the defensive square. He remained vigilant though, ready to shoot any of his own soldiers who might attempt to sneak off in the night.

Unsurprisingly, Drenart's men rested now and the Hounds of R'ti and the Seekers of C'ps had not returned. Navi scoffed at the poor combat ability of their 'Allies'. It was little matter though: soon the snoollab reinforcements would pass over this position and the mission would be a success.

A lone figure walked up the trail from the southwest. The human was dressed as a Karlist, one of those softer versions of Bolshevism that Helltowne often found so useful in destabilizing various settlements. Navi was confused though: he was not aware of any Karlist Cult in Walstock. Perhaps he was an Unassigned Agent looking to assist Uncle Steel Dwarf?

"Oh look! A bunch of Anti-Proletarians Pretending to Be True Socialists!"

On second thought, Navi ordered his soldiers to prepare to fire.

"Is this how we do Committee Meetings now? Well, I'll give you My Vote, if you'd put down your firearms! And why are none of you Bearing Your Sacred Hammer and Sickles?"

A deep roar from the opposite direction, like the one heard earlier when they had first reached the top of Tower Road, startled the Helltowners from the Karlist's long-winded diatribe. The Hospitaliers were roused as well. Navi turned to see what was happening. The red dwarves and fell men fumbled with their weapons to fire.

Suddenly, the woods erupted with tumultuous sound again-this time, a yell.

"IS IT SALTY!?!?"

From the north, the Dinglesfuhrian lady led the screaming savages upon the now-shaken Helltowners. An amazon warrior spearheaded another group that rushed in from the west. A furious witch hunter launched his own attack from the south upon the Hospitaliers. And, to Navi's horror, the large barbarian had returned, now riding a 10' tall carnosaur that rushed in from the east.

Another crossbow bolt shot out from another treetop at Navi. Hunters rarely missed their prey twice.

Chapter 30

Some Sunny Day

Dawn began to peak over the distant mountains to the east, far beyond even the Nuttens that bordered the Vale. Light from those distant lands showed the approaching snoollab fleet, another invasion from Helltowne at least thrice as large as before. The many combatants upon Tower Road stared at the spectacle for a moment and all was quiet.

Elfriede dodged behind a tree just before a group of red dwarves fired upon her; the quiet now ruined by the blast of firearms. She avoided most of the barrage of nails and lead, though she caught some in the arm and the Fjord Vallee savage standing next to her was slain. Elfriede intoned the ironic words that Mistro had taught her and the affected dwarves fell. The Dinglesfuhrian lady wondered at how much longer the wand would work and whether her arm injury was sufficient sacrifice to the Gods for her use of such magic.

Brymanah crushed a Helltowne man's throat between her thighs and shot another through the chest with her strong bow. Tepson dodged a red dwarf's hand axe, only to nail the soldier in the head with his own pickhammer. Halfdan knocked Cherries out of the way before another group of Helltowners fired at her.

With the Odinnic staying clear-minded, the soldiers forgot about them for a moment and Cherries's pyromania was also held in check.

Seeing Farhred fell two Hospitaliers with his tyrsword, Drenart readied his lance, but was distracted by a vivacious Freyan priestess beckoning to him from the forest. Now preoccupied, the Hospitalier did not see the Minervan nun and the accused warlock charging him from behind.

Navi struggled to compel his injured leg to move from the cold autumn ground. Some marksman had crippled him, ensnaring him to the spot with a crossbow bolt. The soldiers in front remained too fearful to fire at the large mulleted barbarian upon the huge carnosaur steed. So the commissar pointed his own firearm at his men, a pistol given to him by Uncle Steel Dwarf himself, cast in cold-wrought Hell Iron and engraved with the hammer and sickle within an inverted pentagram, symbol of Helltowne.

"ERIF!"

Kolveig spotted the Helltowne commissar across the battle. The red dwarves and fell men seemed to regain their courage with the threat of summary execution and fired upon Gorm and his pet. The beast had rushed forward and grabbed two dwarves in its mouth, but toppled in the face of the firearm onslaught.

"Oh I see!" he shouted. "And what sort of Committee Meeting came up with that Sort of Response? Seems Pretty Fascist To Me!"

Rather than finish the barbarian and his carnosaur off with another volley, Navi ordered his men to train their weapons at the Karlist instead.

"Who is that madman?" asked one of the savages.

Clutching her wounded arm, Elfriede answered, "That would be our friend, Kolveig."

"You mean the Great Prophet himself?"

Oborren leaned back from his tree position and took in the battle. It seemed that the attack was going well, but it was unclear if this group of Helltowners would be defeated before the hot-air balloon reinforcements arrived. They were roughly a mile away and some were quite large and even shaped like satanic characters and beasts.

The hunter felt sorry for Gorm and his mount, Bitey, but was only grudgingly concerned that thirty Helltowne firearms were now pointed at Kolveig.

Elfriede spoke the words and pointed her wand at the red dwarf commissar. Nothing happened. In desperation, she flung the wand at him, causing the Helltowners to momentarily pause, so that Brymanah, cursing herself for all eternity, sprinted in and knocked Kolveig to cover.

Word that the Great Prophet Kolveig was at the battle spread amongst the Fjord Vallee savages like wildfire. With frenzied reckless abandon, they launched themselves at the remaining Helltowners. Chanting their mantra, many of the lightly-clad savages broke their bodies upon the armor and weapons of the red dwarves and fell men, but many more overwhelmed what was left of the battalion with their primitive weapons and zeal for Powder Doom.

Aelstad and Carsanna began tending to the wounded as a remaining Helltowne squad carried Navi off into the woods to the south in the confusion of the melee.

The snoollabs loomed closer now; the victorious forces of the Fjord Vallee savages and their allies could see the red dwarves above beginning to point their gondola cannons at them. Halfdan turned Cherries in their direction and let his clear-mindedness end.

It was time for the pyromaniac to shine.

* * *

Oborren, Brymanah, and Kolveig raced through the woods to catch the red dwarf commissar and his remaining soldiers. The amazon's many wounds bled freely, giving her own Olympian armor a reddish hue. Kolveig found it tasteful.

"How do you know where they are going?" she asked Oborren.

"There's only one place that *they would go*," he replied as they ran.

Kolveig was about to make Another Cleverly Poignant Remark, when an incredible clamor overhead knocked them all to the ground. A balloon in the shape of an enormous, smiling red dwarf had exploded and its remaining pieces and passengers fell into the forest around them. Oborren ran to the wreckage to see if anything could be salvaged.

"Your lover will be the death of us all," stated the amazon.

And again, Kolveig was ready to reply with the Perfect Retort, but spotted movement out of the corner of his eye. Brymanah spotted it too and signaled to Oborren.

They did not get a good look, but it appeared to be slender and human-looking figures dressed in grey forest garb and hoods.

"They're not Helltowners," reasoned the amazon.

"And they didn't look that Bourgeois," added the Karlist.

"They were elves. Tower elves," stated the hunter.

"Elves?" said Kolveig incredulously. "They're just a Delusion of the Masses!"

296

Brymanah was startled that she had a similar sentiment to the Karlist; yet again, she greatly regretted saving his life.

"You just saw them with your own eyes," explained Oborren. "And luckily for us, they hate Helltowners."

* * *

Enormous blasts filled the sky when the sorceress's magical jets of flame connected with yet more of the flammable Lifting Vapors of the hot-air balloon fleet. One after another exploded. The Fjord Vallee savages cried over their many slain comrades and cheered "Powder Doom!" as the snoollabs were destroyed.

Tepson was glad that this second, larger red dwarf invasion had been stopped, but was still concerned that all this falling fiery debris would cause massive fires in the autumnal forest all around them. Of course, there was an even bigger problem at hand than burning trees.

Standing alone in the battle clearing, Cherries continued to cackle madly as fiery jets of eldritch origin erupted from her hands. Elfriede, Tepson, Halfdan, and Farhred watched from a safe distance. It was obvious that though the sorceress had saved Walstock and perhaps even the entire Vale from this invasion, there was little chance of her coming back to her somewhat normal self again.

Cherries's hair and garb were already inflamed- the former began to turn to pure fire and the latter burned away. Even the frenzied savages started to look at the sorceress in concern as she babbled all manner of obscenity and destroyed an especially large dirigible in the sky. Farhred approached her from behind, clutching his Tyr cross for protection.

The others looked on, hoping and praying that the sorceress's end would be painless and quick.

Quiet Upon Shenbyrg's Dawning

"If you are going to STAB ME, why don't you just COME AT ME WITH SOME GUSTO!" Cherries whipped around and stared at the witch hunter.

Her eyes and other orifices were now erupting in flame. Farhred gritted his teeth and steeled himself to strike, making sure to avoid looking directly at her exposed body. She pointed her finger at him and frowned. Elfriede and Tepson got ready to leap for cover; Halfdan readied his spear.

Whether from the fire or from some other agency, Cherries's skin began to take on a reddish hue. Her eyes grew white hot and a snakelike tongue of flame erupted from her mouth. Little red horns sprouted from her head. She began in her strange, deep voice, *"You witch hunters are ALWAYS SUCH PAINS IN THE-"*

A large, strong hand landed upon the sorceress's shoulder. She turned startled and the barbarian bonked her on the head with the haft of his axe, knocking her out. Halfdan put his spear between her and Farhred, blocking his execution.

"Cherries can look too hot sometimes," said Gorm

* * *

The party gathered with the surviving savages to have lunch upon the Tower Road. The remaining snoollabs were retreating to Helltowne, having lost nearly half their number. Based upon Oborren's report on the nature of hot-air balloon crashes, few if any Helltowners would have survived. As for the remaining Helltowners from the land battle, the party agreed that they would be useful prisoners for interrogation at least or serve in work details back in the Fjord to assist the savages.

For their part, Oborren and Elfriede had met with Gorm two days ago and enlisted his tribe's aid, following Mistro's advice. Since Dinglesfuhr had already begun to fall, the hunter stuck to the back-up plan and led Elfriede, Gorm, the Carnosaur "Bitey", and the many Fjord Vallee savages that thought Kolveig was some sort of a prophet to the mountaintop to rendezvous with the party in Walstock. Whether it was really the Will of the Gods or just dumb luck that they had happened to engage the Helltowners at nearly the same time as their other party members, Oborren could not say. Gorm seemed to think that it was simply the Will of Kolveig.

Meanwhile, Halfdan and Farhred had put their differences aside to attack the Helltowne battalion as well- from the opposite side- an action that granted them all victory. Their timely arrival helped Oborren and his group to overcome the superior red dwarf arms and armor, though Walstock remained held by the remaining red dwarf forces and Allied Cults.

As for Oborren, Brymanah, and Kolveig's retrieval mission, they only recovered Navi's head from an Ancient metal tower. All the rest was gone- vanished into the forest somehow; perhaps the Tower Elves truly were real.

As the group finished their rations, the sky grew clearer and a cold wind blew from the north, signaling the approach of winter. The group had many decisions to make: where to go to next, who would go where, and what to do with Cherries.

Kolveig strutted back from being intensely groomed by his many adoring Fjord Vallee followers. Though he was saddened by what had happened to his lover, he was looking forward to another Debate Over Their Next Course Of Action.

* * *

Emhild browsed through the merchandise at the Strass Hill Trading Post. The place was empty and reminded her of a certain department store from her youth. Ragennar looked on from the far wall, though he and the other Helan guards had already cleared out any shoppers who had not already fled, knowing that the Minas-Ninona nursemaid was coming.

Quiet Upon Shenbyrg's Dawning

Tales of the infamous Bride of Death had begun to circulate the town almost at the same time that Luce announced that he was the new Jarl. Emhild might have found the variations in Norse culture between this land and hers to be fascinating- that he would be called Dróttning in Winnonar, but Jarl in Strass Hill or that warriors wore bull-horn or hornless helms in her homeland, but only ram-horn helms here, for example- if she didn't feel so awful about all those local warlords who died in her bed nearly a week ago. Even the sight of goods from Amland and Metros at the Trading Post did little to assuage the dark sadness within her heart.

"Dontchya think ya could find something to buy hjere, Em?" asked the grizzled warrior.

"They don't seem to sell any new hjearts hjere in Strass Hjill," she replied ironically.

Ragennar looked downcast, feeling grief for Emhild.

A commotion outside the store snapped them to attention. They hurried outside with Ragennar leading the way. The many Helan guards in Em's detail had stopped a large group of travelers. She spotted many unusual people: a strong woman, a black-clad hunter, a midget, a blonde woman, a man with a big beard who carried on about 'Fascist Checkpoints', a devilish-looking redhead, and another man who walked beside her. He was an aging, slender man who carried a makeshift spear and bore a symbol of Odin. Something about him seemed very familiar.

They locked eyes for a moment and something passed between the two of them. The slender man and Em felt a deep love of a life past and a better world from which both of them had come. For a moment, all stood still and they were ready to embrace each other again. But then they averted their eyes, for they guessed that such love might not be for them in this world.

"What is this? More Authoritarian Anti-Migrationalism?" The bearded man remained outraged at the Helan guards.

300

Em grinned. "Let them pass."

Her detail obeyed and made a path for the travelers to continue. The strong woman grabbed the bearded man by the collar as well, so that he would not insult the guards as they moved on. The slender man looked at Em and smiled; she smiled back. Perhaps their paths would cross again someday?

"We've hjeard that the road up ahead for ya is dangerous," said Ragennar to the black-clad man.

"I know," said the man. He patted the grizzled warrior on the shoulder as he passed by. "We're going to Helltowne."

A flying thing watched them head north and east from her rooftop perch. She remembered the hunter who had tried to stop her tasty meal nearly two weeks ago. She also recognized Halfdan as that horrible tutor who she was not able to destroy completely last year. She had half a mind to try now, but had the Count to save in Mauriatown first.

Nevertheless, she knew that she would eventually be successful in getting her revenge. Even though she was now turned into a harpy, she always gave her 187%!

Glossary of Select Terms, Places, and Personages

Amaranthine Wizard- ruler of Dinglesfuhr a century before the story begins, instituted the destruction of the Mountain Folk who possessed some great treasure.

Amercia- land in which the story takes places. It once held a technological society, which predictable fell roughly 400 years ago (Lights Out), bringing on the New Dark Ages. Its people ironically returned to cultures and lifestyles of their ancestors (from the Old Dark Ages). Includes such regions as Minas-Ninona in the north central, Alban in the northeast, the Shenbyrg Vale in the central east, and many others. Also known as Vinland by the Minas-Ninonans.

Amercian- language of most in the story. Like its people, it returned to more archaic speech forms and more noticeable regional dialects. The gentle reader is reminded that all narrative and quotes within this work are grammatically correct within the *Amercian context* or if not, because the grammatical laws of Reality may have shifted since its initial writing.

Beast-heads- men (and possibly women) with the heads of various animals. Quite savage and vicious. Unclear if they are actually a true race or come from some sort of fell ritual as did Oborren's brother in the first novel. Also known as bestial men or as per type (e.g. stagman, goatman, horsehead, etc.)

Beneglushio- sage lord of Fairfacts Lordship.

Bitey- Gorm's pet carnosaur.

Bjartar- henchman of Oborren, from a village in Strass Hill that was plagued by a *winged flying-thing*. Oborren made the mistake of learning his name, which is often fatal for most henchmen.

Brotus- large Walstock thug, rumored to even have orc blood. Friends with Burb and Ivnok.

Brymanah- brown-haired, muscular amazon warrior-woman from Stephania. She has a particular dislike for Kolveig the Karlist.

Celts- encountered in Alba and in other places, they tend to be more red of hair and green or grey of eye. Their dialect also includes the replacement of "my" with "me", "you" with "ye", as well as adding an "a-" before certain verbs, adverbs, or even adjectives, because they are often fans of large quantities of alcohol and mirth.

Cherries- red-haired, cherry-color-everything(!) sorceress and former pupil of Mistro Tsar Huk. Fan of fun, magic, and footwear!

C'ps- Demon Lord of child-snatching to ostensibly prevent child-mistreatment.

Cult of R'ti- bizarre Demon Lord faith that blames tutors for all of society's ills, among other things. It gained a foothold in the Schoolhouse in the first novel and now has come to dominate all of Walstock.

Diogenes- pre-Ancient Olympian philosopher who espoused poverty by living in a wine barrel.

Drenart- a Hospitalier (q.v.)

Dróttning- Norse lady/ queen.

Dróttinn- Norse lord/ king, called 'Jarl' in Strass Hill.

Eind- dark haired advisor to Mekla and proponent of Underreign (q.v.)

Elfriede- blonde lady from Dinglesfuhr, former scrivener at the County Castle in Walstock, fan of riding bareback in Fjord Vallee.

Emhild- yet another blonde, this one a former nurse-maid from the town of Bjeiland in Minas-Ninona and possible another time and world. Cursed by Hel so that none may be with her romantically (or attack her) and live. A gentle heart, she struggles with minimizing the tragedy of her curse. Also known as Em.

Farhred- aging black and white-clad witch hunter of Tyr. Has an understandable penchant for burning heretics. His assistant is Freundel, a witch hunter of lower rank.

Freya- Norse Goddess of love, magic, and battle. Wife of Odin.

Funbox- Enchanted boxes that show illusory images to the Cults in Walstock.

Gaeswyn- red haired, voluptuous woman from the ruins of the Alban Capitol. She is apparently a psychic.

Goblins- short, ugly humanoids with hides of unusual colors. They are quite wicked and cunning, though lack human intelligence and the occasional ability to cooperate.

Gorm- great (struggling) philosopher and barber-barbarian. Now head of the Deer Watcher tribe in Fjord Vallee.

Gottschalk- a Dinglesfuhrian salt miner

Halfdan- aging, slender, ex-tutor, cleric of Odin (an Odinnic). Believes that he is originally from the past and another reality entirely. Apparently cursed with women, perhaps due to a past-life event of a blonde woman dying in his arms.

Hel- Norse Goddess of death. Also noted for disease, sloth and pestilence, though those aspects are not as noted in her contact with Emhild- so perhaps they belong to a different denomination.

Helka, Esmerre, and Frollicke- other advisors of Mekla (q.v.)

Hospitalier- knight-executioners in the service of Shield Ghul (q.v.). They wield syringe-like lances.

Hounds of Vigilance- politicized enforcers in service to the Cult of R'ti. They often wear white tunics and carry clubs.

Hymnir- half- frost giant leader of the Glowing Spectral Personhood cult.

Insolitus Novus- the New Strangeness that had begun the party's quest in the first book.

Quiet Upon Shenbyrg's Dawning

Kalla and Gudre- beautiful blonde friends of Elfriede.

Kolveig- bearded Karlist cleric, intent on defying any Autocratic, Authoritarian, Counter-Revolutionary, and/or Capitalist influence that he encounters

Krampus- Dinglesfuhrian staghead-type creature, possibly related to beast-heads or actually mythical only

Ley Lines- conduits of great power that span both above and below ground. Their intersections are known as nexi, nemetons, etc. Useful for translocation rituals apparently.

Life- series of mysterious events that can be labelled as a story, though it is essentially just a series of perceptions, sensations, and apparent phenomena within a field of consciousness. Suffering apparently seems to end when one focuses on the I-sense. Also known as Reality.

Lloyd Dingle- Sheriff's deputy during the very early days of Lights Out.

Luce- (pronounced: Loo-kay) blond ponytailed trickster and skald. Dresses strangely, has a fondness for regional cuisine, and sings sundry eccentric songs of the Ancients. He is apparently quite old and potent.

Magic- a mysterious force that some seem to use in various ways and with divergent approaches. Magical emanations are generally only visible when underground, if it all. Unlike in other fantasy realms, magic in this world remains quite secretive, unpredictable, and elusive. Nearly every magical act requires some sacrifice or something in return, otherwise Reality itself might become undone.

Melyssa- Queen of the Kernazons.

Mekla- leader of Dinglesfuhr, who becomes wracked by her people's past misdeeds.

Minerva- Olympian Goddess of justice, learning, and other traits, depending on regional variations. Also known as Athena in the Hellenic tradition.

Mistro Tsar Huk- eccentric dark-haired wizard that dresses in magenta and blue and has a megalomaniacal letter M marked on his chest. Dwells in a white tower just west of Walstock. Has little patience for simpletons and speaks in an eccentric and sibilant accent.

Mohee- strange old hick who claims to know the Party of the Vale. Now dwells with Gorm's tribe in Fjord Vallee.

Navi- red dwarf commissar, from Helltowne naturally.

Norse- a taller, blonder, and bigger-boned folk. Found in Minas-Ninona, Strass Hill, and elsewhere. Those from different areas might have different facial features, such as wider chins and more pronounced cheekbones, while others might have less pronounced features. Fond of chain mail, nasal helms (with adornment that also varies by location), wooden shields, battle axes, longswords, and other 'long'-items. Their dialect of Amercian shows the replacement of "you" and "yes" with "ya", as well as inclusion of "j" after their "h's" for a "hy" sound. Those from Minas-Ninona are also apt to say "dontchya know", as well as other bizarre colloquialisms.

Nuttens- mountain range that borders the Vale to the east. It generally runs north-south.

Odin- Norse God of insight, travel, and the runes. The version of Odin that Halfdan follows seems to be less overtly warlike than in other traditions and more focused on insight and journeys, both within and without. Husband of Freya.

Oborren- dark-ponytailed hunter, who also dresses in black (with a colorful necktie) and works to slay the unnatural horrors of the world.

Old Sieg- proprietor of a foodhouse in Walstock.

Olympians- a darker-haired and more tanned folk. Found in Caelum Mount, Claw Island, and other places. Fond of breastplates, plumed helms, metal shields, spears, short swords, columns, and grapes.

Orcs- pig-nosed humanoids with dark hides. They are quite brutal and foul, being innately evil-spirited. They are generally larger than but less clever than goblins.

Quiet Upon Shenbyrg's Dawning

Poy and Jeg- Stephanian Dames who have apparently been *changed* during a visit to the Hold of Kern, the Kernazons. Dames are a caste of amazons who take pride in dominating, belittling, and enslaving males, unlike other females that do so less often.

Procrustean Giant- giants who stretch out or cut away their victims, so that they are all the same size (when put in a bed). Derived from the pre-Ancient 'Procrustes': one of the first Karlists.

Ragennar- Grizzled, rust-bearded, Norse warrior and follower of Luce.

Remus- Monitor Director of the Schoolhouses around Walstock, now also the new Count. He appears to be a loyal devotee of the Cult of R'ti.

Shield Ghul, The- Demon Lord of getting possible healing at ridiculously high prices and long waits. The Hospitaliers are his knightly order.

Snik Snak- deposed yellow goblin Chieftain, who led an attack on Walstock the previous year.

Tepson- biologist gnome (midget- not 'a little person'), who believes that he was cryogenically frozen and is therefore from the distant past.

Teutons- the 'generic' folk encountered in the Vale and elsewhere. They tend towards generally fairer skin and fairer hair with other regional variations in culture, language, and mien. Worship a mixture of the Norse and Olympian Gods, though true Teutonic deities may be worshipped instead.

The Ancients- the technologically advanced people who lived in Amercia before Lights Out occurred. 'Pre-Ancients' would be the ones who came before even them and their Technological Revolution.

The Druid- a Celtic holy man from the Shenendehowa tribe in the land of Alba

The Gaol- place of imprisonment in Walstock. Later fittingly known as the Gaolag.

The Gods- mysterious beings who represent various aspects and concepts of Reality, some say a God Almighty rules over or is even beyond them all. Most Gods noted in the Vale thus far are Norse or

Olympian. See <u>Divinities & Cults</u>, q.v., by this same author for more details.

The Shell Oracle- gregarious leader of the Stephanian amazons, whose divinatory abilities and fair treatment of men set her apart from her subjects.

The Shenbyrg Vale- a Valley nestled in the eastern central portion of Amercia, noted for its scenic mountains, good soils, locally neurotic populations, and fairly pleasant climate. Select towns and areas include (listed generally from north to south): Middlechest, Gore (to the west), The Hold of Kern, Stephania, Fairfacts Lordship, Pentagram Tannery, Strass Hill, Helltowne (further east), Mauriatown, Walstock, Calvary (further west), Caelum Mount, Dinglesfuhr and Fjord Vallee (both further east), Monjaksen, Narquay, and Madisonburg.

Tyr- Norse God of justice, purity, and order. Patron of many witch hunters in the Vale who like to burn heretics first and practice coexistence later.

Underreign- the Dinglesfuhrian policy of surrendering their national sovereignty, welfare, and safety of their own people in order to signal their own guilt over some apparent transgressions in distant memory.

Van Dwick- Fieldmarshall of the Army of Dinglesfuhr, Elfriede's onkel (uncle).

Vertagern- giant who dwells in Fjord Vallee and doesn't care for bad haircuts nor traveling salesmen.

Wilstrin- yet another fellow who believes he travelled from an alternate reality.

www.ingramcontent.com/pod-product-compliance
Lightning Source LLC
Chambersburg PA
CBHW061129200626
46817CB00016B/460